HER *Good* NAME

OTHER BOOKS BY JOSI S. KILPACK

Sheep's Clothing
Unsung Lullaby

HER Good NAME

JOSI S. KILPACK

DESERET
BOOK

SALT LAKE CITY, UTAH

Library of Congress Cataloging-in-Publication Data

Kilpack, Josi S.
  Her good name / Josi S. Kilpack.
    p.   cm.
  ISBN 978-1-59038-965-2 (paperbound)
  1. Single mothers—Fiction.   2. Identity theft—Fiction.   I. Title.
PS3561.I412H47 2008
813'.54—dc22   2008015777

Printed in the United States of America
Worzalla Publishing Co., Stevens Point, WI

10   9   8   7   6   5   4   3   2   1

To my sisters—Jeni, Cindy, Lizz, and Crystal

Mom: "One day you guys will be best friends."
Us: "Mom's nuts!"

Fast forward twenty years:
"Wadayaknow, Mom was right!"

ACKNOWLEDGMENTS

*T*hanks again to Willard Boyd Gardner, a talented author and retired police officer, who helped ensure my storyline rang true. I had several pre-submission readers, namely: Erin Klingler who helped with making Idaho Falls sound and look like Idaho Falls; Annette Lyon for going grammar-Nazi all over me; and Carole Thayne Warburton, Heather Moore, and Julie Wright for pointing out the multitude of overall plot and character issues that needed more attention. Thank you to my writing group partners: Ronda, Jody, Becki, Anne, Janet, Carole, and Jolynne. Getting feedback throughout the writing process is priceless.

Big thanks to LDStorymakers—my family of writers—and to Deseret Book: Jana Erickson for overseeing the entire process, Lisa Mangum for her editing and feedback, Tonya Facemyer for typesetting, Shauna Gibby for cover design and a whole team of folks for marketing and PR. With groups like this behind you, how can a girl go wrong?

Thanks to my fabulous sister, Cindy, and my mucho-coolness brother, Sam, who used their fluency in Spanish to keep me from sounding like the translation web site I thought would be good enough. They also gave me some insights into Latino culture, conversation, and personality that helped a great deal in fleshing out my Latino characters. I tried very hard to follow their advice, but if I fell short it is surely my own deficiency and nothing to do with them.

Thank you to the readers who take the time to share their thoughts; they help more than you know as I approach each new project. Thank you to my kids who are the cutest cheerleaders you've ever seen and to my wonderful husband who loves me despite the fact that I live in a world of my own making far too often. Above all, thank you to my Father in Heaven for the people in my life, the stories in my life, and the love that surrounds me every day.

CHAPTER 1

Idaho Falls, Idaho
Wednesday, February 20

I need an ID."

"General?" Tony asked the caller, reaching for his notebook. Freddie was a pretty basic client, buying general IDs every few months; nothing fancy. Tony didn't know specifics but he assumed Freddie used the IDs for quick fixes, a few thousand on a couple cards, maybe clean out an existing account if he could get access fast enough. Two weeks and he'd be done with the name, discarding it along with the others and moving on to the next. It wasn't a bad business model so long as you could keep from being discovered, which, thus far, Freddie had been able to do quite well.

"Custom."

Tony smiled, glad to see Freddie was moving up in the world. He flipped open his notebook to a clean page and picked up a pen. Custom IDs were just that—customized to fit a specific purpose— a very different animal than the quick fix. "Okay, I'm ready."

"Female, thirties or forties, South American, good credit history, legal. I'll need a full workup as soon as possible. With documents."

1

Tony finished writing then reviewed the specifications. He let out a breath. For a buyer who had always been so low-key, this was a huge change in MO. "Dang, Freddie, this is tripped-out custom." He wondered how he'd find that kind of ID in Idaho Falls—his current city of harvest. Bringing in ethnicity was unusual and meant his hunters would need to target a different demographic than they usually did. Quite frankly Tony wasn't sure a custom ID like this would be worth his time. "How much?"

"Seven grand if I get it within ten days."

Tony's eyebrows went up. Seven thousand! Visions of Florida danced in his head. After four months of brutal winter he was ready for the beach. Seven thousand could make that happen.

Freddie kept talking. "You're not the only trader I've talked to. The first one to get back to me with a verified ID gets the job."

"Got it," Tony said, eager to get off the phone and round up his contacts. He never found the initial ID himself and wouldn't be able to do anything until he had that name.

"The sooner the better," Freddie added.

"I'm on it," Tony said before ending the call. Then he typed up a text message to send out to his taps. He'd have to hurry if he was going to beat out the other hunters. He proofed his message before hitting send.

Mexiwmn—30 2 40—solid—NOW

CHAPTER 2

*C*hrissy walked through the door of the café and paused long enough to scan the room and find the guy she'd been set up with. Amanda, her best friend since junior high, had said he'd be wearing a Boise State baseball cap. Sure enough, on the other side of the restaurant was a man sitting by himself, wearing a bright blue hat with a blazing orange Bronco's logo. He was already watching her.

She put on a polite smile and made her way toward him, asking herself yet again why she'd let Amanda talk her into this. Oh yeah, Amanda had promised her a pedicure. Chrissy adored pedicures but could rarely afford the luxury. She looked away from him in an attempt to distract herself from what lay ahead. Gingham curtains contributed to the forgettable nature of the café, which seemed appropriate since she had no expectation of anything but a forgettable date—well, other than the hat maybe. She'd likely remember that.

She reached the table and slid onto the vinyl-covered bench, adjusting her long denim skirt so that it didn't get bunched up underneath her. Skirts were her thing, as were high-heeled shoes of every variety. The skirts accentuated her curves without drawing attention to thighs that were on the thick side, and the heels helped disguise just how short she was—come spring they would also show off her calves, one of her best features. Chrissy was all about focusing on the positives.

"You should know up front that I haven't been on a second date with the same guy in two years," Chrissy said as she unwrapped the scarf from around her neck and shrugged out of the coat that was supposed to keep the freezing temperatures at bay. February in Idaho was certainly a force to be reckoned with.

Once sufficiently unwrapped, Chrissy crossed one leg over the other, folded her hands on the table, and finally made eye contact with her date for the evening. *Nice eyes,* she thought immediately. *Bummer.*

"Maybe that has something to do with your approach," he countered, and she felt a thrill of anticipation rush through her at his challenging comeback. This might not be so bad after all.

She spread her hands as if to show her imaginary cards. "Well, I spent over a decade playing games and quite frankly, I'm tired of 'em. These days I figure it only makes sense to be completely open right off the bat, then we can both decide whether we're up to this, or pack our bags and go home before it gets ugly."

He looked at her and she had no choice but to hold his gaze as his eyes peered out from under the bill of his baseball cap. To go along with the hat, he wore a long-sleeved T-shirt and jeans. Apparently he wasn't much into dressing up to impress his dates. His blue eyes had little star patterns and he wasn't bad looking—not like the last guy Amanda had said would be *perfect* for her. *And* he wouldn't look away, forcing her to do the same and study him in the process. He had a round face, but a strong jaw and a small cleft in his chin. Her eyes started to burn, yet he still didn't blink. *Dang, he is good.*

She wondered if a bribe had been involved on his side as well. He was nothing like her last few dates, all of whom had exuded desperation.

"You're quite self-defeating, ya know," he said, a smile turning up one side of his mouth.

"Only in that I still meet men for blind dates." She blinked. The other side of his mouth pulled his face into a smile. *Shoot!* He'd won the staring contest.

He finally dropped eye contact and leaned back against the bench, folding his arms over his chest as if cross-examining her. *Nice arms too—and shoulders.*

"So, no games, huh?" he asked, cocking his head to the side just a little.

She nodded sharply and straightened in her seat, trying not to squirm amid this new set of circumstances. She'd counted on an awkward, but free, meal where at the end he'd hurry to his car and she'd never have to see him again. What was this guy's name? Matt? Michael? Melvin? She should have written it down when Amanda called her. In her own defense, however, she didn't think she'd need that kind of information.

"I can ask you anything and you'll tell me the truth?"

Chrissy nodded again. "I have nothing to hide."

"How much do you weigh?"

She was speechless. He didn't bat an eye, still staring her down as his smile slowly grew. Three seconds ticked by as she argued with herself. *Completely inappropriate and rude. What kind of guy asks about a woman's weight?* And yet, why not? She agreed that he could ask anything. "One hundred thirty-three pounds as of last month. But I think I'm down a little this week, since I usually lose a couple around the time I'm ovulating."

His face jolted the tiniest amount. She couldn't hide a smirk of her own as she gave herself two points—one for being so quick on her reply, and another for having upped the ante.

"Divorced?" he asked a second later.

An adolescent waiter with a bad complexion interrupted them with water and a basket of rolls. He pulled out his notepad and asked for their order. Neither of them had looked at the menu, but Chrissy suspected that he, like her, had eaten at places like this enough to know what was on the menu without having to look— burgers, a pot roast dinner, chicken cooked four ways, and a pasty white sauce used as the base for everything from gravy to Alfredo.

"Double cheeseburger—no onions—french fries and a root beer," he said.

"Me too," she said. "But extra onions, steamed veggies instead of fries, and lemon for my water." He held her eyes again as the waiter left. *What was with the watching?* she wondered. And shouldn't it bother her?

"Divorced?" he asked again.

She shook her head and reached into her purse, pulling out a stat sheet she'd typed up last year just for fun and kept on hand for moments like this. Amanda would be furious. She handed him the paper before using her fork to fish out all the ice from her water glass. Ice cubes tinkled as they piled up on her bread plate.

He glanced up from the paper to see what she was doing.

"I have very sensitive teeth," she said as if he'd asked for an explanation. "Ice tends to really tick them off." Had the waiter asked about drinks before bringing them out she'd have specified.

"Right," he said, looking at the paper again. "You made a list?"

She shrugged and grabbed a roll. "Like I said, no games. You want to know, you've got it." She stole a glance at the cheap plastic clock on the wall above the sign that said *Restrooms*. She was sup- posed to pick up Rosa at eight—an hour from now—which made time of the essence. Her niece was at her very first Young Women's activity, and Chrissy's stomach was in knots over it. She hoped and prayed and begged that Rosa would like it now that her mom, Chrissy's sister, had given permission for her to go.

He began reading the stat sheet out loud. "Chres-y-aid—"

"*Chressaidia*—Cress-aid-ee-uh—but you can call me Chrissy."

He nodded and kept reading. "Chressaidia Josefina—"

"The *J* is an *H* sound in Spanish."

"Josefina," he said again, emphasizing the *H*. " . . . Salazar, thirty-five, Mexican-American, never married, no kids, convert at sixteen but not baptized until eighteen." He looked up at her and raised his eyebrows.

"My parents wouldn't give permission."

"Oh," he said, turning back to the paper in his hand. "Five-foot-one without size seven shoes on. Owns a home. You help take care of your niece and nephews who live a few houses down the street from you. Work as office manager at Almo Insurance company." He looked up at her.

"And I have to pick up my niece by eight," she added, smearing butter across the jagged edge of the torn roll. "Your turn," she said, looking at him and taking a bite.

"My turn to pick up your niece?"

She pushed the bite of roll into one side of her mouth and smiled at his purposeful misinterpretation. "No, your turn to give me your statistical rundown. How else am I to know what I'm dealing with?" She glanced again at the clock on the wall. "I've only got forty-eight minutes."

He put the paper down and for the first time didn't meet her eye as he spoke, which she found interesting. "Divorced, three kids, forty-one years old . . . Caucasian."

His discomfort was proof that she was still earning points,

though she wasn't sure what the prize was. The part about three kids definitely caught her attention, but she continued forward. "Height, shoe size, living arrangements?"

He sat forward and picked up a roll—stalling, she figured. She inspected him a little closer. He was very white and likely one of those men who should shave twice a day, as he already had a reddish beard dusting his chin. Judging by his muted-red eyebrows, she assumed his hair, hidden under the baseball cap, would be the same color. She looked at his arms again, the way the muscles pushed against the sleeves of his T-shirt when he was only buttering a roll. *Brazos muy agradables*—Very nice arms. He either worked out or was employed in a labor-intensive job. He looked up at her, and she went back to her own roll in hopes that he wouldn't realize she'd been checking him out so thoroughly.

"I bought a fixer-upper in Iona last year," he said. "I'm *six*-one, wear a size eleven shoe. I get my kids every other weekend and for six weeks in the summer." His eyes shifted when he talked about his kids, indicating to Chrissy that he was not a man comfortable with his past.

"And you're in Cam and Amanda's ward, right?" she asked.

"Right."

"Are you active?"

He hesitated. If she'd really thought this date might go somewhere, alarms would have gone off in her mind. She wondered if he'd answer or if she'd pushed too far. Then again, he'd asked how much she weighed. Fair was fair.

"I go when the kids are with me."

At least he was honest. "Why not every week?" she asked, taking another bite of her roll and finally realizing why the first bite had been unsatisfying. The restaurant used unsalted butter. She scowled. That was the problem with these American-fare restaurants—the food was so bland—down to the butter apparently. She grabbed a salt shaker and sprinkled salt over her roll. He watched her closely as she took another bite, meeting her eyes with a confused look. "Unsawted utter," she explained around the roll in her mouth. "Why on't you oh oo urch evey week?" Ha! Talking with her mouth full ought to scare him off if nothing else did.

"I don't like my ward very much."

She swallowed and then laughed, covering her mouth so as not to blow crumbs. He looked annoyed. "What does the ward have to do with it?" She'd been in a lot of wards in her life, and there was always something to like about them—if you were looking for good things, anyway.

"What's wrong with unsalted butter? We all have preferences."

"I never promised to eat unsalted butter," she said. "Covenants count for something."

He paused, and she smiled at her victory. "I'll take that into consideration. Cam's my home teacher. I like *him*."

Under the table, Chrissy wiggled her toes inside the heeled boots she was wearing tonight. She wished she could kick them off, but that would make running for the door much harder to do should she decide an escape was necessary. However, so far she was actually enjoying herself.

They were silent for several seconds, but he didn't take his eyes off her. "You called yourself a Mexican. I thought Hispanic or Latino was more politically correct."

"In the same sense that you're North American or Caucasian, yes—though I'm a Latin*a,* not a Latin*o*—but if a Hispanic is from Mexico, *como yo.*" She put a hand to her chest. "Then they are Mexican, but if they are Dominican, or Puerto Rican, or Colombian, you'll blow that whole PC thing out of the water by calling them

Mexican. *Hispanic* or *Latina* keeps everyone happy—hence the political correctness factor."

"Are you full Mexican?" he asked. She took that to mean he was looking at her at least as closely as she was looking at him—enough to notice that her skin wasn't very dark, but more of a brown sugar color. Her eyes were also a dark gold, not brown. She tried not to focus too deeply on his attention to detail, even though it did intrigue her.

"My dad immigrated when he was a child. My mom's white and grew up in Arizona. They somehow met in Idaho Falls—I never did hear the whole story about how that happened. Anyway, they divorced when I was eight and then Livvy and I bounced between them and Abuelita until we were old enough to figure out our own course."

"Abuelita?"

"Abuelita means *Little Grandmother.* She's actually my dad's aunt—his mother died when he was little—but Abuelita was like a grandmother to us and an amazing woman. A couple years ago she moved back to New Mexico to live with her daughter. She'd had enough of Idaho winters."

He nodded and seemed to have run out of questions, so she chose one to keep things going. "What do you do for a living?"

"I'm a loan officer."

"Sounds boring," she said, eyeing the rolls and wondering if she dared have another one. She was getting older, and the five pounds she used to worry about had turned into ten over the last year, reminding her to be careful about carbs. However, she *had* ordered veggies instead of fries with her burger.

"Boring *and* tedious," Matt-Michael-Melvin agreed. "But I'm good at it, and it pays the bills. You work at an insurance company, right? That sounds pretty boring too."

"Yeah, well, I'm good at it, and it pays the bills," she said, smiling as she echoed his words. "The agent I'm working for retires in fifty-four days though, and I'm trying to decide what to do next." Brandon, Kent's son, would be taking over the office, but she wasn't sure she could stand working for him. "I also do consignment work for Lupe's Dress Shop—I'd do that for a living if I could."

There was silence again. It probably wasn't a good sign that Matt-Michael-Melvin couldn't think of anything else to ask her. However, she had plenty of questions to fire at him, and she wasn't all that worried about signs.

"So, why did you get a divorce?" she asked, then raised her finger to point at him and squint one eye. "No games."

He looked at her over the rim of his glass and swallowed as he put it down. *Now* he looked uncomfortable. "Natalie had a reality problem and I had a temper problem."

"You hit her?" Chrissy sat up straighter. Half-active *and* abusive? Check please!

"No," he returned quickly. "I never hit her. We had some hard years and neither of us handled it very well. She shopped, I yelled. We got a divorce, and she found herself a wealthier man to marry."

The meals arrived and they busied themselves with prepping their food and then chewing for awhile—half-time without a show. The hot meat and crisp veggies rejuvenated Chrissy, but she didn't want to stop the info dump they had found themselves in the middle of. Feeling magnanimous, she waited until he put down his half-eaten burger and took a drink before asking her next question.

"How long ago was your divorce?"

"Eleven years."

"How old are your kids?"

"Nineteen, sixteen, and thirteen. Two girls with a boy in the middle."

She smiled, a bit hung up on the fact that his kids were all teenagers. But he *was* forty-one—strange to think he was only six years older than she was. What had happened to the fancy-free twenty-two-year-old girl she'd been just yesterday?

She wondered how she could find out his name without tipping her hand. Matt-Michael-Melvin was a mouthful. Maybe she'd just call him *Mmmmmm*. Her eyes moved to his thick arms and bright blue eyes. She decided *Mmmmmm* fit him just fine.

She did the math in her head. "So you didn't serve a mission?"

He paused, but seemed relaxed when he spoke. "Much to my parents' displeasure. They were even less impressed when I later divorced the girl I thwarted the mission for." He shrugged as if it were no big deal. By the way he didn't meet her eye, she suspected it was a very big deal, even now. He returned fire. "Why haven't you been married?"

She attempted to be nonchalant in her reply as well—so much for not playing games. "You'd have to ask the guys I date."

"The guys you only date once?" he asked, smiling and popping a fry in his mouth. A drop of ketchup landed on his chin. He didn't notice.

"Yeah," she said, lifting her burger again and finding her thoughts going in a direction she hadn't felt them wander into for awhile.

Would she want to date this guy, Mmmmmm, again? Strangely, the answer wasn't the solid *no* she'd been counting on. "Must be something in my approach." An approach that so far seemed to actually be working this time.

"Or the guys you date."

Mmmmmm held her eyes as he took another bite, smearing the chin-ketchup. She couldn't look away from those eyes, and though she tried to ignore everything she'd ever heard about chemistry between two people, she suddenly wished she'd worn the red top instead of the blue one. Bright colors accentuated her figure, though her shape was hard to hide no matter what she wore. Blessing or curse, she was busty and hippy, which at 5'1" could be less than complimentary if a girl didn't make it a priority to dress in such a way that showed she still had a waist, but she hadn't done anything special tonight.

On the heels of that thought was the reminder that Mmmmmm was an Idahoan, white, divorced with kids, lifelong Mormon. She was a never married, converted Mexican-American woman from a broken home. Calculating differences had always been a part of Chrissy's life and although she liked to give people the benefit of the doubt, it was impossible to ignore that chances were good he thought Mexicans were only good for cleaning toilets. And yet, he didn't talk to her that way. He didn't look at her that way, either.

He was watching her again. She found herself sitting up straighter and wondering if he liked what he saw, blue top not withstanding.

The chorus to Shakira's "Hips Don't Lie" shattered the moment and sent Chrissy grabbing for her purse, trying to find the phone before it sent the caller to voice mail. She was glad for the distraction. Her thoughts were getting away from her. The number on the phone was unfamiliar. She offered Mmmmmm an apologetic smile as she pushed the talk button and lifted the phone to her ear.

"Hello?"

"Can you come pick me up?"

Rosa. Chrissy's heart sank. Was she not having a good time at Young Women's? "What's the matter?" Chrissy asked, dropping her head a little bit, as if that would keep her conversation private.

"They're all done," Rosa said, her tone sounding insecure. "It started at six."

"Six?" Chrissy asked. "I thought it started at seven."

"I guess they changed the time but didn't know they should call me. It's over now. Please come pick me up."

Several options ran through Chrissy's mind. The Young Women's leaders could drive her home, but Rosa didn't know them very well yet. Livvy had gone to parent-teacher conference with the boys so Chrissy didn't want to call her. Plus Livvy was already somewhat hesitant about her children's involvement in the Mormon Church and making her leave the conference early would not work in Chrissy's favor. And the fact was that Rosa had called Chrissy— no one else.

"I'll be there in five minutes," Chrissy finally said. She hung up and looked at her date of the last twenty-two minutes. He quickly looked away.

"I'm sorry," she said, wishing she hadn't started things out so aggressively. She'd thought it would be like the other dates, and now wished she'd gone about things different since Mmmmmm was . . . well, different. She didn't know what to say.

Mmmmmm shrugged and took another bite of his burger, not making eye contact. "You warned me."

She pulled her nicely waxed eyebrows together. "Warned you?"

He looked up and met her eyes again, but they were harder, keeping her out, not looking at her the same way as before. "You don't do second dates," he said.

He made it sound like she'd planned this all along. "It's just my niece. She needs a ride home."

"Sure," he said, picking up a ketchup-soaked fry, looking embarrassed and a little angry. Chrissy bit the inside of her lip, vacillating between defending herself and just letting it go. It sounded cliché, but no one understood what her life was like.

"I'm really sorry," she said as humbly as she could, pulling her debit card out of her wallet in preparation to pay for her own dinner. It didn't seem fair for him to pay when she was leaving early. "You seem like a really nice guy." It sounded terribly trite and she hated how the tempo of their banter had been replaced with tension.

He raised his eyebrows. "Nice guys finish last, right?"

"It's not like that," she said, an edge creeping into her voice. Why was he being so difficult? Could it be he'd been enjoying things as much as she had? Maybe he didn't want it to end, either. "If you want, we could, uh, try this another time."

He finally met her eyes. "If *I* want?" He shook his head and looked even more annoyed. "You don't need to do me any favors."

Chrissy sat there.

"No big deal," he said before she could think of a reply. He raised his other hand and waved her away. "I'm working on remodeling my bathroom, and I've got tile to rip out. Drive safe." He gave her a dismissive look and took another bite.

She didn't know what else she could say that he wouldn't twist around, so she simply nodded, stood up, and headed toward the cash register. She hated leaving her leftovers behind, but didn't want to draw things out by asking for a box.

"I need to pay for my meal," she said to the gothic-looking girl at the register. The server was fetched, the check split up, and Chrissy glanced toward Mmmmmm as the gal took Chrissy's card and license to the back office. Apparently the front credit card machine was broken. Chrissy hoped they'd finish before Mmmmmm caught up to her. She might be outspoken and quick on the draw with banter or retorts, but that didn't mean she welcomed open confrontation. She also knew that if it had been *his* cell phone that sent him running, she wouldn't want to face him at the register.

"Here's your card and license," the cashier said, her hands shaking just enough to be noticeable. Must be all the Coke she drank while working; Chrissy had downed soda all shift long when she'd waitressed.

Chrissy glanced at the twenty-something clerk only long enough to notice the ring in her eyebrow and the name tag that read "Sid."

"Thanks," Chrissy said as she shoved the cards into her purse and hurried toward the door.

She slid into the driver's seat of her car, a red two-door that had hit 180,000 miles a few months ago. She'd gotten in a car accident last summer and had to replace the hood and front right fender with black counter-parts. She glanced at Mmmmmm through the window as he paid and wondered, if under different circumstances, things would have worked out between them. But there were no different circumstances. Ignoring the slight pang of reality as she pulled out of her parking space, she reassured herself that Matt-Melvin-Michael was hardly the man who would change her life—nice arms or not.

CHAPTER 3

She knocked twice and removed the "Sid" name tag from her shirt. Her clothes and hair smelled like the café—grease and ranch dressing. Gross. She'd forgotten her coat, but it didn't matter since she was sweating anyway.

The big metal door opened and she slipped inside. "I've got six," she said to the only other person in the room—Tony—as soon as the door thudded shut again. The flickering fluorescent light overhead had a kind of strobe effect that nauseated her. She handed over the photocopies she'd made of that night's credit cards.

"Did you get my text this afternoon?" Tony asked as he took the papers. She always met him in the same place—an empty office at the back of a bar. The loud music on the other side of the wall, coupled with the lights and her queasy need for a hit, made the walls seem as if they were moving.

"Yeah," she said, nodding toward the papers. "She's in there."

"Six at thirty bucks apiece is one-eighty. Plus an extra fifty for the one I requested," he said with a pleased smile. He tapped the side of the bag he always carried with him. "Do you want it in cash or in product?"

"Product," she said decisively, her eyes already trained on the pack. It hung around his neck and over one shoulder, lying against his left hip like a big purse. "I've still got a paycheck." Though it wouldn't last long, she was sure. It would only take one person to trace the card thefts back to her before everything blew. She knew those thoughts *should* bother her, but they didn't. The people whose information she stole would get their bad debts removed, and the banks and credit card companies made so much off of the interest on their loans that they barely felt the loss of a few dollars. It was the perfect crime, and besides, all she did was find the info.

"Tell me about her."

She swore he was dragging this out only to annoy her. "Um, she was, like, old, like forty or something. Brown hair, dark skin—*Mexican*." They all looked the same. But she knew he wanted details, so she did try to pay attention. "She paid with a debit card, so she's got a bank account and she was dressed nice." She kept to herself that the woman's car was a total hunk of garbage.

"Wedding ring?"

"Um, no, she was with a guy, but she, like, ditched him."

"Good," he said, finally unzipping his pack and removing a plastic bag with several smaller drug-filled baggies inside it. Before handing it over, though, he unzipped another compartment and put the papers inside.

She clenched her teeth, sure he was moving slow on purpose. It had been more than a week since she'd last brought him any names. He knew she was desperate.

"When will I see you next?" he asked.

"I work again on Friday, but weekends are harder. Too many people around."

She finally snatched the drugs from him and turned them in her hand, counting each hit, verifying that she'd gotten her money's worth. He handed her two more baggies—the extra for the specific ID she'd found—and her heart rate sped up even more. Her hands were shaking—had been all night—and her breathing increased just knowing that relief was so close. She put the extra hits in the bag and put the bag in her pocket before immediately removing it again to count the hits a second time.

"Just get me what you can," Tony said with a smile. "You did good for me tonight."

But she'd already turned toward the door, desperate to be alone with her addiction. She headed into the cold night without a backward glance. She'd worry about Friday when Friday came. For now, relief was only a hit away.

CHAPTER 4

Tony watched the girl disappear out the door. When he was alone, he pulled out his cell phone and dialed. He had to walk to the far corner of the room and plug his other ear in order to hear over the music. As soon as Freddie said "Hello" in that slightly accented voice of his, Tony started talking.

"I got one for a Chressaidia Josefina Salazar. I haven't worked her up but she sounds good. Just wanted you to know."

Freddie was silent for a moment. "I'll throw in an extra grand if you can get us a full workup within the week. We really need that name. We're also looking for a few other IDs. Details don't matter."

"Sure. How many do you want?"

"Two men."

"I've got a Daniel Dorado and a Micah Heet, both with copies of their driver's licenses."

"Perfect. Five hundred apiece."

He frowned. Five hundred was nothing, but Freddie was good, always paying fast and easy. Tony wasn't about to screw it up by making demands for more money. Besides, this Salazar workup would cover the difference. "I'll fax them in the morning and have Salazar for you by next week."

"The sooner the better."

"Got it."

Tony hung up and smiled. "Florida, here I come."

CHAPTER 5

Idaho Falls, Idaho
Thursday, February 28

*I*t was nearly dark when Micah pulled into his driveway Thursday night. On the way home from the office he'd stopped to pick up a bottle of grout sealer he needed for the bathroom—assuming he'd ever finish the project. He was new to laying tile so the job was moving slowly, but at least he had something to keep his mind and hands busy.

The cold took his breath away and he missed the heater of his truck as soon as he opened the door to get out. He tucked the bottle of sealer under one arm, shut the driver's door behind him, and headed toward the house by way of the snow-packed sidewalk.

Once inside, he shook off the cold and put down the sealer. He felt guilty for being glad the kids weren't coming this weekend. They'd made him promise he wouldn't spend his weekends with them working on the house, yet he hated being haunted by half-finished projects.

After flipping the switch on the gas fireplace he'd had installed in July—when the price was low—he shrugged out of his coat and threw it over the back of the couch. The orange Post-it note Amanda

22

had given him on Sunday was still stuck to the wall where he'd put it after church and it caught his eye for the two hundredth time.

Cam had been the first one to ask how the date had gone, but it had been Amanda who had forced the number into Micah's hand and committed him to at least think about calling Chrissy again. He'd tried to explain that he wasn't interested, but Amanda wouldn't take no for an answer. The orange Post-it had been haunting him ever since. Micah wished his stomach didn't get so fluttery every time he saw it.

Why haven't I thrown it away?

He had no answer and it made no sense, but part of him was riddled with curiosity as to how a second date with Chrissy would go. Did that mean he was stupid or just bored? She wasn't anything like the other women he'd dated. She was . . . color and energy . . . unique in a somewhat frightening way.

He unclipped his cell phone from his belt, wondering if he ought to throw caution to the wind and just call her. He looked around his living room—white walls patched with white mud still in need of sanding. Plain, boring—safe. Was that why he hadn't called? Was he afraid of adding color, of perhaps *feeling* something he hadn't felt in such a long time? The thought scared him a little. He didn't like the idea that he was afraid of change. If that was true, then he would live *this* life, *this* way, forever.

Kayla was attending her first year of college in southern Utah, Blake had just turned sixteen, and Mallory would be fourteen in a few months. Micah had been alone for eleven years and the emptiness inside him not filled by the house and the kids wasn't going away. He wanted more—longed for it. He looked at the Post-it again, his stomach filling with butterflies. Calling her wouldn't be the dumbest thing he'd ever done, and maybe his existence needed a little spin cycle. It's not like one more date would require a lifetime commitment. He felt a smile tugging at his mouth, and the rush of anticipation at a second date with Chrissy was impossible to ignore. *I'm gonna do it,* he said to himself. *I'm going to give it another shot.* His thumb was hovering over the number pad when the phone rang in his hand, making him jump.

He recognized Blake's cell number and lifted the phone to his ear, unsure of whether he was relieved or annoyed by the interruption.

"Hey, Blake," he said as he leaned against the back of the couch and took off his ball cap, rubbing the heel of his hand against his forehead and feeling guilty for wishing his son had waited just two more minutes.

"Dad, I'm sick of this," Blake said, his voice thick with adolescent temper. "She's making me crazy."

Even though he had visitation only two weekends a month, he talked to the kids a few times a week, and Blake complaining about his mother was becoming a common theme. Micah kept his voice calm and neutral. "What's going on?"

"She won't let me take that job," Blake spat. "She says it'll *'distract from my studies.'*" The last part was said in a high falsetto voice that Micah assumed was an attempt to impersonate Natalie. He smiled slightly, glad Blake couldn't see him.

"How are your grades?"

"Great," Blake said as if offended Micah had to ask. "Nothing lower than a B, just like I promised. So I turned in my application, and Pizza Hut called back for an interview, but she won't let me go."

Micah let out a breath, already formulating what to say to Natalie. "Is your mom there?"

"She's downstairs. I'll go get her." There was a triumphant quality to Blake's voice that Micah didn't like, but he didn't know what to do about it either.

He hated being pitted against Natalie, but wondered if she didn't make these decisions on purpose, knowing Micah would be pulled into it and thereby giving her someone to vent to.

"Of course he calls you," Natalie said right off the bat.

"Why shouldn't he?" Micah countered. "I was there when *we* made the bargain. We can't back out now, Natalie. We told him if he got his grades up—"

"They are *barely* up," she cut in. "And it's only the end of the second term. Dennis and I talked about it and we just don't think—"

"Dennis is not Blake's father," Micah interrupted, trying to keep his voice calm. "He does not have a say in this and you know it. Do we have to argue about that *again?*" Dennis and Natalie had been married for almost eight years. They had two children—boys Micah had only seen fleetingly and in pictures. Dennis was a good-enough man—he treated the kids well and kept Natalie in all the shoes and purses she could want—but Micah resented it when Dennis tried to do his job for him. Natalie knew that and had agreed to keep decisions about *their* children, between the two of them. "Blake didn't get anything lower than a B, right?"

"Barely Bs."

"Barely *is* a B. It's enough. We don't have the luxury of changing our minds."

"Oh, I most certainly do," Natalie replied before launching into her other complaints, a million reasons why Blake couldn't handle a part-time job. Micah let her go on about dirty laundry, sleeping in on the weekends, and how hard it would be for her and Dennis to drive him back and forth. His frustration grew with every item on her never-ending list. He couldn't take it anymore.

"None of that matters." Micah was pacing now; his ex-wife had that kind of effect on him. "We promised. If his grades fall, he'll have to quit but until then—"

"Oh, so you want to set him up for failure?"

Micah's jaw clenched and fire shot up to his head. "No! I want us to follow through. We told him—"

"*You* told him," Natalie spat back. "You're the one who made the deal."

Micah stopped in the middle of the floor. "That's not true!" His other hand clenched into a fist. "We were both there. We *both* agreed."

"But it was your idea."

"And you agreed!" Micah yelled back, finally losing his cool. "If you didn't want him to do this, you shouldn't have agreed, but you did, and . . . and maybe I can find him a cheap car or something so that it's not such a burden on you and Dennis."

"Oh, that's perfect!" Natalie said. "Buy him something—that will make it all better. You know what? I'm sick to death of him, of you—of everything. Since you're so sure you've got all the answers, he can come live with you and you can make all the decisions."

Micah paused, but only for a moment. No way would he let her hang up the phone and tell Blake that Micah had hesitated. "I'd love to," he said, though the idea was a bit frightening. He hadn't been more than a summer-weekend-holiday dad for a very long time. Taking on that much daily responsibility made his mouth go dry.

"Fine," Natalie said. "I'll bring him over in an hour." She hung up.

Micah scrubbed a hand over his balding head again as his stomach sank. How would he keep tabs on a teenage boy? Micah survived on cold cereal and frozen burritos—except for every other weekend when he stocked the fridge with yogurt and hamburger in an attempt to make his kids think he lived something like a normal life. What would happen when he made a decision Blake didn't like?

Would Natalie rescue Blake the way Micah just had? He didn't like the way his son suddenly felt like a commodity, traded when the market wasn't looking good.

Not for the first time, Micah wondered what he'd expected almost twelve years ago when he'd gone to an attorney and filed for divorce. Back then it seemed as if the new-found freedom would make up for all the difficulties that might lie ahead. He'd had no idea how hard it would be.

He picked up the orange Post-it one last time before crumpling it in his hand and launching it toward the box by the fireplace he used for a garbage can. Wanting color and longing for companionship was no longer an option. Life was about to change again, with less room than ever for someone else. He sat on the edge of the weight bench he kept in the living room, knowing he should work out or do something to take his mind off the fears rising in his chest. Instead, he stared at the box for a long time, thinking about all the details of his life that had just been shifted.

Almost an hour later, headlights swept across the window. He looked up, panic closing his throat.

Blake was here. It was time to be a dad.

CHAPTER 6

~~~~~~

*C*hrissy looked at the clock again, noting that it was after nine and Livvy *still* wasn't home. She wasn't answering her phone either. Chrissy had told Rosa her mom was working late, but that was hours ago and besides, the kids knew Livvy never worked past seven. It was a school night, and though Chrissy loved having the kids over, it was late, and they were all getting tired.

Chrissy was trying to pay some bills, sure that the gas bill should have arrived by now. Had she put it somewhere other than the desk where she threw the rest of her mail? She'd been through everything four times and still couldn't find the statement. Weird.

When her cell phone rang, she instantly thought it could be Micah—turns out that was the name of the guy she'd referred to as Mmmmmm. She wasn't sure which name she liked better. Amanda had told Chrissy she'd given Micah her number and even though she'd been telling herself not to expect a call, as the days went by she'd still found herself hoping he would. But then the caller ID told her it was Livvy, and all thoughts of Micah were pushed away.

"Liv, where are you?"

"Hi, Chriss," Livvy said. "I thought I better call and let you know I won't be home 'til later. Some gals at work invited me to go out with them. It's Maria's birthday."

Were her words slurring or was Chrissy imagining things? She turned away from the kids and tried to keep her jealousy at bay. It wasn't fair that Chrissy watched Livvy's kids while Livvy hung out with friends.

"Liv," she said, trying to sound diplomatic. "Why didn't you call me?"

"I did—I told Rosa."

"You told Rosa you were working late. The kids were already here when I got home. They'd been here alone for three hours."

Silence.

Chrissy took a breath, trying to keep her tone even. "Why didn't you call my cell instead of telling Rosa? I could have left the office early. *I'm* the one who needs to know when I'm watching the kids, not Rosa."

"Sorry," Liv said. "I didn't think it was a big deal. I haven't been out for so long. I just needed a break." There was loud music and laughter in the background, meaning she was likely at some bar.

There had been a time when Livvy was the consummate party girl—it was how she had met Rosa's father when she was still in high school, and later how she'd met Marius. But after Marius left her and she became a single parent, she'd calmed down. Around that same time, Chrissy had moved back from California and lived with Livvy and the kids for a few months. Chrissy made a spontaneous offer on a house down the road when she realized the house payment wouldn't be that different than if she rented an apartment. She was shocked when a month later she found herself a home owner.

Living so close to Livvy and the kids was wonderful—most of

the time—and though Chrissy was usually optimistic about her sister, she didn't like that Livvy was dipping her toes back into the nightlife scene. She wondered if Livvy was with the new guy she was seeing, and the jealously pitched a little higher. The last thing Livvy needed was a new man—she'd proven twice over that she wasn't any good at choosing the right kind.

"I need to know when I'm being left with the kids," Chrissy finally said. "You have to check with me. What if I'd had something going on tonight?"

"Did you?" Livvy challenged.

Chrissy paused. Was her life so insignificant? "That's not the point. What if I had?"

"But you didn't." The line was silent. "I'll be home in a little while. Just take the kids over to the house and put them to bed. They'll be fine," Livvy said. "Thanks."

Chrissy clenched her teeth when the line went dead. It wasn't enough that she constantly helped out with one thing or another, but now Livvy was hanging up on her too? Amanda's familiar lecture about doing too much for Livvy came to mind and she couldn't chase it out no matter how much she wanted to. But now wasn't the time to work through it. She didn't want to burden the kids with her anger so she set it aside and got down to the task at hand. It wouldn't be the first time the kids had fallen asleep alone—it was just that it usually happened when their mother *was* working late.

Chrissy unlocked the door to Livvy's house a few minutes later and went through the nightly routine with the kids. When the boys finished brushing their teeth and slammed the door to their room, Chrissy turned to Rosa. Her eyebrows were pulled slightly together, and her dark eyes reflected worry beyond her years.

"Are you okay here?" Chrissy asked. Rosa usually didn't have a problem with nights when Livvy was working and the kids were on their own. But Rosa, like Chrissy, seemed to realize there was something different about tonight. "Remember to lock up after I go. Your mom will be home soon."

"Where is she?" Rosa asked.

Chrissy hedged. Rosa had been through a lot in her young life—no father, her mom's failed marriage to Marius, and taking on responsibility for her twin brothers. "She's not at work, is she?"

Chrissy didn't know how to answer that. Rosa looked away, her face looking tight and pinched. Livvy had lied to her own daughter to avoid having to tell Chrissy the truth. How was Chrissy supposed to explain that without making Livvy look even worse?

"It was a friend's birthday, that's all."

Rosa nodded and looked at the floor. "His name is Doug," she said, her voice soft as a secret. "He calls her all the time now."

"Oh," was all Chrissy said, trying to keep her disappointment under wraps. She stayed in the doorway a few more seconds, before admitting to herself she didn't have anything else to say. She hadn't been around the kids much until a few years ago when she'd moved back to Idaho Falls. Livvy's divorce from Marius had just become final and Livvy was taking her new role as a single mom very seriously. But sometimes Chrissy wondered what Rosa had been exposed to through her mother's life before that. It was obvious she didn't like her mom dating any more than Chrissy did.

"You guys can stay at my place, if you'd rather," Chrissy offered.

Rosa lifted her chin and met Chrissy's eyes again, trying to look strong. "We're okay," she said as if offended by the insinuation that she wasn't. She *was* thirteen after all.

"All right, but lock the door behind me and call if you need anything, okay?"

Rosa nodded.

Chrissy grabbed her puffy red coat from the couch where she'd put it and pulled her beanie cap back over her head. She shut the front door a minute later, and waited for the sound of the lock clicking into place before she turned to face the night. It was really cold, and she pulled her hands into her sleeves as she walked down the front steps. The night was clear, a billion stars breaking through the darkness. The three-quarter moon gave everything a polished look.

She'd found her place well enough in Idaho—in the Mexican community and the Mormon one. But she still felt like a bit of an outsider everywhere she went. She was Mexican—but not Catholic or surrounded by a large, loud, and loving family. She was Mormon—but not white or married with kids, even though her own children would have been teenagers now if she'd gotten an early start on her family like so many Mormon women did. In some ways she felt like a parent to Livvy's kids, but she wasn't, not really.

A breeze picked up, taking her breath away and sending her curls behind her shoulders. A dog started barking. Someone down the road slammed a door. Life sounds, proof that people were living life, just like she was.

She hurried to the sidewalk of her own house and up the steps to her wide, cement porch, but then paused and turned to face the night, avoiding the dishes waiting for her, avoiding the stillness of the house—wishing she could avoid her own thoughts as easily. She'd been anxious for Livvy to return home and take care of the kids half an hour ago, but now she wasn't longing for her own company so much. She sat down in one of three patio chairs she kept outside, thinking that maybe if she stayed outside long enough, the cold would either numb her worries or spur her to make a decision. About what, she couldn't be sure. But she'd felt a growing unrest these last few months, like something wasn't right, something was out of place. She didn't know what it was, but often found her mind circumventing it—like when someone's car broke down in the middle of the road. She'd just ease to one side or another to avoid it and continue on her way. Tonight, with Livvy's night on the town, that car felt too big to get around. Perhaps it was time to stop looking for shortcuts.

From her porch, she could see into the Parkers' living room. They lived across the street, a nice white family with four kids squeezed into a home built for two. The big picture window glowed like a television screen in the darkness. She couldn't help but watch them. It looked like bedtime for the Parker kids, too. She felt bad for spying, as if she were some kind of Peeping Tom, but she didn't feel bad enough to look away. Other people's lives seemed so full sometimes, so . . . necessary.

Brother Parker had his youngest son, Terrance, tucked under one arm, and as he walked past his wife he let his hand brush across her shoulder blades. She looked up from whatever it was she was doing and smiled until he and the kicking feet disappeared through a doorway. Such simple intimacy brought a sharpness to Chrissy's chest and for a moment Chrissy allowed herself to delve into that old fantasy of having her own family, her own children. She tried not to anymore, but sometimes she couldn't help it. Was that the unrest? Was she realizing how far away from that life she'd traveled? Was the banging of each tick of her biological clock finally taking its toll?

The fantasy played out, and she couldn't help but be pulled along with it. What would it be like to have a husband to cook for, a shoulder to cry on, a hand to hold throughout her life? But those things weren't her life, never had been, and as every birthday passed she had no choice but to accept that it may never be. It wasn't as if these thoughts were new ones. For years she'd been trying to find joy where she was, even if it wasn't her plan A, or B, or even D, E, or F. She knew she needed to get away from the status quo path to happiness and focus on her situation, her actual circumstances. What did she really want? What did she really need?

It took almost a minute to narrow down her thoughts. "Help me allow myself to be at peace with the direction my life has taken," she whispered. Chrissy knew the power of peace—she'd felt it when she first realized she wanted to be baptized. The feeling came again two years later when, on her eighteenth birthday, she entered the waters of baptism, despite her family's wishes. The same feeling had made itself known dozens of times since, the silent calming of her fears when some aspect of life threatened to overwhelm her. She needed it now, needed this unrest to be quelled. "Let me do the right thing, and know what the right thing is."

Every time she'd spoken to her Father in Heaven this way, He'd answered her, and despite the cold, she felt the warmth of His arms around her, reminding her that she was His child, that He loved her.

That she was exactly where she was supposed to be.

Really? she asked in her mind. *This is where I'm supposed to be?* In this house, with Livvy's children instead of her own? She wondered if she'd missed some opportunity and was now being punished for it.

Trust me.

Those two words couldn't have been more powerful if someone had yelled them in her ear. She felt the questions begin to settle.

The image of piercing blue eyes staring at her from under a Boise State baseball cap passed before her, and she sighed. Amanda had said he might call and Chrissy had allowed herself to get her hopes up. But it was Thursday, more than a week since the date-gone-bad. Some things just couldn't be fixed.

Trust me.

She let out a breath and nodded into the night pressing around her. Brother Parker returned to the living room, kid-free, and sat down while Sister Parker scurried around, trying to undo the day's damage on her living room. They were just two people, after all. A couple, yes—parents, certainly—but here at the end of the day they were just two people, with individual, though connected, paths to navigate in life. Chrissy had her own path, and wishing it were a different one simply kept her from moving forward.

Trust me, she repeated to herself, finally understanding where the discomfort had come from. She'd questioned Him, wondered if He'd forgotten her. She couldn't expect to have joy if she wasn't looking for the path He *had* created for her.

I can do that.

Brother Parker went to the side of the window and began pulling the blinds shut. Just as Chrissy felt like maybe she should apologize to them for her watching, the phone began ringing in the house and spared her further consideration. She hurried inside, the warmth of her home a sharp reminder of how cold it really was outside. Who would be calling her? She glanced at the clock on the microwave. It was after ten. Would Micah call her this late?

"Hello?" she said when she picked it up on the third ring.

"Chrissy," Rosa said, her small voice shaking. "I'm scared to be alone."

Chrissy hesitated a moment, but a warmth coursed through her, reminding her of what she'd just been told. She was exactly where she was supposed to be. She turned her thoughts to her blessings, to all the good things she had in her life, and felt even more peace make its way into her mind. "I'll be right there."

CHAPTER 7

❧

*T*ony's phone rang at almost midnight, an answer to the message he'd left earlier. He was feeling rather smug about all he'd accomplished and looked forward to sharing his good news—the information he'd found through a basic online background search, looking through some public records, and going through the woman's mail.

"What do you have for me?" the faceless voice asked.

"She's got a house. Based on how much she owes and how much other homes in the area are selling for, I'd guess she's got at least fifty thousand in equity. She doesn't have a car loan, her credit is good, she's got very little debt, and she's single."

The voice on the other end was silent, and for a moment Tony thought they'd tell him they didn't need the workup anymore. He held his breath. He'd worked so hard on this ID, and she was a perfect target. If it was all for nothing . . .

"Docs?"

"I've already ordered a replacement license, and I've got a birth certificate." It had taken a rather complex story about his girlfriend being in the hospital and needing an official copy for the lawsuit against the trucking company that had hit her before someone finally gave him a copy. Lucky for him he had a face people trusted.

"How soon can you get them to me?"

He calculated. Tomorrow was Friday. The weekend would slow him down. "I could overnight the stuff I already have tomorrow morning, but the rest of it will take about a week."

"I'll forward you half the amount we agreed on as soon as I get the first mailing."

Tony's mood became even brighter. He thought about how easy it had been to intercept her mail. What were the chances she also locked all her doors and windows when she went to work? A checkbook, an old bank statement, maybe even pin numbers if she was like ninety percent of the population and kept them written down within a few feet of their computer. "You won't be disappointed," he assured his contact. This was a slam dunk. Maybe his focus on the drug trade was putting priority on the wrong profession. ID peddling was a much hotter business than he'd thought.

CHAPTER 8

Idaho Falls, Idaho
Wednesday, March 12

"Hi, my name is Linda. Please note this call is being monitored for training purposes. How may I help you?"

"Yes, hi, this is Chrissy Salazar," she said, holding the phone between her ear and her shoulder as she shuffled files into alphabetical order on her desk. Chrissy had been meaning to make this call for two days but kept leaving the bill at home. Finally, she was getting around to it. "I've got a question about my bill."

"Do you have your account number?"

Chrissy read off the number, listening to Linda's fingers click across the keyboard as she entered it in.

"Can you verify your address, please?" Linda asked.

Chrissy rolled her eyes at the ridiculous hoops she had to jump through—she'd already gone through an automated menu before talking to Don who had forwarded her to Linda. "Five-four-six Evelyn Street, Idaho Falls, Idaho."

"Thank you, Ms. Salazar, how can I help you?"

"Yeah, I've just received my March gas bill and I'm wondering if I can get the late fee taken off since I never got a February statement."

More clicking. "Our records show that your statement was mailed on February eighteenth. Are you sure you didn't receive it?"

"I'm sure," Chrissy said with a nod. She wasn't nearly as organized at home as she was at the office, but she'd made note of the fact that she'd never seen her gas bill—then forgotten to call about it until receiving the new one complete with two months worth of charges and a late fee.

She finished alphabetizing the files and moved them to the other side of her desk in order to concentrate on the call. Brandon, Kent's son and soon-to-be successor to the business, came out of his office and winked at her. She looked away and told herself he didn't mean anything by it.

"If I had received it, I'd have paid it, and you can see from my history that I always pay and I'm always on time. I never received the statement. Therefore it didn't get paid."

"So you're not claiming to have sent payment that wasn't received?"

"No," Chrissy said, realizing this was the weak spot in her argument. If she hadn't received her statement, she should have called and requested another one. "I just never received the statement. You're certain your records show it was sent out?" Then again they only had two bazillion accounts, it wouldn't be far-fetched to assume one went astray now and again.

"According to our records it went out," Linda said. "But hold just a moment while I check something."

Chrissy agreed and straightened her desk while she waited for Linda to get back on the line. Brandon returned to his office but he kept the door open and moved his chair so that he could make a phone call and watch Chrissy through the open door. What was his problem? He'd always been kind of flirty, but over the last few months he'd moved to flat-out creepy. She turned in her chair so her back was facing him and wondered if she could work here once Kent left for good.

"Ms. Salazar?" Linda asked.

"Yes," Chrissy said. "I'm here."

"I spoke with my manager and he agreed that due to your excellent history with us, he would waive the late fee this one time. However, in the future should you not receive a statement be sure to let us know before the next billing cycle."

"I sure will," Chrissy said with a smile. "Thank you very much."

She hung up and let out a breath of satisfaction. She looked at the situation as if she'd made fifteen dollars in less than five minutes—not bad.

CHAPTER 9

Idaho Falls, Idaho

"Thanks, Dad," Blake said as he put his new track shoes on the checkout counter.

"You're welcome," Micah said, but as soon as Blake turned away, his smile fell. *Eighty bucks for running shoes?* It was highway robbery, but Blake had wanted the hundred-and-twenty-dollar shoes. At least Micah had talked him down from those.

"Track?" the clerk asked. Micah looked up at the flirty tone in the woman's voice. Or rather the girl. About seventeen, she had her eyes on Blake as she scanned the bar code on the box. Micah stood behind his son, and saw Blake's neck go pink—just like Micah's likely would have should the clerk have been twenty years older and looking at him that way. However, that kind of thing didn't happen to him very often, and it was just starting to happen to his athletic, tall, good-looking son. Micah hid a smile and nudged Blake with his elbow so he'd speak.

"Uh, yeah," he stammered as Micah pulled his debit card out of his wallet. "I, uh, run the four hundred and the sixteen-hundred relay. I'm really fast."

Micah pinched his lips together to keep from chuckling, but the girl seemed very impressed. *Ah, the innocence of youth,* Micah thought. When you didn't even know what baggage was let alone have any. He and Natalie had started dating when he was Blake's age. Neither one of them ever imagined how things would end up.

"Where do you go to school?" the girl asked.

"Skyline."

Her face took on a slight pout. "Oh, I go to Idaho Falls High. But maybe I'll see you at one of the meets." She smiled brightly, and Blake nodded like the starry-eyed, sixteen-year-old boy he was. Micah nudged him forward again so he could run his card through the machine bolted to the countertop.

"Do you run track?" Blake asked.

"No, but I have a friend who does. She runs the eight hundred."

The register beeped, and the girl had to tear her eyes away from Blake to find out why. She looked instantly uncomfortable. "It says the card is denied."

Micah furrowed his brow. "I'll try it again. Maybe I did the wrong pin." He scanned it again and this time, they all watched. After about ten seconds, it beeped, and the word "Denied" showed up on the little screen. It was Micah's debit card, tied to his checking account, into which he'd just deposited two loans' worth of commissions last week.

"Um, maybe you have another card?" the clerk asked.

"Yeah," Micah said. He pulled it out and ran it through the machine, watching the screen. When "Denied" came up again he felt his face getting hot. He looked up at the girl. "Are you sure there isn't something wrong with your machine?"

"Um, it worked on the last lady who used a card." She started looking around, saw someone at the other end of the bank of cash registers, and called him over.

"I'm Paul, the manager. Can I help?"

Micah explained the situation as the guy behind them in line let out a breath and crossed his arms over his chest. *Believe me, buddy,* Micah thought. *I'm the last person who wants this.*

"Is the credit card off the same account as the debit card?" the manager asked.

"Well, yeah, but the credit line is separate from the debit."

"If there's a problem with your overall account, often none of the cards will work."

"But there isn't a problem with my account," Micah said, his words clipped. Blake had walked a few feet away. He shifted from one foot to another and looked around as if not wanting anyone to know he was with the guy getting all irate at the check stand. Seeing Blake's embarrassment was even more humiliating to Micah.

"Okay," Micah said, calming down and trying not to let his head run away from him. "I'll write a check."

"We do electronic check filing, so if there's a problem with your account a check won't go through either. I'm afraid we'll need another card or cash."

"I don't have any cash," he said. And though he had other cards, he kept them at home—it wasn't safe to carry too many at one time.

Paul made an uncomfortable face and shrugged before turning to the young clerk, who also looked uncomfortable. Blake had backed up until he was almost out the door.

"Laura," Paul said. "Let's hold on to these for twenty-four hours." He turned back to Micah. "Just let the clerk know when you come back."

Laura smiled as if trying to tell him it was okay. Who was he that he needed some teenager to reassure him? Micah nodded tightly and hurried from the store. Blake was quick to lead the way.

They drove home in silence. Micah went straight to his office and logged onto his credit union's web site. The moment the account came into view, he inhaled sharply at the balances. Blake called to him from the kitchen.

"Hey, Dad, there's a message on your voice mail from the bank. They said there are some charges they'd like you to verify. What's the deal?"

CHAPTER 10

~~~~

Antigua, Guatemala

*I*f she had been born a son, this would not be her fate. She'd be staying with the soldiers, fighting, and furthering the cause of freedom as her brothers did. She would be a warrior. But fate had made her a woman, a creature of limitations.

She turned her face toward the rain falling in the Antigua jungle, wanting to remember the smell of it, the feel of it on her skin. It would be a long time before she would feel it again. She didn't imagine that rain in America was anything like this.

"*¿Estás lista?*" her father asked from behind her—*Are you ready?*

"*Sí,*" she said, inclining her head to show both her respect to him as her father and her subservience to him as her leader.

He continued in Spanish. "You will wait for your new identifications in Mexico City. Frederico is making all the arrangements."

She nodded again and hoped her father didn't notice how her body stiffened at the sound of her husband's name. Frederico, the father of the child she was carrying—a man she barely knew.

She focused her attention on the chaos around them as the men broke camp. They moved as if the sky were clear, pulling up tents, wrapping supplies in banana leaves and loading them into the back of the trucks. The government army had been tipped off to their location, and even though the People's Army for Freedom had only been camped a few weeks, it was time to move. It was a natural time for her to begin her own journey as well.

Her father placed a hand on her shoulder, and the hint of tenderness caught her off guard. She looked up at him in surprise, and then narrowed her eyes. She was not weak. She pulled her shoulder away, an action that would be interpreted as disrespectful in any other circumstance, and looked at him steadily.

"I am ready," she said in English, the primary language she would speak once she reached her ultimate destination—once she was reunited with Frederico. He did not love her any more than she loved him, but they both respected the dreams of their fathers—a Guatemala free of foreign dominance and suppression. Their marriage had been one of politics, and the mixed blood of their offspring would join two of the largest militia groups in the Guatemalan rebellion. It was how tribes had made treaties many years ago, an old tradition of sharing power that, though she respected, she found to be very primitive.

Her father smiled and she realized he'd been testing her, seeing if she was softening due to the advancing pregnancy. Nothing could be further from the truth. If anything, the more this child grew within her, the more her thirst for this war grew as well. Perhaps because, as they all hoped, it was a son. Or perhaps the child simply served as a constant reminder of her limitations and therefore increased her anger and resentment of her current role.

The rain began to fade, the pattering of drops on the jungle leaves getting softer, more spread out. Only two trucks were left. One would take her father and her oldest brother, a prominent leader of the army, to join their soldiers in the new camp. The other truck would take her away from this life. It was all she could do to keep herself from refusing to do it, refusing to go.

"It is better this way," her father whispered, also in English, the words not as crisp and properly pronounced as when she spoke it. He had not attended Brazilian boarding schools eight months out of every year as she had, and so his English tones were muted and soft, the words strung together as if still trying to make Spanish music from the bulky English words. "This is your contribution."

"I just want to do what I must so that I can return." She stared at him, wishing she dared to suggest she stay, wishing she could find a way to make her own place in this war without the swelling in her belly. What would she do with a child anyway? She didn't know how to be a . . . *mother*. The word was foreign to even think about. Her own mother had produced three healthy sons, only to die in the jungle hours after birthing her only daughter. Her mother's weakness was a curse that had followed her all her life. "This is where I belong," she said, waving her hand to encompass the jungles of Antigua, Guatemala, the trucks coated in thick mud.

"Bring me an heir," her father said. "Through your sacrifice, you may yet create a place for yourself among the generals of this army."

No matter how hard her father or the other generals tried to convince her she was a queen—and set apart for a different kind of greatness—she could not overcome the insult of her role. They said she would usher in the next generation, raise the men who would rule the country once their agendas were fulfilled and the current government was uprooted. However, she was not stupid enough to fall for their false divinity. She was nothing more than a broodmare, a fact made even more apparent when her father had brought Frederico into the camp all those months ago and told her that he would be the father of her children. He had stayed only long enough for them to be sure she was carrying his child, then he left—returning to his life in the U.S., waiting for her to join him.

"You are ready?" her father asked again. His tone showed that he was tired of the discussion. They both knew she would fulfill the role assigned to her; but it was up to her whether she would fulfill it with honor.

"*Sí,*" she said, taking one more look at the rain-sodden jungle, so green, so comforting. "I am ready."

She would be a different woman when she arrived in America, with a different name, a different life. She feared and resented it, yet she would embrace it as well.

It was her calling, and she would make her father proud.

CHAPTER 11

~~~~~

San Ysidro, California
Wednesday, April 16

*S*he'd chosen to walk over the Tijuana border crossing, rather than fly, due to her pregnancy and security issues. At the entry point, she gave the birth certificate and replacement driver's license of the real Chressaidia to prove she was a U.S. citizen. The advancing pregnancy had softened her own features to better match those of the real Chressaidia, and she'd worn her hair down so the similarities were even more apparent. However, she'd still held her breath until her documents were back in hand and she was allowed to continue out the doors and up the ramp that would lead her over the highway.

When she emerged from the corridor, she looked beyond the buildings at the cars and the people. *This is the United States?* she thought as she made her way down the ramp. It didn't look much different than the Mexico she'd just left with the noisy and heavily fenced freeway, desert landscape, and overflowing garbage cans—but it represented so much more.

Decades earlier, America had convinced the Guatemalan leadership that democracy was the only way to have peace. Since then,

Americans, along with others like them, had been slowly taking over her country. They moved their companies to Guatemala City. They took the people from their fields to work in the factories. In the name of democracy, they were slowly enforcing a different kind of bondage on her people. It made her angry to be on American land, to be in any way dependent on her enemies, but she took comfort in knowing that her being here was one more step toward an end in which Guatemala would be returned to the people who had lived there for centuries.

Frederico stood on the sidewalk next to where a Hispanic family watched the portal that led the pedestrians from Mexico to America. Her *husband* was pacing and looking up every few seconds. She squared her shoulders and took confidence that thus far the identity procured for her was flawless. For all intents and purposes she now *was* Chressaidia Josefina Salazar, a Mexican-American woman who was returning *to* her homeland rather than fleeing from it. The story she'd come up with was that she had been traveling with a group of friends but wasn't feeling well so she was coming back early. No one had questioned her. Why should they?

The simple reminders calmed the anxiety that had grown during the hour-and-a-half wait in the customs line. Legitimate border crossers surrounded her: Hispanics in the U.S. on work visas, college kids still hung over from their weekend in Tijuana, and Americans who lived south of the border because of the cheap rent and free beaches.

The wind was blowing, and though not cold, it wasn't warm either. A white woman passed by, cursing about the wind ruining her hair. Her husband rolled his eyes and tightened his grip on the bag he carried, overflowing with cheaply made blankets and souvenirs. He walked faster, probably wishing he'd left her on the other side. Spoiled, arrogant, selfish people. Dipping their toes in a country they despised in the name of entertainment.

Frederico looked up again, a guarded, cautious look on his face until he saw her. There was the slightest recognition in his stern features, but almost instantly, his face tightened again—the exact way she remembered him.

When she reached the bottom of the ramp, they fell in step together. He barely looked at her, treating this as a transaction rather than a reunion. She'd expected as much. His cartel needed drugs and her father needed guns. Together they would fulfill the needs of both their interests and further both agendas by bringing their child into the world under the best of conditions.

"No problems?" he asked in English, his voice quiet to be certain they would not be overheard. He nearly sounded like an American after so many years of living here. He even dressed like one, smelled like one. It disgusted her. Did he even understand what their fathers were fighting for anymore? His shoes were shiny, made of tight, solid-looking leather. She scowled at them before forcing herself to turn away. The soldiers made do with whatever shoes they could find, or steal—or kill for, if necessary.

"None," she said, concealing her judgments. "You?"

"I've already set up the bank account and half a dozen credit cards in your name. The home equity loan should fund by Monday. Ms. Salazar has been a great asset to us. She even has health insurance. I've already sent in a change of address form. It's all in place. I was able to use other IDs to get this one set up so there's no trail. We'll be married at a courthouse tomorrow."

"Again?" she said, hating that she'd have to go through it a second time.

"The child must be of legitimate birth here in the U.S. as well— my father demands it."

Even if the mother has a different name? Frederico was the only person in this country who knew who she really was. On all the records, the baby would be born to Chressaidia Salazar. But one more pointless and loveless ceremony was not worth fighting about. "While I am here I want to manage my own affairs—these accounts you've set up in my new name."

"Good," Frederico said. "I have enough to do already." His long strides forced her to nearly run to keep up with him, and she had to put a hand under her extended belly as she did so.

It felt heavy and every day seemed to get worse. Thank goodness they'd lined things up in time. The grandson of the most powerful man in Guatemala would not be put at risk by being born in the mountains—and she, unlike her mother, would not bleed to death in a makeshift tent. All her hatred of this country aside, it was a relief to know she would get the care she and this baby needed. With so much hostility toward the growing militia groups there was too much risk in a Guatemalan hospital.

"I want to be clear," Frederico said as they reached the car, a shiny automobile that, again, was American. He stopped walking, and though she wouldn't have admitted it, she was grateful for the rest. "I have a life here." Frederico glared at her from underneath heavy black eyebrows. "I do not want it interrupted."

"And I have a life in the jungles, fighting for freedom." She met his glare with one just as heated. "I did not want it interrupted either. I will be here only a short time, then I will leave without regret."

He walked to the driver's door, pushing a button on his keychain to save himself the effort of putting a key in the lock.

Spoiled, arrogant, selfish.

CHAPTER 12

Idaho Falls, Idaho

J have faxed the letter and the police report to you twice already," Micah said, trying oh-so-hard to keep his anger and frustration in check.

"Deed you sent eet to 1–888–555–9834?" The customer service rep on the other end of the line had such a thick accent that Micah could hardly understand what he said. He shouldn't be surprised that his credit card company had farmed out its call center to India like so many other businesses had, but it sure didn't make this any easier.

"Yes, that's the number." He read the notes he'd written on the last notice he'd received. "I faxed it last Friday and then I faxed it again yesterday."

"Cun you fax eet wone more time?"

"I can do that, but how can I make sure you'll receive it?"

The customer service rep went on to assure him that even though the fax had been lost twice now, he fully trusted he'd get it that afternoon.

"Can I call back and see if it was received? Can I talk to you about it specifically?"

"Yeahs, sir, of course."

"Okay," Micah said, hitting *send* on the fax machine. As the machine hummed, the customer service rep asked if there was anything else he could do to help.

"Yeah, get this figured out!" Micah said, banking on the fact that his call was being recorded. "I've been contacting you people for weeks now. I want the bills to stop and I want it removed from my credit."

"We wheel do our best. Tank you for culling us todeey."

Micah hung up, checked his watch, and quickly put the growing pile of bills, notices, letters, and log items back in the file he'd titled "Bullcrap." He put the file back in his drawer even though he knew he'd be working on it again this afternoon. Then he grabbed his laptop and headed out the door. He hoped the traffic gremlins would be on his side and help him make it to the office in time to meet with his clients for a few minutes before the closing. He'd spent countless hours this week trying to get items removed from his credit report and he was running out of patience. He was the victim, yet proving his innocence was taking over his entire life.

He pulled out of his driveway and cursed under his breath when the first light he came to turned yellow two cars in front of him. Tapping his thumbs on the steering wheel he tried to think happy thoughts—it was getting harder and harder to do so, however, when he felt like the puppet at the end of someone else's strings.

CHAPTER 13

❦

*Y*ou're sure you won't reconsider?" Brandon asked as Chrissy scanned the bottom drawer of her desk for any other personal effects. She saw a bit of pink and shuffled some folders out of the way to reveal a stack of Post-it notes. Printed in the lower left-hand corner were the words "Just do it my way and no one gets hurt." The notes had been part of a gift basket Kent had given her for Secretary Appreciation Day more than a year ago. She smiled and put the notes in her box, almost forgetting Brandon was there until he continued with his thinly veiled begging. "This office won't be the same without you."

It's certainly not the same without your father, Chrissy thought. She tried to come up with something polite to say and looked up, but immediately realized that, by leaning over, she'd afforded Brandon a direct view down her shirt. She tried very hard to dress in a way that was modest, yet flattering. However, being well-endowed made it nearly impossible sometimes. She sat up quickly and adjusted her top. In the weeks since Kent had officially retired, she'd become the recipient of too much attention from her new boss. She was tired of wearing turtlenecks but wished she'd donned one yet again today.

"It's time for me to move on," Chrissy said, shivering under his gaze, which was still directed at her chest. "But Carla will do great."

He finally looked up to meet her eyes. "You do yourself a disservice to think you're so easy to replace." His eyes moved back down. *"Te voy a extrañar,"* he continued—*I'll miss you.* He often switched to Spanish when talking to her, another thing that made her uncomfortable. It wasn't the language he used; rather it was the presumed intimacy that seemed to lace his words when he used it.

"That's very nice of you to say," she said as politely as she could. Chrissy was always respectful to her employers. It was something Abuelita had taught her—to have respect and not cause problems at work.

She stood up, lifting the box, anxious to get out and be free of this. The upside of Brandon's behavior was that it convinced her of the need for a change in her career path. She had always been a meticulous saver and had almost six thousand dollars in savings for just such a circumstance as this. Though she didn't look forward to living off of it while she decided what to do next, it was a better option than staying here. Maybe she'd look into becoming a hotel desk clerk. That sounded fun. Or maybe a massage therapist. She'd always had strong hands.

She forced a smile and looked at him until he met her eyes, working hard to hold in all her evil thoughts of him. "Good luck," she said, then hurried to the door without looking back. It was raining, hard, and she bent her head over the box she carried, but didn't slow down.

Once inside the car, she put the box on the passenger seat, leaned her head back and shouted, "I'm free!" The door didn't seal completely, so rain dripped down the inside of her windows. It was why her car always smelled faintly of mildew, but air fresheners masked most of the smell.

With a grin, she started the car and headed home, turning on her lights just to see them flip up from the hood—it was one of her favorite things about the car. Tomorrow morning she'd sleep in, take a walk if it wasn't still raining, clean out a closet or two—whatever she wanted. She wasn't certain how long it would last, but for now, life was good!

CHAPTER 14

Chula Vista, California
Saturday, May 3

The pains were getting closer together and Chressaidia let out a deep, low breath. She put a hand on her belly—tight as a drum—and looked around the room as if something within the walls of the beach house could help her, but she was alone. She'd called Frederico hours ago, and he said he'd be back in time to take her to the hospital. But he wasn't here yet. It was frightening to face this at all, much less to face it alone.

He hadn't spoken to her in the days since her arrest and she was sure this silent treatment from him was supposed to be part of her punishment. Her face still throbbed from where he'd hit her after picking her up from the police station. He was the one who had sent her out to contact a few of his dealers; he was the one who had told her she needed to earn her keep. But she hadn't known what she was doing, didn't fully understand the way things worked. Luckily, the police had taken pity on the poor pregnant girl, though she'd still been charged with possession.

In the aftermath of her arrest, Frederico was angry, and yet, so was she—missing her father and the comfort of her homeland more than ever. In their silence to one another she'd tried to learn even more about what he did, determined to not make any more mistakes, and had even followed him a few times to high-end clubs. When he came home, she knew he had been entertaining himself with more than women and dancing. He was using the drugs he was supposed to be selling, she was certain of it. When the time was right, she'd take her revenge and tell his father. It would not be taken lightly. But for now, their paths were separating quickly. She had stopped seeing this child as his son. The child would belong to *her*, be raised and trained by her. Frederico had done his part eight-and-a-half months ago. He would take no glory from her now.

She was packing a bag when another pain came, this one causing her to bend forward over the bed. She clenched her teeth and willed it to go away, then moved faster, trying to push away the panic. When her mother had given birth to her, she was hours away from her own death. But she hadn't been alone, and she'd already borne three other children. Chressaidia knew nothing of what was ahead. Her ignorance terrified her.

She threw a nightdress and some underwear into her bag, as well as a red-and-yellow woven blanket to wrap the baby in. The red represented the blood and heritage of her people; the yellow represented the illumination her child would help bring to his country. She had made the blanket herself, on a backstrap loom in the Antigua mountains before she prepared for her journey here. And though she was not a sentimental person, her heritage defined her as her son's heritage would define him. Perhaps by the time he was grown, he would run the government of Guatemala instead of fighting against it.

She looked at the clock and walked carefully into the foyer of the beach house. What if Frederico wasn't coming? He'd told her to wait for him, and she'd agreed that would be best. Yet, now she was feeling foolish and hated the dependency. After a few minutes, and another pain—they were only minutes apart now—she pulled open the door. She'd spent the last few weeks driving around the area, finding Frederico's dealers, making introductions. She could find the hospital. Even if the idea of driving in her condition frightened her, at least she could use Frederico's neglect against him in the future.

She closed the door and hurried as fast as she could to the parking garage where her car was waiting—a silver Toyota she'd bought right after her arrival. As she slid awkwardly behind the wheel, another contraction seized her and a warm rush from between her legs announced with even more certainty that her time was short. With shallow breaths, she put the key in the ignition and swallowed her fear. This was her role; it was her mission. And it was only the beginning.

CHAPTER 15

✦

Idaho Falls, Idaho

Micah stood on Cam and Amanda's porch and rang the doorbell. Mallory had spent Saturday morning at their house while Micah worked on a loan that absolutely had to close next week. He hated working on the weekends, especially when Mallory was there, but he was doing everything he could to keep his head above water these days and putting in a sixty-hour workweek was only one part of the equation.

The front door swung open to reveal Cam—his home teacher.

"Oh, I'm so glad you're here," Cam said, holding the door open and inviting Micah inside. "I'll holler for Mallory to dry off—they ended up in a water fight—but can you help me with something?"

"Sure," Micah said.

"It's so stupid," Cam said as Micah followed him into the kitchen. Cam opened the back door and yelled to Mallory that her dad was there while Micah assessed the situation. The cupboard under the sink was empty except for a detached garbage disposal. The dish soap, kitchen cleaner, and an array of sponges and rags littered the floor in no semblance of order. Cam lay down on his back and scooted until his head, neck, and shoulders were inside the cupboard. He lifted the disposal off the cupboard floor as Micah got down on his knees and poked his head into the small space next to Cam. The cupboard smelled like mildew and Lysol.

"Okay," Cam said, turning the disposal slightly. "I can get the connection lined up until right about . . . here, but I can't hold it up to tighten it."

"You want me to hold or tighten then?"

"Uh," Cam said. "Hold."

Micah nodded and within a few minutes they were done. They both got up and Micah washed his hands in the sink.

"Thanks," Cam said, stretching his arms and back. "Amanda's been after me for weeks to get that fixed. The gasket was shredded and leaking."

Micah was rinsing his hands when he looked out the window into the backyard. Mallory was on the patio, drying off with a towel, but her eyes were following the water fight still in progress. Amanda sat reading something at the picnic table, and a passel of kids chased each other on the grass. His hands stilled in the running water when he recognized Chrissy. He'd only met her once, after all, and that had been months ago, but his stomach flip-flopped anyway.

Chrissy was embroiled in the heart of the battle. If not for the fact that she wasn't in a swimsuit, he'd have likely thought she was one of the children. No, he corrected himself, in a swimsuit it likely would have been far more obvious that she was a full-grown, well put-together woman.

What is she doing here? The feelings from all those months ago rose up. As time had passed, he'd forgotten what he liked about that evening and simply thought of her as the last date. Last as in *final,* as in the straw that broke the back of the camel named "maybe I'll find someone." In his mind that night had become a symbol of why dating was off his radar. And yet, he couldn't help but watch her.

She wore short Levi pants that came down to the middle of her calf—they had some kind of special name but he couldn't remember, Cappies or something. She also had on a red-and-white polka-dot blouse. Her hair was gathered into a thick knot on top of her head, and she was dripping wet as she ran after a small Mexican boy. She caught him around the waist and wrestled him to the ground. Micah could just hear the sounds of squealing laughter through the window. After a few seconds she let the boy go, but remained prostrate on the ground, smiling, laughing. Micah could only stare, not liking how beautiful she looked or that he'd noticed at all.

"Dad, do I have to go?"

Micah turned to Mallory, her wet hair clumped and sticking to her face. Her shorts and T-shirt were completely soaked, and she held a towel around her shoulders. She'd be fourteen in a few weeks. How had that happened so fast? She'd only been a toddler when he and Natalie had split up.

"It's almost two o'clock," he said. "You've been here most of the day."

"Please?" Mallory whined, bouncing up and down slightly on the balls of her feet.

"Ah, let her stay," Cam said, throwing soaps and sponges back into the cupboard; Amanda would be thrilled with his organizational skills. "There's a bunch of kids out there. We won't even notice her."

Micah looked back out the window. This time, Chrissy was being chased by three or four children. She was fast, and now that her wet clothes were clinging a bit tighter, Micah noticed her curves were in all the right places. He felt his cheeks heat up at having put it into words, even if only in his mind.

"Please, Daddy?" Mallory asked again, bringing his thoughts back to the kitchen. Her eyes were pleading and therefore looked twice their natural size. It had been beautiful weather all week. Today was one of the warmest days they'd had all year and everyone knew the break in the weather wouldn't last very long.

"Well, I—"

"It's really okay as far as we're concerned," Cam said, standing up and surveying his work before kicking the cupboard closed, a smug smile on his face. Micah knew he couldn't wait to boast about his disposal-fixing success to Amanda. "She can stay as long as you want. I did the soccer game circuit this morning, so we're home for the rest of the day. Besides, other kids keep ours from demanding so much of our attention."

Micah looked back at Mallory. "Go ahead."

Mallory brightened, dropped her towel in the middle of the floor, and disappeared. Micah looked out the window expecting to watch Mallory re-enter the battle, but his eyes were drawn to Chrissy instead. She dove under the trampoline and crawled out the other side, circling back to the hose and picking it up. The screams of the kids came through the window. He couldn't take his eyes off her face. There was just something about her.

"Micah?" Cam asked, watching him.

Micah tore his eyes away from Chrissy. "Well, I'd better go," he said with a smile. He managed one more glance out the window in time to see Mallory dump a bucket of water over Chrissy's head. She jumped, dropped the hose, and turned on Mallory, whose long legs made her escape a quick one. A dark-haired girl who looked to be about Mallory's age, picked up the hose and got Chrissy in the back. The wet shirt clung to Chrissy's curves even more. Micah swallowed.

Cam took over the position at the sink. Micah grabbed a paper towel and turned his back to the window so he wouldn't be tempted to look anymore. The Sunday after Micah had said he'd think about calling Chrissy, Cam asked him about it. Micah had said he'd thought it over and decided against it; he wasn't in a position to have a relationship, so there was no sense in pursuing a bad start. Cam didn't push it. He must have said something to Amanda because she'd never said anything about it either.

After Blake moved in, Micah began going to church every week. Blake played ward basketball, got the job at Pizza Hut, made a few friends, and was doing great. Micah had even been called into Scouting last month. A lot had changed since the phone call he'd never made.

"Thanks again," Cam said, looking out the window just as Micah had done. He paused, then turned, a knowing look in his eye and a hesitant smile on his lips as he seemed to realize why the window had drawn so much of Micah's attention.

Micah didn't give him a chance to say anything about it. He threw his paper towel in the garbage can and hurried toward the front door before the moment became even more awkward. But the image of a dripping wet, smiling Chrissy was relentless.

"I'll be back in a couple hours," he said, reviewing all the things he needed to do at home today. "Thanks for letting Mallory stay."

CHAPTER 16

*W*hew!" Chrissy slid onto the picnic table bench and tried to catch her breath. "Good thing I wore waterproof mascara today," she said with sarcastic sincerity as huge drops of water dripped from her hair, now tightly curled. She reached up and removed the elastic so she could redo her bun. The dark, wet tendrils fell halfway down her back. She scooped up her hair in one hand, twisted it on top of her head, and secured it with the elastic once again. Then she grabbed a napkin from the leftover Happy Meals and dabbed it on her face. The napkin was soon covered with foundation and eye shadow—all non-waterproof, apparently.

The weather was such a relief, a day of summer amid a spring that was stubbornly refusing to release its hold. When Amanda and Cam had moved in about six years ago, they had lined the cedar fence with lilac bushes and now the shrubs were tall and seemed to cocoon the yard in blessed green. The blossoms would open in another few weeks, turning the yard into an even stronger haven, soaked in the scent of flowers. Chrissy's yard, on the other hand, stood as a tribute to naturalism. She mowed, now and again, but the weeds had taken over the grass years ago. She wasn't big on working in the dirt like Cam and Amanda were. Even Livvy tended a few rosebushes. Zealots; the whole lot of them.

Amanda eyed her with amusement. "You are such a child," she said, shaking her head and sending her new haircut—a chin-length bob—brushing against her jaw. It looked nice, but maybe a little too soccer-Mom for Chrissy's tastes. "Hasn't anyone told you to act your age?"

"Ah, but which age?" Chrissy said, lifting one eyebrow. "The age written on your birth certificate, or the age written on your face?" She lifted her chin and moved it from side to side, using her hands to frame it. "Just last week the woman at the Clinique counter told me I have the skin of a college girl."

"And what was she selling?" Amanda asked, dipping a cold fry in a smeary blob of ketchup.

"To me?" Chrissy said with a hand on her chest. "Nothing. You know me better than that. I just go for the free facials and makeup tips." She turned around and watched the kids, who were still spraying one another with the water guns she'd made out of surgical tubing and clothespins—86 cents apiece. Amanda provided lunch; Chrissy provided the weaponry.

One of Amanda's neighbors, Mallory, was close to Rosa's age, and the two seemed to have hit it off. Chrissy was glad. Rosa wasn't very social, carefully approaching new people as if afraid to expect too much. In fact, she hadn't even wanted to get wet today. But Mallory had convinced her that they could join forces against Trevor and his friend. At one point Cam had said it was time for Mallory to go home, but she must have used her pretty blue eyes to their best advantage because she came back out a few minutes later. She was a cute girl.

Chrissy turned back to Amanda, eager to brag about her latest find. "I did, however, find an entire eight yards of green terry cloth at a yard sale last week for three bucks—ten percent the price the Clinique woman wanted to charge me for just one lipstick—*ay, ay, ay.* I'm going to make Rosa a swimsuit cover and maybe a robe."

"Cam would give his left arm for me to have half your domestic skills."

Chrissy made an exaggerated motion of flipping her hair—despite it being caught up in a bun on top of her head—and gave Amanda a movie-star smile. *"Gracias, Señorita,"* she breathed, batting her eyelashes. "I do try." In truth, she'd been raised in an environment where learning to cook and sew and take care of your own home wasn't a hobby; it was survival. As an adult, she took great satisfaction in making something great out of something so little. Amanda, on the other hand, filled her time with PTA and book groups rather than traditional homemaking. All good things, but different from Chrissy's perspective. However, their differing interests ensured they always had a lot to talk about.

"So how's the unemployed life going?" Amanda asked. "Are you loving it?"

"Absolutely," Chrissy said, letting herself bask in the glorious three weeks she'd had. "But I'm actively pursuing the quest to find yet another grindstone to put my nose to." She sighed dramatically and looked at her friend. "Poor me," she said with sarcasm and a pouty look.

"I thought you were taking a few *months* off?"

Chrissy shrugged. "Well, I've managed to catch up on nearly all the projects I'd planned to do, and it's killing me to live off my savings. Maybe I've grown out of these vacations of mine. I put in an application with Bedis last week."

"Bedis?" Amanda repeated, her eyebrows lifting in surprise. "That's like . . . career work."

"I know," Chrissy said, shaking her head as if disappointed in her own conformity. "It's wacky weird stuff for me, but I think I need to start planning my future. You know, get a 401K, sick leave, maybe a free turkey at Thanksgiving. I was with Almo for almost four years, longer than any other job, and it was kind of nice until that dingbat took over."

"Bedis *is* a great company to work for, but they don't give out free turkeys." Amanda spoke from experience, since Cam was one of the many engineers who worked at the nuclear test facility. The site was located about thirty miles out of town and employed over five thousand residents of Idaho Falls, Rexburg, and Shelley, through various companies contracted with it. "Cam said that the background checks on engineers are thirteen months out right now. All the Homeland Security issues have made the government clearances an absolute nightmare. Did they say how long the wait would be for you to even hear back?"

Chrissy shook her head. The closer you actually worked with the nuclear waste or sensitive documents, the more in-depth the application process. Chrissy had applied to be in Office Management, located in Idaho Falls, but the position still required a detailed poke and prod into her past. If she'd thought there was anything at all to hide, she wouldn't have bothered. But other than a somewhat eclectic work history, she couldn't think of anything that would stand out.

"They said it would only be a few weeks, since I want to work in the city. The pay's better if I get clearance to work at the site later, but the days would be longer because of the commute." She paused before continuing. "Lupe's been sending me more dress orders. I wish I could make a living off that, but there are no benefits to consignment seamstress work."

"That stinks," Amanda said.

Chrissy shrugged and lifted the wet fabric of her shirt off her skin. It made a squelching sound, and she smiled, disappointed the boys weren't close enough to laugh at the sound with her. "What are ya gonna do?" she said, then turned around, leaning her back against the table and watching the water fight.

The older kids were playing King of the Hill—on the trampoline—and Rosa and Mallory were the current rulers, squirting the boys in the face every time they tried to get over the metal frame. Rosa's water gun was almost empty; a real battle would soon ensue. "You gonna get in there and pretend you remember how to have fun?" Chrissy asked, sending a sparring look over her shoulder.

"You really get into this stuff, don't you?"

Chrissy laughed. "I might not be able to find a man willing to put up with me, but kids are a whole 'nother story."

The comment fell flat as Amanda's face showed her insecurity about finding the right response and the obvious loomed heavy between them. Without a man Chrissy would never have children of her own. It wasn't the first time such thoughts had intruded on her attempts to find peace, but it stung a little more than usual on a day like today—when she was enjoying other people's children so much.

Amanda recovered and saved the moment by making a face and responding to Chrissy's earlier request. "Getting blasted in the face with ice-cold hose water is hardly my idea of fun." She picked up the magazine she'd been reading and snapped it open. "I'll read about cooking with tofu, thank you very much."

CHAPTER 17

San Diego, California

Jon Nasagi looked at the chart and read the patient's name, Chressaidia Josefina Salazar, then looked at her lying in the hospital bed. She didn't act as though he were there at all. She was turned toward the wall, her back facing him. He tried again.

"It is very difficult when a parent has to accept circumstances other than what they expected," Jon continued.

She still made no response. He considered whether another approach would be more effective. Mrs. Salazar was certainly not the first new mother he'd tried to help in the six years he'd worked at University of California, San Diego Medical Center, but she was by far the least interested in what he had to say. How was she supposed to care for a special-needs child if she was this closed off? She wasn't even crying.

"The important thing to keep in mind is that this is not your fault. With today's technology . . ." He trailed off as Mrs. Salazar pulled the blanket over her head like a child. He had seen her face for only a moment, long enough to see the bruise the nurses had told him about. No one had come with her to the hospital, and she wouldn't answer any questions about the father of her child. Although she did say she was married, she didn't use her married name. The nurses insisted she spoke very good English. She'd come in dilated to an eight and delivered her baby within the hour. At first, they wouldn't allow her to see the child while they did a general assessment. When they did show her the baby, she had refused to hold him. Certainly a shocking experience all the way around.

After almost a minute of silence, hoping she'd respond to him or get angry or sad or . . . *something,* his beeper went off. Jon stood and placed the grief pamphlet on her bedside table. "I'll come back later," he said as he headed for the door. "If you decide you want to talk before I return, just tell your nurse. She'll page me."

He left the room, updated the nurse at the nurse's station, and called his secretary about his latest page. Two parents in the pediatric wing had just learned their son's cancer had spread to his spine, and they needed someone to help them work through the heartbreak of realizing their child would not get better. It was going to be a difficult afternoon.

Almost two hours later, overloaded by the heaviness of the day, Jon headed for his office. He had some notes to enter into the computer before leaving for home. Tomorrow would be his first day off in more than a week and he was looking forward to it. That's when he remembered Mrs. Salazar. He paused mid-step, and then went to the elevator and pushed the button for the maternity ward on the fifth floor. He was exhausted, but he'd told Mrs. Salazar he'd check in on her. She was due to be discharged sometime tomorrow, though the baby would need to stay for another week at least. His mother needed training on how to care for him, and she needed to understand the follow-up care he would need as well. Jon worried she might not be up to it, but it wasn't his job to make that assessment. At least not yet.

"Dr. Nasagi," one of the nurses said as soon as he turned the corner into the maternity wing that held the patient rooms. "Thank goodness you're here. Dr. Larsen wanted to talk to you about Mrs. Salazar."

Jon noticed a different kind of tension in the air. Something had happened. "She wouldn't talk to me," Jon said. "What's going on?"

"She left, and I think you were the last one in the room."

He raised his eyebrows. *"Left?"*

The nurse nodded. "I went on my rounds forty minutes ago and she wasn't in her room. I thought she was at the NICU, but when she wasn't back in time for her medications, I called down there. They hadn't seen her."

Jon let out a breath. "Any idea when she left?"

"Sometime between two-twenty and four o'clock. Security is checking the videos." She shook her head and met his eyes. "I'm getting tired of mothers like her."

Jon knew the sad truth was that hundreds of babies born in hospitals all through Southern California never went home with their parents. Usually it was because of drugs. Sometimes the parent needed some help before the baby could be released, and sometimes, like this, the mother just left—unable or unwilling to care for her child.

But something about Mrs. Salazar didn't fit this situation. She had health insurance. She claimed to be married. *Maybe she'll come back,* he told himself, but was unable to take much comfort in the possibility. A woman who wouldn't hold her own baby and wouldn't stay in the hospital twenty-four hours wasn't likely to be up to the role she would need to play in the life of this child. Once a mother left, the chances of the child being reunited with her was very slim and because of the Safe Haven laws that protected mothers from any criminal charges, it wasn't a police matter to try to track her down. Jon visualized the process of dealing with an abandoned child. And not just any child either.

"Dr. Nasagi?" the nurse asked.

He turned to look at her, moving on autopilot. "Yeah?"

"Dr. Larsen still wants to talk to you."

CHAPTER 18

Idaho Falls, Idaho
Thursday, May 8

Chrissy was not perfect. She had a vice, and Thursday morning found her watching *General Hospital* to the pattering sound of rain on the windows. It had been almost a week since the water party at Amanda's and the traditional May showers were in full force. Now that Chrissy wasn't working, her past weakness for the soap opera had woven its way into her daily life, and it had only taken a couple days for her to understand all the new twists and turns of the show. She loved rainy spring days like this, when there was nothing better to do than curl up on the couch and watch sappy soap operas or read a book . . . or, as was the case today, hand-sew the beading on a bridesmaid dress. Chrissy was grateful for the extra income and for something to do. Idle hands were the devil's playground, after all.

Apparently she'd grown up since her last stint of unemployment; it wasn't nearly as fun as she'd thought it would be. Last night her dishwasher had gone on the fritz and her home teacher had come over long enough to assure her it was not eligible for resurrection. It was fifteen years old—practically an antique—but knowing she needed a new one put her finances into even sharper perspective. She knew she needed to make a plan—but was putting it off today in favor of Carley and Jason and the secret that could destroy them both! Intense drama made Chrissy feel better about her own life, or so she told herself.

When she heard the sound of footsteps on the porch, she paused for just a moment. The mail. She stood quickly, placing the dress on the couch and securing the needle before heading for the door. She'd had to buy new contacts a few weeks ago, and the fifty-dollar rebate check should be here any day. She could really use the money to take some of the pressure off her savings account.

She reached the door in time to make the postman jump when she pulled it open. "Sorry," she said, offering a smile.

He smiled politely, but his gray eyes remained guarded. Chrissy imagined it was days like this that would send many a postal worker to the Help Wanted section of the newspaper.

"It's okay," he said as he held out a stack of mail, rain dripping off the slick sleeve of his poncho. At least she had a covered porch.

She took the stack of mail. "Thanks," she said as she shut the door with her foot while thumbing through the stack of envelopes. Phone bill, junk, junk, junk—she paused when she encountered a letter from Bedis.

"Already?" she said, sitting down at the kitchen table and ripping open the envelope as her excitement built. She hadn't expected anything regarding her application for another week at least. She took a deep breath while pulling the paper from the envelope. She read the opening line with a smile on her lips, expecting good news, but then stopped and went back to the beginning to read it again.

Dear Ms. Salazar,

After a thorough examination of your application for employment, we regret to inform you that we are unable to approve it. Because of our federal contracts, we can only accept the most impeccable employees, which is why, even in the early stages, we conduct such an extensive background check . . .

She read through the letter twice, her heart rate increasing each time, then picked up the phone. They couldn't just send a cryptic letter like this and leave it at that. Something was wrong.

"There isn't anyone I can talk to?" Chrissy said several minutes later, pacing and glancing at the clock and trying to keep her brain focused. In a few minutes Livvy's kids would come through her door, and the house would come alive. Now that she was home during the day, Chrissy had been having them come over right after school.

"I'm sorry, we can't tell you any more than what's in the letter."

Chrissy took a breath. "All it said was that my background check was insufficient, but there has to be some kind of mistake. I have a perfectly clean record, and my finances are in order." She hadn't had so much as a late payment on anything for at least three years except for that missing gas bill and the gas company said they didn't report it unless you were sixty days late.

"I'm sorry, I—"

"Please," Chrissy interrupted as her hand fell to her side. "Please give me something. Help me understand what I can do." Her face was tingling and she felt panic rising. Whatever was happening wasn't fair. She wondered if it was some kind of discrimination. But why would Bedis do that? She knew several Hispanics employed there.

"Your federal clearance application has been rejected," the woman said, but there was just enough sympathy in her voice to keep Chrissy's anger in check. "You cannot reapply so there is no help I can give you."

Cannot reapply? Chrissy's eyes widened as the woman continued. "If you have ever had an arrest in any state, or filed bankruptcy or have any other questionable accounts, it will show up in our check and the application will be rejected. We simply have no margin for error."

"But I've never gotten more than a speeding ticket. I've never filed bankruptcy, and I have a near perfect credit score. I don't even have a late payment on my mortgage," Chrissy said. "This doesn't make sense. Can I get a copy of the reports?"

"I'm very sorry, but we're unable to release that information."

They both waited for the other to speak—Chrissy trying to think of some way to talk her way through this problem and the woman on the phone not wanting to be rude and hang up.

The front door burst open, with Carlos pulling on Nathan's backpack and both boys arguing about something while they dripped water all over the entryway. Part of her was grateful for the interruption.

"Thank you for your help," Chrissy said before hanging up and trying to force a smile. She turned to the boys, but her thoughts were still on the rejection. She felt . . . guilty. As if she *had* done something wrong. Only, she hadn't. "So, how was school?" she asked the boys.

"Horrible," Carlos said, dropping his backpack and sagging into a kitchen chair. "Monson tripped me at recess and then Nathan took my reading book and said it's his." He glared at his brother and she turned her eyes on Nathan.

"Is that true?" Chrissy asked, trying to care about their petty argument.

Nathan gave her a bored look, cocky as usual. He was three minutes older than Carlos and used it to his advantage as often as possible. He shrugged one shoulder and then collapsed onto the couch. "Who said life was fair?"

Who indeed.

CHAPTER 19

Chula Vista, California

"Come home," her father said into the phone.

Chressaidia stood at the window of the beach house, watching the waves, almost able to believe she was back on the beaches of Guatemala and full of youthful vigor for her father's campaign. Back then she'd been so eager for the day when she'd be old enough to help him. How little she'd understood.

Her head still throbbed, and her bones ached from the birth and from the beating Frederico had welcomed her with once she finally returned home a few days after leaving the hospital to tell him the baby had died. But her body would heal, and with it, her spirit and her mind. Sometimes it was necessary to be broken in order to heal. It was something she believed about her country—that it had been broken by years of corruption and now it was up to the People's Army for Freedom to rebuild.

"I will not come home a disgrace," she said. "I want a different mission to prove myself."

"You have already failed us."

His words stung. She'd told everyone her child had died. Had he no compassion? No, he didn't. Compassion would get in the way of his goals. As it would her own. "Which is why I need redemption. Give me another task."

"You were only meant to be there two months," her father reminded her. "There is nothing left for you to do."

"That's not true—give me another task!" she shouted into the phone as the anger overtook her. "Do you want your daughter to return dishonored? Do you want your generals to know that my being here was a complete waste, that all their work was for nothing?" She'd learned a great deal about what Frederico was doing, and she knew she could do it better, but she didn't dare get too close too fast. Not now. But she had other options. She only needed to convince her father to let her stay.

"You were to give us an heir—*me* an heir."

"And I did not do it, but I will try again. Right now I am here. Your operations are still in need of repair. Do you really think breeding is my only ability?"

"It is your calling."

"You are the commander—give me another calling. Pretend I am a son and not a daughter. Let me prove to you and to the other generals that I am capable of the power that is mine." She paused for a moment, gathering her courage. She had never spoken to her father this way, so strong and so determined. "Let me find Mr. Holmes."

There was a pause. She knew her father was not used to being surprised. "Frederico has looked for him," her father said carefully.

"And he failed. Let me try." Mr. Holmes had disappeared months ago and the generals had given up on recovering his shipment. She'd overheard her father and his generals discussing it on several occasions, but their battle was too fierce to spare anyone to go after it and so they had given the task to Frederico. When his search turned up nothing, they had no choice but to let it go. Since returning to the beach house she'd studied Frederico's files even more, desperate for a way to redeem herself, and learned that Frederico had actually done very little in his search. If she could find the man they knew as Mr. Holmes, she would not only prove her worth, but perhaps trump Frederico in the process. "I am not needed with the army." It stung to say those words out loud. "Let me find him, Let me restore my honor—and yours."

Her father was silent for a moment. Chressaidia kept staring at the waves, every muscle tense as she waited for an answer. Surely he could see her reasoning. Surely there was room for another chance.

"Do you think you can find him?"

She relaxed just a bit. He still had some faith in her. She still had an opportunity. "Yes."

"I will not tell the others unless you succeed. You do not have much time. Has your new identity been discovered?"

"No," she said, surprised to learn he didn't know about her arrest. Or maybe he did and, like her, did not see it as a problem. "The identity is flawless."

"You have one month," he said finally. "Then you will return to us, with or without the shipment."

Chressaidia nodded, then winced at the stabbing pains the movement erupted in her face and neck. "I will bring the shipment with me when I return," she said.

I have to.

CHAPTER 20

~~~~~

Idaho Falls, Idaho
Sunday, May 11

"Where is it?" Chrissy muttered through clenched teeth as she dug through her church bag in search of the visual aid for today's Primary lesson. She'd woken up with a headache that Tylenol hadn't touched before it was time for her to round up the kids and make a dash for church. As was usually the case, being in a bad mood seemed to attract more frustration. It was also Mother's Day, which was second only to Valentine's Day in lousy holidays if you were a single Mormon woman. It hadn't been the best of weeks and it was by far not the best of sacrament meetings.

Rosa leaned over. "What are you looking for?" she whispered. Nathan and Carlos were busy coloring in their notebooks.

"The Liahona," Chrissy said, still digging. "I need it for class today."

"Is that the Christmas-ornament thing you made?"

Chrissy paused, did it really look like a Christmas ornament? She hadn't thought of it like that but she supposed it did. "Yeah, I swear I put it in my bag." Chrissy had been teaching the seven- and eight-year-old kids in Primary for almost four months now and loved it. As they prepared for baptism, their excitement kept her enthusiasm high for the covenants she had made and now lived. She felt sure the reason she'd been called as a Primary teacher was because Nathan and Carlos were in her class, and they were by far the most . . . *spirited* kids that age. But she liked that, too. Having never learned the gospel from someone in her family, it was exciting to teach her nephews herself. Or, at least it was when she didn't feel like stale toast.

"It was on the table when we left," Rosa whispered.

Chrissy's head snapped up and she looked at her niece. "Really? I thought for sure I put it in here."

Rosa shrugged. "I saw it on the table."

Chrissy let out a breath and glanced at the clock. There were still fifteen minutes left in sacrament meeting. She let her eyes move to the boys. If she made them get up and go with her, chances were good that they would want to stay home, but for now they were occupied. She turned her eyes to Rosa and gave her a pleading look.

"Fine," Rosa said with a dramatic sigh. "I'll watch them."

"Muchas gracias," Chrissy whispered as she dug her keys out of her bag. "I'll hurry."

She smiled at the other ward members as she left the chapel and got into her car. She could be back in five minutes. Maybe she'd take another Tylenol before coming back. Too bad she didn't drink. Abuelita had always said tequila was the only treatment for headaches.

Once home, Chrissy ran inside, and sure enough, the Liahona model she'd made from a Styrofoam ball, Popsicle sticks, glitter, spray paint, and bric-a-brac was lying on the table. "It does look like a Christmas ornament," she admitted as she picked it up and headed back to her car.

She was on the bottom step, scowling at her mangy lawn and wondering if she should just gravel it over completely, when something down the street caught her eye. She looked to her left, to Livvy's perfectly manicured, postage-stamp lawn—she even had flowers in the flower beds—and froze. A man was hauling a box out of Livvy's house and loading it into the back of a pickup truck. Was Livvy being robbed? In the middle of a Sunday afternoon? She watched for another moment until Livvy came out, carrying a garbage sack. Chrissy's stomach sank.

It was worse than being robbed.

Livvy must have seen Chrissy marching toward her because she paused mid-stride, then brought her foot down and stumbled forward. She caught herself, but Chrissy had almost reached her by then. The man was back inside.

"What are you doing?" Chrissy asked, the panic in her voice impossible to hide.

Livvy continued to the bed of the truck and put the garbage sack inside it. Her thick black hair was pulled into a high ponytail and she was dressed in jeans and a black top Chrissy had sewn her for Christmas. Her wide hazel eyes showed her discomfort as she shifted her weight from one foot to the other. Livvy had the kind of figure Chrissy had always wanted—tall and willowy rather than short and squat. Unfortunately, being as beautiful as she was had gotten Livvy into a great deal of trouble and seemed to be doing it again. "I was going to tell you tonight," she said, turning to face Chrissy but avoiding her eyes. "We're, uh, moving in with Doug."

Chrissy froze, then crossed her arms over her chest and clenched her jaw. "Oh, really? You've known this guy for a few months and you're moving in with him? Never mind that you have a house of your own and three children!"

Livvy continued to look at the ground. "Doug works with me

at the hospital. He does maintenance," she said as if that explained everything. "And we've been talking about this for a long time. A couple weeks ago a realtor friend of his said now was a great time to sell. I knew you'd freak out if I told you so I—"

"Are you out of your mind, Livvy?" Chrissy said, taking Livvy's arm with her free hand and shaking her. "You are not really doing this."

"I was going to tell you tonight," she said again, as if the upsetting part was finding out about it in the afternoon instead of later today.

"Do the kids know?"

"Not yet. I thought I'd tell all of you when you got home."

Movement on the porch caught Chrissy's eye, and she looked up to see the man—Doug, she assumed—coming their way. She'd avoided meeting him, praying that the relationship between him and Livvy wouldn't last long.

"Move it." His words were rude, but his tone was light. Chrissy stood there looking at him, wishing she had a frying pan to hit him upside the head with. Maybe he'd be easier to knock some sense into than Livvy was.

"Move!" he said more sharply. Chrissy complied, more out of surprise than anything else. She had to let go of Livvy, and as he passed by, she took a good look at him. He was white and wore an auto parts T-shirt tucked into the waistband of his skinny-man jeans. Scuffed and faded cowboy boots were a perfect match for the faded chew can-shaped mark on his back pocket. The man was a walking redneck cliché, except for his striking face. Bright green eyes and a perfectly shaped jaw. Livvy had always been a sucker for a good-looking man. Chrissy, however, was not. As soon as he passed between them, Chrissy looked at her sister again.

"*Creo que no estás pensando con la cabeza,*" she said—*I think you're out of your mind.*

"*Él me quiere,*" Livvy countered—*He loves me.*

"*Estás embarazada?*"—*Are you pregnant?*

"No!" Livvy said. Now she was mad.

"Ain't good manners to speak so as other people can't understand ya," Doug said as he came up and draped one overly-tanned arm across Livvy's shoulder. He had a tattoo of the Ford symbol on his forearm. Chrissy looked between the two of them, then held her sister's eyes, thinking, rather than saying out loud, how horrible this was.

"You must be Christy," Doug said. He smiled, and it was every bit as beautiful as Chrissy would have guessed. Dazzling even.

Chrissy glared at him and his loveliness.

"I'm Doug."

"You're trash," Chrissy said, because that's exactly what she thought, and she saw no reason not to be perfectly honest with him. He didn't seem fazed by her assessment at all, which only proved he was also an idiot. Chrissy continued, cutting off Livvy who had opened her mouth to defend him somehow. "Livvy has three children. How could you ask her to do this?"

Doug shrugged his shoulders and ran a hand through his hair—perfectly disheveling it. "We love each other," Doug said. "And people in love ought to be together. Besides, we can get enough from this house to pay off my truck and the tractor both."

She was selling her house and putting the money into his things? *I'm being punked,* Chrissy thought to herself, staring at her sister and this mutant hick and wondering what planet she was on. *This has got to be a joke.* She'd seen a TV show once where an actor played the part of the most annoying fiancé in history. If the family didn't catch on, they got like a million dollars. But she was just being optimistic to think that's what was happening here. This was real—and exactly something Livvy would do, at least the old Livvy would. Chrissy thought her sister had learned a thing or two since then. She looked at her sister. *"¿En seria?"—Are you serious?*

"No Spanish," Doug said, making a face. Just then, Hector, the neighborhood guy who'd had a crush on Livvy for years, drove by in his low-rider truck. It thumped as he passed. He waved at them as if Livvy didn't have another man draped all over her.

Doug watched the truck and laughed. "Know why Mexicans like them low-rider trucks?" he asked, grinning like a fool and not waiting for an answer. Chrissy's whole body tensed. "They make it easier for them to pick cabbages." He laughed again, then leaned in to kiss Livvy on the temple before heading back inside.

Chrissy could only stare at her sister, her stomach tight. Livvy was looking at the sidewalk. She wasn't going to react at all? What had happened to the part of her sister's brain that had once made rational decisions?

"He doesn't mean it bad," Livvy defended. "He's just trying to be funny."

Chrissy had never felt such disappointment in her little sister. Was not having a man that impossible? When she spoke her voice was softer, the anger having given way for the absolute sorrow. "That's what you want for your kids, huh?"

Livvy looked away and rubbed her arm. "I'm not moving until next weekend, and we'll drive the kids to school so they can finish up the year. Doug had the day off and so we thought we'd get a head start while you had the kids at church." She looked back at Chrissy, her eyes begging for understanding. "Once you get to know him, Chrissy, you'll see he's a really good guy. And he treats me better than anyone I've ever been with."

Chrissy's brain was on the verge of explosion. "He just told a Mexican joke in front of two Mexicans!"

"He doesn't mean it that way," Livvy said, waving it off. "And he says I don't even look like a Mexican. Not really."

"*That* makes it better? That you don't *look* like a cabbage-picking Mexican? What about Rosa and the boys? *They* look Mexican. What kind of jokes will he tell in front of them?"

Livvy's mouth tightened. "You don't understand. He makes me feel—"

"Well, you're right about that. I don't understand this at all. After all the chaos you have gone through—and put your kids through—I cannot believe you would do this. I thought you were smarter than that." Chrissy turned on her heel before she started to scream or cry.

This couldn't be real, and yet, it was. She whimpered slightly as she thought of what this meant. Livvy, gone? The kids, gone? How would Rosa and the boys ever learn about marriage and commitment and values if they were raised with this?

Her head tingled with an emotional buildup she didn't dare release. How could this be happening?

It wasn't until she got back in her car that she remembered her Primary class was likely waiting for her by now—including Carlos and Nathan, who had no idea the sharp left turn their mother had taken in their lives. The differences between Chrissy and Livvy had never been so stark. She felt sick, betrayed, and so very, very sad.

CHAPTER 21

San Diego, California
Thursday, May 15

*C*hressaidia pulled into the Burger King parking lot. She was meeting with one of Frederico's dealers—Eduardo Algra. Frederico hadn't let her do anything in the weeks following her arrest and the baby's death, but he'd finally relented. His father wanted his trade lines increased and Frederico didn't want to do it himself. Chressaidia had volunteered and he'd acted as if he were doing *her* a favor to let her be involved. Little did he know the plans she had for the little bit of power he'd given her.

Eduardo's territory covered six blocks of downtown San Diego, and he seemed to be a reliable dealer, but they had never met. She scanned the building and finally saw him leaning against the south wall, watching her. The Lakers shirt he wore was the only indication he was the guy she was looking for. He was tall, with short hair and glasses—clean-cut rather than rough-looking. Nothing like she'd expected, which put her immediately on guard. She pulled her car into a parking space, and he walked over to her and slid into the passenger seat.

"You're Frederico's chica?" he asked, looking her over.

She wouldn't answer; she just stared at him. Was this a setup? Was he a cop? The other dealers she'd met with had looked the part, acted the part, and with the promise of receiving a larger cut of the profits, were more than happy to go over Frederico's head and look to her as their authority. But there was something different about this guy. Chressaidia didn't like surprises.

He held her eyes as the silence elongated, until finally he let out a breath and shook his head. "You're just like him, aren't you?" he said in Spanish, reaching into his pocket for a roll of cash. She watched his every move as he turned to face her, holding out the money. "You're looking for junkies—guys who live on the beach and spend every other night in jail. I'm not that kind of dealer. Now Freddie's sending some chica to do his trades, and she's looking at me like I'm some stupid kid." He leaned toward her. "I spent more than a year in your jungles," he hissed, his dark eyes burning with indignation. "I saw what was happening there, and I joined up with Freddie to do my part to help his people—*my* people—find freedom. I knew weeks ago that Freddie was using, and that meant everything was going to fall apart."

He threw the money into her lap and put his hand on the door handle. "I'm not supporting freedom anymore. I'm supporting Freddie's newest habit, and now he's sending some girl to do his dirty work. Some girl who probably doesn't have any idea how big this is."

He got out of the car but leaned back inside to deliver a few final words. "Tell Freddie I'll find another way to support his little army." He slammed the door and stalked away. Eduardo didn't look back.

Chressaidia followed him with her eyes, reviewing his words. He knew about the army? He was a sympathizer with their mission? Frederico hadn't said anything about *that*.

Once Eduardo turned the corner of the building, she stowed

the cash in the jockey box before picking up her phone and dialing the number for Carbon, the dealer in Imperial Beach. She'd met with him on several occasions and trusted him as much as she trusted anyone.

"Do you know Eduardo Algra?" she asked when he answered.

"Sure, college-looking kid up in Old Town. Sells to the University crowd. I've met with him a couple times when Frederico couldn't get up there."

"Is he reliable?"

Carbon snorted. "Yeah, he's built up a good line far as I can tell."

"How long has he been in the trade?"

"Almost a year now."

"And he's not a cop?"

Carbon laughed. "A cop? That kid? Algra plays to his audience, but he sure ain't no cop. His mama's Guatemalan like Freddie—and you, too, I guess. I think dealing makes him feel closer to his cartel roots." He laughed at his own joke.

Chressaidia turned the car around and started heading in the direction Eduardo had taken. "I'll see you Wednesday," she said to Carbon and hung up. Two blocks later she saw Eduardo walking down the sidewalk. He might be just the person she was looking for.

CHAPTER 22

Idaho Falls, Idaho

$\mathcal{M}$icah heard someone pull into his gravel driveway and looked at the clock as he removed another fact sheet from his file. After each loan closed, he typed up a fact sheet on the customer and filed it. When work got slow he could call past clients to see if they were interested in refinancing. He absolutely hated making those calls—hated begging for more work—and yet work had slowed down and he hadn't quite caught up with his bills. A car door opened and shut. Blake was at school for another hour and a half so Micah wasn't sure who it could be.

The doorbell rang a few seconds later and when he pulled the door open a few seconds after that, his eyebrows lifted in surprise. His ex-wife, Natalie, stood there, the expression on her face showing how uncomfortable she was being on his front porch. A light, but cold, rain was falling, and she shivered under the leather jacket that matched her boots.

"Hi, Micah," she said, trying to smile, but it wouldn't stick to her highly-glossed lips for more than a moment. She lifted a manicured hand to tuck a lock of hair behind one ear. "Can I come in and talk to you?"

He couldn't remember the last time she'd come to talk to him in person—had she ever? Since the divorce, if she ever needed to talk to him, she called. Now and then she'd asked him to come over to her house so they could discuss an issue in person. He moved aside so she could enter. After he shut the door behind her, he motioned toward the couch and settled himself into his recliner, watching her intently. She held her hands in her lap and kept her back perfectly straight.

"Dennis and I are having some trouble," she said after a few awkward seconds. "Things are really tense right now."

Micah waited for her to add the part where this involved him. When it didn't come, he figured he ought to say something. "I don't think your marriage is any of my business."

She nodded. "It's just that a lot of the trouble is related to . . . money and the kids."

Money? Dennis always made a point of advertising how well he did. Then again, Natalie was a professional-level spender, so it wasn't too far-fetched that she could burn through his money the way she'd once run through Micah's. "The kids as in *our* kids, or the kids as in yours and Dennis's kids?"

"*Our* kids," Natalie said. "Kayla wants to go on a study abroad, but it costs almost five thousand dollars. Mallory's on that dance team, and it seems like that's costing hundreds of dollars every month. My kids—I mean, *Dennis and my kids*—are getting older, and raising five is taking a lot out of us. Then there's the tension with Blake, and the tension between you and me, and things are just so crazy." Her chin trembled but, if anything, Micah felt himself becoming more defensive. She'd spent years manipulating him with her tears and her "Poor Natalie" games. He was not inclined to give in to her, yet he wasn't so hard-hearted as to not have any sympathy.

"I can imagine things are pretty crazy," he said. "Things are hard to keep up with here too."

She grunted slightly. "You've only got Blake."

He stiffened, then took a long deep breath. He needed to stay calm. She'd come here for a reason, and he needed to get to it. But he hated that he was always on the defensive with her. "Don't talk down my problems, okay? It's not fair and it's not helpful. What are you doing here?" He was sorely tempted to tell her about the identity theft and the resulting chaos, but resisted. Opening up to her had never been safe.

"I'm sorry," she said quickly. She went quiet. Micah took a minute to look at her. She was getting older—she'd be forty next month. The lines around her eyes were deeper, the skin on her face thinner. She wore more makeup than she used to and her hair was a very natural-looking strawberry blonde, except Micah knew she was a natural brunette. She was still a beautiful woman and, despite the lingering animosity between them, he was sad that she was having problems with Dennis. He'd thought they were a perfect fit, making Micah just a speed bump in Natalie's journey toward happiness. He couldn't imagine what it would feel like to have another marriage teetering and for a moment was grateful he'd not faced that issue.

"I need a favor," Natalie said, looking up and meeting his eyes. "That's why I came. Could Mallory come stay with you until your summer visitation time starts in June?"

"Before school gets out?"

Natalie looked down. "There's a bus from her school that comes out here, and she could take that for the last few weeks."

Micah let out a breath and reached up to scratch his head as an excuse to stall while he put his thoughts together. He was still getting used to having Blake around so much, but instantly felt guilty for being selfish. He'd played Dad a few days a month for most of his children's lives while Natalie had taken on the lion's share of parenting.

"Of course she can come stay here," Micah said after a few seconds. "Are you sure that's the best solution though?"

Relief softened Natalie's face. "She likes it here, and I really think that Dennis and I need more time with just the four of us, ya know, to be a family."

Micah bit back a sharp retort. And Mallory was the expendable one? Natalie almost made it sound as if Mallory was the reason for all the problems, that having her leave would make it all better. But he didn't want to make things worse, and he didn't want Mallory to be somewhere she wasn't wanted.

"What reason will you give Mallory? I don't think she needs to know about your marital problems," he said, trying to be diplomatic and getting back to the important part.

"I won't tell her that," Natalie said. She fidgeted with one of the buttons on her jacket. "And, well, I had hoped maybe you would just ask her to come. If you asked, it wouldn't seem, you know, um, bad or anything."

Ah, back to living pretenses. Natalie was an expert at that. Micah had no idea what kind of reason he'd come up with for why Mallory should move in with him for the last few weeks of school. He'd have to ponder that one. "Does Dennis know you're here? Telling me how bad things are?"

"Of course not," Natalie said and her cheeks turned slightly pink—though it was hard to tell under all the makeup. "I'm just not sure what else to do at this point."

"I'll call Mal tonight," Micah said. "I'll talk to her about it, and then I'll ask to talk to you."

Natalie's face relaxed as she stood up. Micah took in the leather jacket again, the boots, the designer jeans, the hair. She'd said money was tight, yet she had likely spent the equivalent to his monthly truck payment just on what she wore today. But that's how she operated—always had.

"I hope things work out for you guys," Micah said. "For everyone's sake. The last thing our kids need is another broken home." He bit his tongue to keep from pointing out the details of what she was wearing and how screwed up her priorities were. He thought instead of the kids. This needed to be about them.

She looked up at him and met his eyes. "You know, Micah," she began, adjusting the strap of her purse on her shoulder. "Sometimes I think back to you and me and I wonder why things ended the way they did. You've been a good dad to our kids, and sometimes I think if I'd just—"

"Don't," Micah cut in, though part of him strained to hear it. In all the years since their divorce she'd never made the slightest insinuation that she might share some of the blame for the failure of their marriage. Her saying it now, however, was completely inappropriate. "You're married to Dennis. Don't say something to me that would hurt him if he heard it. Make this work with him."

She held his eyes a moment longer and looked embarrassed. "I'd better go," she said. "I still have to stop at the store."

Micah nodded and led her to the door, shutting it behind her without saying anything else. He closed his eyes and let out a breath, falling forward a few inches until his forehead hit the door, knocking his hat off in the process.

If I'd just—

What would she have said if he'd let her finish?

CHAPTER 23

~~~

Idaho Falls, Idaho
Saturday, May 17

*I*t had been a very long week for Chrissy, full of job hunting, sewing some summer dresses for Lupe, tension with Livvy, and far too much time to think about everything that wasn't going right. When Saturday morning finally came—moving day—Chrissy held on tight to Rosa's hug, maybe too tight. But her niece held on too, trying to hide the fact that she was crying. Chrissy looked up and met Livvy's eyes over Rosa's shoulder. Livvy quickly looked away and swallowed, shifting from one foot to another. The boys had already gone out to sit in the car idling behind Doug's horse trailer, which was stuffed full with the rest of their possessions. Finally, Rosa released her grip and Chrissy pulled back, trying not to cry—really trying—but a few renegade tears crept out anyway.

She wanted to say a hundred things. *You'll be okay—I'll miss you—I'll still see you anytime—What your mother is doing is wrong.* But she couldn't form the words, so she just smiled and adjusted Rosa's hair around her shoulders. *"Te quiero"—I love you,* she finally said. That summed it all up anyway. Doug hated it when Chrissy spoke Spanish. Would he let the kids speak it anymore?

"We're only in Ammon," Livvy said, but her tone was cautious, which supported Chrissy's theory that as much as Livvy wanted to pretend this was okay, she knew it wasn't. That she was willing to do it anyway was no consolation.

"Too far," Chrissy said, still looking at Rosa. It might only be five miles in distance, but it changed everything. The kids couldn't come over any time they wanted to; Chrissy couldn't see them every day. They'd be living under the roof of a stranger, a man with low enough morals to have a woman and her three children move in with him. The gamut of fears Chrissy had traveled through this week had built upon the stress of not being able to find a job and had left her depressed and angry.

Rosa nodded, tears in her eyes, and finally turned and ran outside, leaving Livvy and Chrissy alone.

The tension hung thick until Chrissy couldn't hold back. "This isn't right, Livvy," she said. "What kind of man is he? How do you know he won't hurt your kids?"

"Don't preach to me," Livvy replied as she turned to the door. "Doug loves me."

"Then marry him."

"I've done that, and I'm not doing it again unless I'm sure it will work out."

"Then what kind of commitment is this?" Chrissy said, unable to hide her exasperation. It wasn't that she *wanted* Livvy to marry this poor excuse of a man, but she needed to make a point. If Livvy loved him, then she should do it right. If she didn't do it right, then maybe she didn't really love him. "Do you remember how disgusting it was when Dad would bring women home? Do you remember laying awake at night, knowing what was happening in the next room? And to sell the house—*your* house—to pay off *his* stuff? He's taking advantage of you, Livvy." It seemed ridiculous that she even had to say that out loud. It was so painfully obvious, and yet Livvy couldn't—or wouldn't—see it that way.

Livvy looked up, her jaw tight and her eyes showing her frustration at Chrissy's lack of understanding. "You don't know what it's like to raise three kids by yourself."

"By yourself?" Chrissy erupted, her arms flying into the air and startling Livvy. "I have been like a second parent to those kids, Livvy. I'm here every day. They know me; they trust me. They are safe with me."

Livvy was shaking her head as she turned toward the door. "It's not the same. They have been raised in a family of women. They need a man around."

"Not like this they don't," Chrissy said, feeling desperate to do *something*. "What will they learn about relationships if this is what they see?"

"They'll learn that love is good," Livvy said. Her eyes were pleading, as if searching for validation Chrissy would never—could never—give her. "Love is what makes life worth living."

"Then love *them* enough to not cheapen yourself like this."

"You have never been in love, Chrissy. You don't understand."

The words were like a slap across her face. "Because I don't find my self-worth in a man's bed, I don't know what love is?"

"Stop judging me!" Livvy finally screamed, her hands balled into fists at her sides. "If I wanted a sermon, I'd go to Mass!"

"Maybe if you'd go to Mass, you wouldn't need a sermon!"

Livvy shut her mouth and glared at her sister. "You are so jealous of me," she finally said, her voice soft and slithery.

Chrissy couldn't dispute the truth. In many ways Livvy had everything Chrissy wanted and it killed her to see Livvy treat her life like this.

"They are not your children, Chrissy. And you can just stay

here, be kept warm by your Bibles, and take comfort in your righteousness. The kids and I are starting a new life with Doug."

The door shut, and Chrissy moved to the window in order to watch the truck pull away from the curb. She closed her eyes slowly, just in time for the tears to come again. Livvy was gone. The kids were gone. She was more alone than she'd ever been before.

CHAPTER 24

Oceanside, California

Chressaidia pushed open the fading wooden door and strode into the office, stopping just a few feet away from the desk, where a heavy white man with a graying beard sat talking on the phone. It was a Saturday, but they'd suspected they might find him here, and they'd been right. No need to wait out the weekend.

She'd found Mr. Holmes.

Her body was healing well, but taking long, fast strides reminded her of her lingering tenderness. She would be grateful when all the reminders were gone.

"Yes, on Monday. Bye then," he said into the phone before hanging up.

She stood there and stared at him.

"Well, well," he said. "Is it my birthday already?"

She didn't smile or show in any way that she'd even heard his depraved joke. Instead she extended her left arm and pulled back her sleeve.

He stared at the black-and-red tattoo located a few inches below the crease of her elbow. His face fell and the lascivious look in his eye turned to one of fear.

The image inked on her skin was of a red cornstalk winding around a black cross. The corn, a foundational element of survival, represented the Guatemalan people. Red represented the blood shed in behalf of the country. The cross symbolized the holiness of their calling to defeat the current government and save the Guatemalan people from the poverty forced upon them by the upper class. It was a symbol all generals received at the time of their appointment. She'd had it done early in order to help her attain her goal, and she was counting on her father overlooking the presumption of her self-appointed rank.

Mr. Holmes mumbled an apology in Spanish and averted his eyes as she dropped her sleeve, glad he hadn't noticed how freshly-done the tattoo was.

"English," she said. "Where is my product, Mr. Holmes?" He had accepted payment for five hundred assault weapons that were supposed to have reached her father's army months ago. As tensions rose on the front lines, the missing Mr. Holmes and his guns were put aside. Most of the generals agreed that the shipment had been lost. She and Eduardo had tracked him down, however, and it had only taken a week. Eduardo had proved himself to be very valuable.

"I have them in storage, but I'm being watched. After the sting in November, I don't dare go near them. I lost three of my men and more than a hundred M-1 rifles in that raid."

She knew all that. It had been in the report he'd sent a few days after the raid on the loading dock, a few weeks before he'd disappeared for good. She'd heard the details discussed among the generals. "And yet, you hold the rest. Because of that, our armies are dying."

"But if I am caught, you have no one to gather them for you. I can't be reckless."

"It's been six months!" she hissed, leaning forward slightly and putting her hands on the desk. "It is only the commander's mercy that has kept you alive this long, and you dare argue with me? I have come for them."

His eyebrows came together, but only for a moment. His face went red. "They sent a girl to do my job?"

"They sent a general," she said calmly, removing the small .22 derringer from her purse. Though the caliber was small—only a two-shot capacity—the gun was easy to carry, and she was well trained. A bullet was a bullet, after all.

She did not point it at him. Instead, she pressed the barrel sideways against the left side of her chest, the sign made at the time every soldier pledged their allegiance to the People's Army for Freedom. It was clear she would not hesitate to act upon part of her pledge, eliminating any person who stood in the way of her mission.

He stared at the gun and swallowed, adequately humbled.

"They sent me because you are failing them, and they are giving you one more chance to preserve your life. Do not give me any reason to doubt their judgment. Do not forget that when you pledged your allegiance, you also pledged the life of your family. To fail us is to fail them. Where is my product?"

The features of his face softened and he looked down, showing his surrender. "It's in a storage unit in National City. But I'm being watched. I can't go near it."

"Which is why I'm here." She sat down carefully. "Write down the address and storage unit number. I need the key, all copies of it, and if anything you tell me is less than true"—she fixed him with a cold look—"I *will* come back and kill you."

CHAPTER 25

"Knock, knock!"

Amanda let herself in, scanning the living room before spotting Chrissy in the kitchen washing dishes. She closed the door behind her as Chrissy said, "Hey."

"Hey back," Amanda said, watching her friend closely. "Cam gave me the day off—let's go do something wild and crazy."

Chrissy snorted and plunged her hands back into the soapy water. "Like what? Go grocery shopping?"

"Ooooooh," Amanda said with sarcasm. "That would be awesome. I hear Smith's has pork loin on sale."

Chrissy chuckled but her heart clearly wasn't in it. Amanda took a breath and leaned against the wall. It was her goal to get Chrissy out of the house today. Livvy's leaving was no small thing and though Amanda hadn't wedged herself into the situation, she knew how hard it was for Chrissy. Unfortunately, she *didn't* know what to do to fix it outside of convincing Cam to do Saturday by himself so she could be with her friend.

"Are you washing dishes by hand?" Amanda said after a moment.

"My dishwasher broke," Chrissy said, moving a bowl to the other side of the sink.

"When?"

"A few weeks ago," Chrissy said. "My home teacher checked it out for me and officially declared it dead."

Amanda moved up behind Chrissy. "Um, you need to get a new one. Automatic dishwashers were the pinnacle of women's liberation. To choose against using one is an insult to your gender."

Chrissy gave her a bemused look. "I'm unemployed and—"

"Horrendously cheap. I know," Amanda finished for her, moving to her side and turning on the tap so she could rinse the dishes piling up in the sink. "But you need a new dishwasher."

"No, I don't," Chrissy said, shaking her head.

"Oh, yes, you do," Amanda said, putting the clean dishes on the rack to drain. "And you need lunch."

Chrissy sighed. "I'm not in the mood. It's been a long day."

"It's one o'clock in the afternoon!" Amanda said. "And you need to get out of here. I'm buying."

Chrissy looked at her and lifted her eyebrows. Amanda was glad to see that even amid the lousy events of the day Chrissy had done her hair and makeup. That meant she wasn't too depressed. "You're buying me a new dishwasher?"

"Um, no, but I *am* buying lunch and then I'm going with you in order to force you into buying a dishwasher, which is worth almost as much as it will cost. Besides, Dennings is having a six-months, no-interest sale on their appliances."

She reached over and unstopped the soapy water, then grabbed Chrissy's arm and pulled her away from the sink. "You deserve a new dishwasher, Chris, and you need to get out of this house and think about something else."

Chapter 26

National City, California

Chressaidia turned the key to free the padlock, removed it from the hinge, and pulled up on the garage-style door. It rolled up and she entered the storage unit, pulling the door shut before turning on the single light, which was barely any light at all. She squinted into the semi-darkness and moved toward the U-Haul boxes stacked along the back wall as her eyes adjusted. The boxes were labeled with tags like "Kitchen cabinets" and "Guest bedroom." She was impressed with Mr. Holmes's attention to detail. She'd fully expected to find wooden crates with "AK-47" written in bright orange spray paint. She opened each box in turn, identifying the different parts that, when assembled, would build the weapons to save what was left of her country. There was only one way to have freedom, and that was to exterminate the enemy.

After each part had been identified, she spent a few hours counting every piece to make sure the numbers matched the invoices Mr. Holmes had sent six months ago. When she finished the last box, she made a note on the paper, closed the box, and stood. The numbers matched; the order was complete. Her father would be glad to hear it.

She let herself out, locked the unit, and hurried back to the beach house. Frederico would be home soon. She didn't want to explain why she hadn't been home all day as she said she'd be. Tonight, after Frederico went out like he always did, she'd come back and move the guns to a new unit—one only she knew about. It wasn't far from this one, but Mr. Holmes would not be able to find his way back to the guns should he try to double-cross her.

CHAPTER 27

Idaho Falls, Idaho

"Fourteen percent!" Chrissy said too loudly, causing a few people to look at her and Amanda to take a step closer to the counter where Chrissy had been working on her credit application with the cashier. "That's ridiculous." She liked to think she was extra-sensitive because of Livvy and the kids leaving, but even if the rest of her life smelled like roses, she'd flip over a fourteen-percent interest rate. So much for Amanda's stupid idea of buying a new dishwasher to cheer her up.

The woman who'd been helping her smiled weakly and shrugged.

"Why is it so high?" Amanda asked in a very reasonable voice.

"Well, for someone with a fair credit rating—"

"My credit is excellent," Chrissy interjected.

"We run all our financing through Guardman, and they reported your credit as fair."

"Then they made a mistake."

Amanda nudged Chrissy with her shoe and gave her a chill-out look. Chrissy knew she was overreacting, she just didn't care. She couldn't get mad at Livvy anymore; she couldn't rage against Bedis; she couldn't shout at Brandon or any of the other guys she'd dated who hadn't married her and given her a family of her own to obsess over. This lady was as good as anyone else.

"Is there someone else we can talk to about this?" Amanda asked.

"I'm sorry, Guardman does all our—"

"Forget Guardman," Chrissy said. "I'm buying from you."

The woman's voice was getting tighter. "But it's Guardman that does the financing, and they rate your risk level as fair."

Risk level? They made her sound like a terrorist.

They all went quiet and looked at one another while Chrissy tried to keep her evil thoughts to herself.

"I don't know what to tell you," the woman said awkwardly. "This is the only credit we can offer, and I'll need a hundred dollar deposit before we finalize the sale."

"A deposit!" Chrissy repeated.

Amanda grabbed her arm and pulled her out of the store. Chrissy tried to argue but finally gave up. She wasn't the one dying for a dishwasher in the first place.

"Okay, that was really weird," Amanda said once they pushed through the front doors. She gave Chrissy a look of reprimand. "And I don't just mean you going nuts on that woman."

"I'm under a lot of stress," Chrissy said tightly. They walked the rest of the way to Amanda's car in silence.

"So what was that all about? Are you no longer the meticulous saver-girl?"

Chrissy looked at her friend. "If I weren't the meticulous saver-girl then I'd have nothing to freak out about, would I? That lady, or Guardman, or *somebody* is off their rocker. I have no debt other than my house. I don't know what she's talking about." She crossed her arms over her chest and muttered under her breath, "Fair."

They drove in silence for a few moments as Amanda navigated out of the parking lot. "Um, have you checked your credit rating lately?" Amanda asked.

Chrissy shook her head. "I don't need to check my credit rating because I don't have any debt and I know my rating is excellent."

"Hmmm."

Chrissy looked at her. "Hmmm, what?"

"Well, I mean, maybe I'm overreacting but Micah—you remember him, right?"

Chrissy started shaking her head, then she made the connection. "Boise State baseball cap guy?"

"Yeah, the one you ditched out on."

"I didn't ditch him."

Amanda waved that off. "Anyway, I guess he had his identity stolen awhile back and a couple weeks ago he did a mutual night activity for the young men on what credit is, how to use it, and how to make sure it doesn't get messed with. He's a loan officer, ya know, and he has software that allows him to run credit reports. He actually ran reports for a couple of the boys and one of the kids had some hospital bill on his record. Turned out it belonged to his uncle who has the same name. Cam got all fired up about it and ordered credit reports on us and all the kids."

"Was everything okay?"

"Well, yeah," Amanda said as if that weren't the point. "But all kinds of things can happen without you even knowing about it. Micah said the first indication is usually receiving a bill you don't recognize or trying to get credit and finding out something isn't right."

Chrissy thought back over the situation at the appliance store.

She felt a tingle go through her as she considered the ramifications of something not being right. Fair credit when she knew it was excellent. "So, you think I need to get a credit report?"

Amanda shrugged. "It wouldn't be a bad idea. I can call Micah for you."

Chrissy instantly rebelled. "No way," she said. "He already thinks I'm a lunatic. I'm not going to ask him for a credit report. Aren't there free ones you can get online?"

"Yeah," Amanda said, sounding just a teensy bit disappointed.

Chrissy knew that not going to Micah's went against every bit of Amanda's matchmaking sensibilities. In Amanda's book of fairy tales, single man plus single woman plus common purpose equaled destiny.

"We *could* go to my house and use my computer," Amanda offered, "but Cam might tie me up and not let me leave again."

"At least we got lunch first."

Amanda laughed. "Or we could use your computer—it should only take about two hours to get onto the web site."

"Don't dis my dial-up!" Chrissy said. "What about the library?"

"Or Micah's, where you don't have to sign up, wait in line, or deal with the germs two hundred people have left behind on the keyboard."

Chrissy groaned. "Give it up," she said. "I'm not going."

Just then Amanda pulled up to a house Chrissy didn't recognize and she realized her derelict of duty in not paying attention to where they were going. Amanda flashed an innocent smile. "Oh look, we're here and he's home. What luck!"

CHAPTER 28

❦

They were still arguing when Micah opened the door, looking adequately surprised to see them there. He held Chrissy's eyes just like he had at the restaurant all those months ago, but this time it made her uncomfortable and she looked away. She was so going to toilet paper Amanda's house for this.

"Hi, Micah," Amanda said before launching into a highly summarized account of what they were doing there. When she finished, she flashed that same innocent smile and waited for a response.

Micah pushed open the door. "Sure, I can get you a credit report."

Amanda looked at Chrissy with an *isn't-that-great* expression and led the way, leaving Chrissy to follow, silent and humiliated.

"Um, do you want to come back to my office?" he asked.

Amanda said they did and Chrissy continued to be obedient, scanning the living room as they passed through. It was big, a good size for a home this old, but it was boring—white walls, brown carpet, mismatched furniture. Piles of tools and other building supplies were stacked along the far wall and in most of the corners.

Smack dab in the middle of the room was a couch, loveseat, and recliner, all at right angles to one another so they formed a small horseshoe. There was also a TV in an entertainment center and a workout bench, with dumbbells littered on the ground around it. It was exactly what she'd expect the living room of a single man with nice arms to look like.

At some point the mantel around the fireplace had been ripped out, leaving a gaping hole. During their poor excuse for a date he'd said he was fixing his house up, but it didn't look as if he'd made much progress. At least, until she got to the study.

She stopped abruptly in the doorway and looked at what she assumed had once been a bedroom. However, it looked nothing like a bedroom now. The lower-third of the walls were covered in a walnut wainscoting that matched the desk and the built-in shelves that ran the length of one side. The walls were textured and then glazed, a technique she'd seen but hadn't dared attempt. She couldn't help but reach out and touch it. The floor was hardwood, with a huge rug that covered most of the floor space. In the middle of the room was a large desk with several chairs.

"Wow," she said, pulled out of her worries enough to admire the room. "This is amazing."

"He did it himself," Amanda said, scanning the room. "But I haven't seen it since right after the paint." She looked at Micah. "Well done."

Micah looked around as well, as if he hadn't taken the time to stop and look at his work lately. "Thanks," he eventually said.

"You did all this yourself?" Chrissy asked, stepping to the wall where a collage of walnut frames formed a pattern for black-and-white pictures of who she assumed were his kids.

"Yeah," Micah said. "It took me almost a year of evenings and weekends."

"I can believe it," Chrissy said. "I claim to be fixing up my house too, but few of my projects take more than forty-eight hours. I don't have the attention span."

Micah smiled when she looked at him. Amanda smiled too and Chrissy looked away. Would it be beyond Amanda to orchestrate an entire false credit scare just to get Chrissy to see Micah again?

They lapsed into silence as Chrissy studied the pictures on his wall. There was one of him as a younger man, with three little faces wedged up against him. They were all in coats and hats, perhaps on a ski trip. It was a beautiful photo. Due to her fragile emotional state it made her eyes water. It had only been a few hours, but she missed the kids so much. Maybe she should put up a picture collage like this. Would it make it easier to have them gone, or harder to have more reminders? As if she would ever forget.

"So," Micah said, abruptly turning her thoughts away from the kids. "You need a credit report?"

"Um, yeah," Chrissy said as he pulled out his office chair and sat down. Chrissy and Amanda took their seats in the two Queen Anne chairs across from the desk. "I tried to buy a dishwasher and they said my credit was rated fair, which isn't right."

Micah held her eyes and nodded, then turned to his computer and started typing. "I need your Social Security number and your date of birth."

She gave him the information and crossed one leg over the other. The black spool-heeled sandal of her top foot slid off so that it was only held on by her toes, and she let it dangle there. After several seconds, she looked up to find Micah staring at her legs. He saw her watching him and blushed before going back to his typing. His attention caused a shiver to run through her, and she put both feet on the floor. Amanda watched the exchange and smiled like the

Cheshire cat. Her absolute enjoyment of this made Chrissy want to be difficult, but she resisted.

Micah's eyebrows came together, but his eyes were drawn to the screen.

"Do you know what your credit score was, uh, I mean is?"

"I think the last time I knew was when I bought my house. That was about three and a half years ago."

"And . . ." His voice was tense now, like he was in a hurry for her answer.

"It was 730-something—the mortgage officer said it was really good. I've paid off my car since then and never been late on a mortgage payment. I don't have any other debt." She rose from her chair and leaned forward in an attempt to see whatever was on the screen that had him so concerned. "Why?"

Micah met her eyes and looked very serious. Amanda stood up too, her eyebrows pinched and her expression reflecting Chrissy's own worry. "Maybe you'd better sit back down."

CHAPTER 29

*C*hrissy pressed the palm of her hand against her forehead and hoped it would somehow help her refocus her thoughts. She took another deep breath and looked at the papers in front of her again. Micah had printed out the report so she could look at it. The proof was absolutely necessary. If she hadn't seen it with her own eyes, she wouldn't have believed it.

"So all this debt has my name on it?" she asked, trying to make sense of what he'd been explaining to her, yet really, really hoping he was somehow wrong.

"Whoever did this has your Social Security number and has, in some ways, become you. I'm so sorry." It was about the thirteenth time he'd apologized. It would be annoying if it weren't so sincere.

Amanda opened her mouth as if she were going to apologize too, but then she closed it. She looked as stricken as Chrissy felt.

"Ninety thousand dollars," Chrissy said out loud, echoing the calculations Micah had done as he read off the amassed debts. She forced a laugh, trying to pretend it was all a joke. Micah didn't smile. "This can't be real." Micah said nothing and she pulled the papers back to her again. "A car? A second mortgage on my house? How is this possible?"

"To most businesses, you are only a number, a birth date, and an address. Your ijacker apparently got those numbers."

"Ijacker?" Amanda asked.

"Another name for an identity thief—it's the fastest growing crime in America, not that it makes you feel better to have so much company."

"Is this what happened to you?" Amanda asked, leaning over to look at the credit report herself.

"Not quite," Micah said, waving his hand to indicate the eight pages of information lying on the desk between them. "I had a few cards and a motorcycle in my name, and they maxed out my existing credit card. The total amount was a lot smaller than yours, but they did use both existing accounts in my name *and* made new ones. You haven't noticed anything funny with your bank accounts, have you?"

Chrissy shook her head. "No, I took some money out last week and everything looked fine." Her head began to buzz.

"Well, that's good," Micah said. "But if I were you, I'd clear your accounts, at least for a while. Existing credit is a lot harder for people to tap into, but you never know—they got to mine somehow."

"I feel so . . . stupid," Chrissy finally said. "What kind of idiot doesn't realize this is happening?" She looked up and met his eyes, only then realizing he was the same kind of idiot. "Sorry."

Micah shrugged it off. "How would you know this was going on?" He looked between the two women. "Unless one of these creditors knows how to contact you—the real you—or until you go in for credit, there's really no way for you to know other than checking your credit report often, which most people don't bother with. And talk about shoulda known, I deal with this all the time with my clients. The first year I was doing loans, I wrote up a three hundred thousand dollar loan for a guy who'd been dead two years."

"Really?" Amanda said.

"I never met the guy in person, just did everything over the computer, fax, and phone. Turned out he was the dead man's son, but his credit was shot so he thought he'd borrow what his dad didn't need anymore. Luckily the title company caught on when he came in to sign the paperwork. Hard to pass for a fifty-two-year-old when you're twenty-seven."

"At least he didn't get the loan," Chrissy said. "Whatever doofus financed this one—no offense—let it go through."

"It's at twenty-one percent, so it's likely a no-doc loan done online. But the ijacker must have a lot of info about you, and your house, to get it to go through. Looks like they got it right before the mortgage laws tightened up." He shook his head. "Perfect timing."

Impossible, Chrissy thought as she tried to collect herself and make a plan. "So, okay, what do I do now? Who do I call to fix it?"

Micah shook his head slowly and waved toward the computer. "Well, I just sent notices to the three credit bureaus to put an alert on your credit. That will hopefully keep new credit from being opened. But I've been working on my stuff for more than ten weeks, and I'm just starting to get results. Even after the credit alerts were on my account, another card was opened up. I was lucky to have found out within a couple of weeks of the accounts being opened. Yours has been active for months."

Chrissy let her eyes drop shut. This was so ludicrous.

Micah leaned forward. "The thing is, all these people and all these creditors—they think this is you. Somehow you have to prove it isn't."

"But that's not fair," Chrissy said, the emotion breaking

through. She opened her eyes again, focusing on his eyes that reflected so much sympathy and determination. Their weird first date and the awkward meeting this afternoon no longer mattered. He understood what was happening. He'd been there, and he could help her. "I don't know what to do next," she whispered.

He opened a drawer and pulled out a notebook, sliding it toward her. Then he plucked a pen from the container on his desk and held it out to her. "You'll want to take notes, and prepare yourself. This is going to dominate your life for awhile."

"Well," Chrissy said. "At least I'll have plenty to keep my mind off the kids."

"Kids?"

"Never mind," she said, not realizing she'd spoken out loud. She took the pen and drew in a deep breath. Amanda reached over and squeezed her arm, offering her support. It gave her strength to know she wasn't facing this completely alone.

She could do this; it could be fixed. She just needed to be centered. "I'm ready."

CHAPTER 30

~~~

*M*icah's son came home at 4:00 and left again at 4:30. It was almost 5:30 before Amanda said she needed to call Cam. Chrissy stood up when Amanda left the room.

"We should probably go," she said, realizing they had been there for more than two hours. Her hand was cramped from so much writing and she had several pages of notes to further overwhelm her once she got home. With Micah's help, they had gone through and sent e-mail notices to each of the fraudulent creditors. Her head was still swimming.

"You'll need to follow-up with them," Micah said. She started to rip out the pages from the notebook, but he put up a hand. "You can keep that."

"Okay, thanks," Chrissy said. She stared at the words on the pages. "I . . . I can't thank you enough for your help. I don't know how I'd have learned this stuff any other way." In addition to sending the fraud notices, he'd also helped her log onto her bank account. Everything looked fine there—thank goodness.

Micah stood up. "I'm glad I could help, but, wow, I'm really sorry. I've run into things like this with some of my loans, and when it happened to me it was awful, but for you, they pulled out all the stops. These guys are real professionals."

"Even better news," Chrissy mumbled, tucking her hair behind her ears and stepping back into her shoes—elevating her height in the process. Her identity thief was a professional, cream of the crop, top of his class.

"You'll want to get a police report as soon as you can," Micah continued, pushing his hands into the pockets of his jeans.

"Right," Chrissy said, not wanting to hear one more thing.

He led her to the living room, where Amanda was finishing up her phone call.

"If there's anything I can do, ya know, to help or anything. Just let me know."

She turned to face him and regarded him for a moment. "Really?" she asked. Even amid all this mess, their first date wasn't far from her mind. "I . . ." She looked down, not sure what to say or how to say it. She cleared her throat, not quite able to push the last few hours from her mind enough to change the subject. She looked up and met his eyes again. "You're a good man to help me like this. I certainly didn't do anything to deserve it."

He looked a bit surprised but didn't get a chance to answer as Amanda snapped her phone shut. "Sorry, but I need to get home, the natives are getting restless."

"That's fine," Chrissy said, turning away from Micah, embarrassed to have said so much. "There's no more room in my brain anyway."

"And I've got to pick up my daughter from a friend's house in a little while," Micah said.

Amanda went out first but then Micah moved ahead and

held the screen door open for Chrissy, making it necessary for her to move past him close enough to smell his cologne. It was very nice. She'd once worked the perfume counter in a department store but couldn't place this scent—musky and yet sweet somehow.

She realized she'd stopped moving in order to identify his cologne and smiled awkwardly, hurrying down the steps and adjusting her purse on her shoulder.

"Well, thanks again," Chrissy said when she reached the sidewalk and turned back to look at him one last time. He really was an attractive man, confident, solid, easygoing.

"You're welcome," he said. She was a few steps away when he called her name. "Uh, Chrissy?"

She turned and raised her eyebrows.

"Do you have a fax machine?"

What an odd question. "Nooo," she said slowly, trying to determine the significance.

"Oh, well, I'm working from home Monday, if you wanted to come over and use my fax machine or get any more help that would be, um, fine."

Fine? Really? "Are you sure? I mean, I already took half your Saturday."

"I'll be here anyway. It wouldn't be a big deal, but, ya know, only if you want to."

Her mind flashed back to their date, when she'd said they could try again if he wanted to. His response had been "If *I* want to?" She wondered if he was remembering the same exchange.

"Well, I might just do that," Chrissy said, smiling for the first time in several hours. It lasted only a moment. Then all the things she'd learned in the last few hours rose back up, taking the smile and the moment of buoyancy away as she realized that whatever she was up against was just getting started.

"I'll call," she said.

Micah smiled and nodded before inclining his head one more time and adding, "Good."

CHAPTER 31

Chula Vista, California
Monday, May 19

Chressaidia was up with the sun—Frederico's door was still shut. The success of having found Mr. Holmes and the guns so fast was intoxicating and in light of her victory she found herself more and more disgusted with the role assigned to her in the beginning. She might not be male, but she was as strong as any man. And she was the Commander's daughter. Her father was proud of her; she could tell from the conversations they had almost daily as she updated him on what she was doing—though she hadn't mentioned the tattoo yet. She needed to prove herself first. But each time she hung up the phone with her father, she was determined to make him even more proud.

A few more weeks and she'd be ready to return to him, her honor restored and her worth proven. Frederico was beginning to notice that something was different, however—even though he didn't yet know what she was doing. He'd recently allowed her to manage most of the southern line, supposedly so he could open up more routes north of San Diego, but she'd gone far beyond the parameters he'd set, contacting other dealers on her own, gaining their confidence and allegiance.

She sat down at the computer and went through her daily routine of checking her e-mail, bank accounts, and credit report.

There were only a few e-mails, one from Eduardo saying that he'd meet her at noon to discuss the details—sending specifics over e-mail wasn't wise. He had once worked as a loader for a transport company, so he knew exactly how this was supposed to happen, and he'd arranged everything with only the most basic information from Chressaidia. She liked that he didn't ask a lot of questions.

Next, she checked her bank account, opened six weeks before she even arrived in the U.S., and made note of the balances. She'd need some funding before she executed the second border crossing and needed to think about what options were available to her. Unfortunately she'd maxed out the credit for Chressaidia Salazar and had been turned down for a high-interest credit card last week. She made a mental note to ask Frederico about getting some more names for funding purposes. He called them quick fixes: two-week runs on bank accounts and credit cards, then shred everything, and start over.

Once she was assured of the bank balances, she checked the credit report for Chressaidia Salazar. She hadn't kept a vigilance the first few weeks. As she used more and more credit, though, and took more liberties with the identity, she'd realized it would be prudent to keep an eye on things—make sure there would be no complications in remaining as Chressaidia Salazar until the mission was over. Even with the credit used up, the name was still sound. It would be complicated to reinvent herself at this point, when so many people knew her as Chressaidia.

She typed in the password to the web site she'd subscribed to and was planning the day in her head when the big red letters on the screen caught her attention. She stared at them and read slowly the words "Credit Fraud report filed 5/17. Do not extend credit without verification."

She cursed in her mind, and immediately pulled open the drawer that had all the information files on the real Chressaidia Salazar. The documents had been included with the purchase of the ID, and it was because of these details that she'd been able to use the ID so fully. How long would it take to get this kind of information on a new name? How much would it cost? The first transport was scheduled for Tuesday. She couldn't believe this was happening right now!

After pausing for a moment, she pulled out a bank statement belonging to the real Chressaidia and considered it. At the bottom of the statement were three handwritten numbers under the heading of "Possible Pins." If the real Chressaidia was already on to her . . .

She had to act fast. She had to buy herself as much time as possible.

CHAPTER 32

Idaho Falls, Idaho

$\mathcal{S}$unday, quite possibly, had been the longest day of Chrissy's life. She taught her Primary class but missed having Nathan and Carlos there. In Primary they talked about the second Article of Faith: "We believe that men will be punished for their own sins, and not for Adam's transgression." She couldn't get it out of her head. *She* hadn't made all those fraudulent charges, but it was up to her to make it right. This wasn't her sin, her transgression, and yet she was the one suffering the consequences. And not only in regard to the identity theft, but Livvy too. When had she made the choices that earned her these results?

By the time Monday rolled around, she was still overwhelmed but was also very, very angry. She arrived at the police station just after 8:00, thirsty for the obvious justice they would help her find. She only waited a few minutes before being led through a maze of brightly lit hallways that ended in an office without a name on the door. The officer was very young and had a brace on his knee, making her wonder if he'd been relegated to a desk job due to an injury.

It would help explain his dour expression and lack of emotion as she explained her situation.

"Before I can issue a criminal fraud report, I need verification from at least one of these creditors that fraud has taken place." The officer looked at the final page of the credit report Chrissy had brought with her before placing it on his desk and looking up.

"Well, I haven't actually talked to any of them yet," Chrissy said. "I'll be making calls today but I need a police report to really get things going."

The officer was shaking his head before she finished. "Standard practice is that *they* verify fraud occurred on their end first, *then* we file a report. Hypothetically, you could rack up some debts, then say someone else did it and get them wiped out. The best I can do right now is file a complaint."

Chrissy blinked. "I need a police *report*," she said, remembering the notes she'd taken. "And I wouldn't do this to get out of paying some debts. You can look at the credit report. I've had terrific credit until February of this year."

"Again, getting credit is easily done—but not so easily undone. Just get one of these companies to say it's fraud, and I'll write up a report." He leaned back in his chair and crossed his arms over his chest.

Chrissy took a breath. Another officer walked behind her and asked Officer Jackson how long he'd be.

"Just another minute," he said, looking over Chrissy's head.

She'd never even been inside a police station and had been intimidated enough just walking through the big glass doors.

"Look, ma'am," Officer Jackson continued. "The fact is that you're asking me to file a report stating that criminal activity has occurred. I can't do that without proof that indeed a criminal act has been committed. However, I can record the fact that you came in and filed a complaint, so we'll be ready when you come back in."

Chrissy leaned forward. "So basically what you're telling me is that even though I'm the victim in this, I'm guilty until I can prove myself innocent." It was discouraging to hear it from a source she'd thought would help her. Her rage, already highly volatile, began rising.

"You haven't given me any reason to believe you're innocent."

"I haven't done anything wrong!"

His expression didn't change. He handed the credit report back to her. "There's also some debate over whether this should be filed here, or where the fraud originated. A fraud report from a creditor will help us establish that, so just get one of these card companies to give you a report. Is there anything else I can help you with?"

Chrissy stood up, holding her purse with both hands and glared at him. "*Anything else* implies you actually helped me with something in the first place."

CHAPTER 33

*N*athan."

Chrissy's head swung to the side even as she realized it wasn't her Nathan being called. *Her* Nathan was at school. But hearing the name gave her a lump in her throat as she watched a young mom coax her son back to her side of the divider that funneled the bank patrons to the transaction counter.

"I can help whoever's next," a cheery voice said, causing Chrissy to plant a fake smile on her face as she walked briskly toward the counter. The failed attempt to get the police report was still fresh on her mind, but she couldn't let it slow her down.

She handed the bank teller her withdrawal slip. "I need six hundred dollars in cash." She tried not to wince at the amount. Every dollar she spent was from her savings, and it was going out faster than she'd hoped. She had to find a job. "And I need to change my pin numbers."

"ID?" the woman asked as she started tapping on the computer keys.

"Of course," Chrissy said, opening her purse and digging

through it for her wallet. She found it, extracted her driver's license, and put it on the glass-topped counter, sliding it toward the other woman.

"Ma'am, I can only give you all but twenty-five dollars of your balance, would you like me to do that?"

Chrissy felt her stomach clench and tried to tell herself she was overreacting. "I have about five thousand dollars. Six hundred shouldn't be a problem."

The woman looked concerned. "Your balance is one hundred fifty-three dollars and eighteen cents."

Chrissy froze and leaned forward. "One hundred fifty-three dollars?" she said, her body heating up with fear. "I had almost five thousand dollars in that account when I logged in on Saturday."

The girl shrugged and turned the screen to face Chrissy. She immediately scanned the numbers. Her heart leapt into her throat. There were two withdrawals for $2400 each, both of them made earlier today. Her chest was tight and when she spoke her voice was too loud. "This wasn't me."

"Um, all I know is what the computer shows me. You can talk to our manager if you'd like." Chrissy followed the teller's eyes and saw the words *Bank Manager* on the door of an office. In sixteen strides she was at the office. She opened the door and walked in unannounced. Her head was spinning. *Not this—after everything that's happened—not this, too.*

"Someone has made unauthorized withdrawals from my account," she said to the hefty man behind the desk, her voice wavering. "And *you* need to fix it."

CHAPTER 34

*Y*es, I need to file a fraud report," Chressaidia said when she reached the desk of the San Diego police department. Eduardo had told her that fraud cases stayed in the precinct where they were filed—not automatically added to the national database where a report could be connected to her arrest that had taken place farther north. Even with such assurance, however, she could hardly believe she was here.

When Eduardo had suggested she file the report, she'd wondered if he was setting her up, but he'd explained the reasons and it made sense. Making a record of the fraud on her own would throw up major roadblocks should the real Chressaidia try the same thing. If she was staying a long time, or trying to establish permanency it could be a disastrous move, but she only needed a few more weeks and that meant this might be exactly what she needed.

"Someone is falsely using my identity."

"Take a seat," the Polynesian woman said, indicating a row of orange chairs.

Chressaidia did as she was told, trying to appear relaxed, but not too relaxed. She was pretending to have had her identity stolen, and that would be upsetting to anyone. She sat there for almost twenty minutes before a desk-cop came over and asked her to follow him. She slid into the chair next to his desk and he fumbled for some paperwork.

"So, what's the problem?"

"Someone's stolen my identity," Chressaidia said. "I've already filed notice with the three credit bureaus, and I've got this." She produced a forged fraud report from one of the credit cards that had been opened in Chressaidia's name. "You need this to file a criminal report, right?"

The desk sergeant, Officer Jeffers, picked up the paper. "Do you have proof you are who you say you are?"

Chressaidia nodded. She'd anticipated this, down to every detail. There was no room for error. She pulled out her driver's license, the real Chressaidia's birth certificate, and a utility bill in her name. She'd gone in to the utility offices that morning and brought the account up to date, asking for a printout of her current statement.

"I moved here about four months ago," she said as he looked over the documents. "And it must have happened right after that. You can see from my credit report that most of this stuff was opened up right after I moved here."

"It looks like you've got all your documentation in place. Let's see what we can put together."

Chressaidia smiled, glad she had cleared this first obstacle. Being polite and personable was not one of her greater gifts. It hadn't served much purpose in her life so far, but since realizing the real Chressaidia was on to her, she'd had to dig deep.

"Um, do you need to take my prints or anything?" This was the part she'd feared the most. If they took prints and for some reason compared them to those taken when she had been booked last month, she'd be in trouble. Eduardo had assured her this wouldn't happen at this point, especially not in an area as busy as San Diego—they didn't have time to process each fraud complaint in such detail.

"Not yet," Officer Jeffers said. "We'll need them later for exclusion when we get closer to the adjudication date."

Chressaidia didn't know what adjudication meant, but at least they weren't taking her prints. She needed all the time she could get. Now that she wasn't so on edge, she hoped this wouldn't take too long. She'd made two transfers from the original Chressadia's account that morning, then transferred them to three other online accounts, which she now needed to empty—and empty fast—in case the bank came looking for the money too soon.

"I'll need you to fill out these forms," Officer Jeffers said, pushing some papers toward her. "Then we'll get it in the computer."

Chressaidia took the papers and began filling in the "Name" field. So far, so good.

CHAPTER 35

Chrissy sat in her car outside the bank and stared ahead. She had insisted on closing her account and the $153.18 was now in her wallet, but the discouragement was overwhelming. Never in her life had she felt so vulnerable, so cheated, and she knew it wasn't over yet. Somewhere, someone was unraveling her life thread by thread and she couldn't seem to stop it. It was surreal to think that just this morning, perhaps at the exact time Chrissy was attempting to file a police report, someone else was cleaning out her account, not taking a credit card company's money this time, but taking her own. She'd spent three years saving that money and now it was gone.

And she didn't know what to do next.

She had pages of notes and a whole list of people to call, but then what? The bank said an investigator would call her sometime that week, that the money would be refunded based on what they discovered. She liked to think the right thing would happen, but the last few days had been such a whirlwind she didn't know what to think, who to trust, how to keep from feeling beaten down.

She closed her eyes and leaned her head back against the seat, praying. What was she supposed to do?

No answers came and she continued to sit there for several minutes, waiting for inspiration, for direction, for understanding. Was that so much to ask? Finally she opened her eyes, blinking at the brightness of the day. Then she picked up her cell phone and dialed the number Amanda had given her.

He answered on the second ring. "Hello, this is Micah."

She felt just a little of the heaviness lift at the sound of his voice. Though she didn't know him well, she knew he understood and he'd offered his help. She'd be a fool not to accept it, even if it meant swallowing an uncomfortable slice of humble pie to admit she couldn't do it alone.

"You still got that fax machine?"

"You still got that cantankerous credit report?"

Chrissy managed a chuckle. "I do, in fact it's gotten worse. They got to my bank accounts this morning."

Micah was quiet for a moment. "Oh, I'm sorry."

Chrissy hadn't expected tears, but his sincerity undid her—and that was saying something based on how unraveled she already felt. She cleared her throat. "I could really use a wingman."

"Well, that just happens to be my specialty. Come on over, I'm here all day."

CHAPTER 36

San Ysidro, California
Tuesday, May 20

*C*hressaidia pulled off I-5, glancing back at the delivery truck that had followed her from the San Diego warehouse and would continue over the border. Eduardo was driving the contents— mostly baby formula, but with fifty pounds of assault weapon parts hidden inside each of the five pallets inside the truck. She'd told Eduardo only last night about the guns. He didn't seem surprised and had helped her pack enough parts to assemble sixty AK-47s. If all went well, the first shipment would reach her father within two weeks, and she'd be right behind it with the rest.

She pulled her car into the parking lot, the same one Frederico had parked in when she'd arrived almost three months ago. As she walked across the border, she watched the truck as best she could. If anything went wrong, she was untouchable. Even Eduardo knew her only as Chressaidia. But she planned on succeeding. If it failed, she would have to find another way across the border with the rest of the weapons—and without Eduardo's help.

She lost sight of the truck as it went under the overpass and bit back her frustration as she pushed through the revolving gate.

Within ten feet, she was back on Mexican soil, or concrete as was the case. Customs required a detailed check to get into America, but anyone could come to Mexico. She walked to the taxi area slowly, stopping every few steps to check on the progress of the truck just thirty feet away. It was a legitimate crossing. Baby formula was not produced in Mexico and was often imported through the Tijuana crossing. The truck was registered to a real transportation company, so the documents verifying its crossing were also legitimate. Only she and Eduardo knew the truth.

The truck wasn't through by the time she reached the taxi area, so she took out her cell phone and pretended to have a conversation, giving herself a reason to loiter while still watching the truck. It was almost five minutes before the truck finally nosed out of its lane. Eduardo picked up a Coca-Cola can and put it on the dashboard, his signal that there were no problems.

Chressaidia smiled to herself and closed the phone. She continued her walk toward the taxi stand and slid into the grimy backseat of a blue-and-white cab. "The old racetrack in Agua Caliente," she said in English. She'd walk to the checkpoint from there and make sure everything was in order before returning to America later that afternoon. Tomorrow, Eduardo would drive the empty truck back and they'd start working on the next shipment.

"*Sí, Señora,*" the taxi driver said.

Only then did she allow herself to relax and take pride in what she'd accomplished.

Sixty rifles down, three hundred and forty to go.

CHAPTER 37

Is it really three o'clock already?" Chrissy said as she heard the front door shut. It had been Chrissy's goal to have left before Blake, Micah's son, came home. For whatever reason, it just felt strange having his kids come home to find a strange woman in their father's office.

"I guess it is," Micah said, looking up from the computer. "Sorry I haven't been much help today."

Chrissy stared at him. "Are you kidding? I'm gonna be making you tamales every month for the rest of my life to pay you back for all this."

Micah smiled. "I like tamales."

"Well, then, you've set your price."

The banter had come easy and it took the edge off. Thank goodness. Today she'd sent another half-dozen faxes, yelled at a few people who didn't necessarily deserve it, and hung up on two people who did deserve it. Having Micah there gave her confidence, even if he told her she ought to be a little more even-tempered. Whatever.

"Hey, Dad."

They both looked up at the doorway and Chrissy finally stood, despite wanting to stay. Being there and having Micah to bounce ideas off of was so much more comfortable than going it alone. But she didn't want to intrude on his family time.

"Hey," Micah said, leaning back in his chair and stretching his arms over his head. "How was school?"

"Lame," Blake said, but he was looking at Chrissy. "Hey, Chrissy."

She smiled. She'd met him twice now, and he acted as if she belonged here. She liked it—perhaps a little too much. "Hey," she said easily.

"You staying?" Blake asked.

Chrissy caught the briefest of looks exchanged by father and son, and it was all she could do to stifle her curiosity and not try to figure out what it meant.

"No, I've got to get home."

Micah stood. "So, have you decided about the job thing?"

Chrissy made a face. "Yeah, it's really my only option." She hadn't told him how much she hated going back to work for Brandon—only that she was pretty sure she could find some work there.

"It makes sense," Micah said.

"Or, hey, Pizza Hut is hiring," Blake said with a teasing grin. "You could try that out."

Chrissy laughed. "It's not *that* bad," she said. "Pizza Hut is about number eighteen on a list of twenty other options." Not to mention she wasn't sure she'd pass their background check either. It didn't take a rocket scientist to figure out that her difficulty in finding a job had to be linked to the ijacking.

"I'm working out of the office tomorrow," Micah said after following her to the door. "Sorry."

"That's okay," Chrissy said. "I'm a big girl and by now I ought to be able to handle a day on my own, don't ya think?"

Micah shrugged. "Keep me in the loop though, okay?"

He held her eyes and she didn't look away for several seconds. Not until a second school bus pulled up and reminded her she needed to go. "I will."

"Promise?"

"Well, Micah Heet," she said, putting a hand on her chest. "I do believe you're flirting with me."

His cheeks went red and then his glance moved over her shoulder. Chrissy turned and saw his daughter descending the bus steps.

"I'll call," she said, hurrying to her car and hoping she wasn't getting to forward. Either way, she found it remarkable that amid all the garbage in her life she could drive home with a smile on her face.

CHAPTER 38

Idaho Falls, Idaho
Wednesday, May 21

*I*t had been three days and there was still no word from an investigator. Micah was working at his office, which meant Chrissy was home alone and giving into despair when Lupe called. She'd received a wedding order for a mother-of-the-bride dress and two flower-girl dresses—was Chrissy interested? Chrissy tripped over her words as she said, "Yes, absolutely, can I start them today?"

Once back home with the fabric, measurements, and pattern in hand, she went to work with a vengeance, gearing up for tomorrow when she'd have to go back to Almo and beg for work. She needed today to get her strength up, and the dress orders were exactly what she needed.

At 4:30, with the flower girl dresses cut out and one of them half finished, the phone rang again.

"Hello?" Chrissy said, her expectations high once she saw the name of her bank on the caller ID. She flipped up the sewing foot and cut off the thread before removing the dress bodice from the machine.

"Hi, this is Teresa Olsen. I've been assigned as the investigator on your National Prime account."

"Oh, thank goodness," Chrissy said, straightening in her chair and shutting off the sewing machine so she could give her full attention to the phone call. "I've been wondering—"

"This recorded message is to inform you that I am committed to giving you the best service possible."

Recorded message? Chrissy frowned. "You have got to be kidding me," she muttered.

Teresa's recorded voice continued. "I will be sending updates via e-mail every few days. After the tone, please say, and spell, your e-mail address so that I might be able to communicate with you at each stage of the investigation. I also encourage you to become familiar with your own credit report. You can purchase one through National Prime for $29.95. Please go to our web site for more information. Thank you for being a customer of National Prime, where your money is our business. Please leave your e-mail address after the beep."

The beep sounded, and Chrissy paused for a moment, her anger roiling. "I don't have an e-mail account. That's "I-space-D-O-N-apostrophe-T-space-H-A-V-E-space . . ."

CHAPTER 39

Chula Vista, California

"Where have you been!"

Chressaidia jumped, the doorknob still in her hand. She wasn't expecting Frederico to be here. He was supposed to be in LA for the week. His high-society friends were demanding more and more of his time, and he was slowly allowing her to do more and more of his responsibility for the trade, something she found very ironic since she'd been operating over his head for weeks now.

"I've been working," she said, closing the door and brushing her hair from her eyes. She was still feeling elated over the successful crossing yesterday, and a small part of her wished she could share it with him. Wouldn't he be shocked? But she couldn't; she wouldn't. This was *her* project, her mission. He had already lost his birthright, so to speak, and she couldn't wait to see him completely crumble to the ground.

"Working on what?" Frederico asked.

She eyed him as she walked to the kitchen and got herself a glass of water. Was he generally suspicious or could he have somehow caught wind of what she was really doing? "It's none of your business. How was LA?"

He glared at her with dead, black eyes set against skin that had taken on a grayish tone. The drugs were taking their toll. Good. That only made him weaker.

"You're trying to pull something over on me," he said when he reached her. He lifted his hand, but she caught it at the wrist, staring him down and feeling her muscles strain against his attempts to pull away. His other hand lashed out at her, and she grabbed it as well, twisting both arms and throwing them down. His drugged-out, Americanized efforts were no match for her lifetime of living in the jungles of Guatemala and being educated at the toughest Brazilian boarding schools. She could have fought him off the other times he'd come at her, but it hadn't seemed prudent.

"You will not hit me again," she said caustically. "I am no longer only good for what I can bear from my womb."

Frederico's eyes turned wild, standing out even more against his dull and tired skin. "You are still my wife. You will not disobey me and make me a fool."

"You are already a fool," she said, glaring at him. "I have proven that."

CHAPTER 40

~~~

Idaho Falls, Idaho
Thursday, May 22

*I*t was barely ten o'clock Thursday morning when Chrissy
walked up to the front doors of Almo insurance company. Every
thing looked so familiar, but she felt very different as she surveyed
the room. That morning she'd finished up the dress order and taken
it to Lupe, shocking the older woman with how quickly she'd finished them. Unfortunately, Lupe didn't have any new orders.
Chrissy collected her cash payment, filled up her car with gas, and
mailed off a portion of her power bill, promising the rest as soon as
possible. Then she'd sat in her car and been forced to make a decision. No matter how badly she hated it, she knew Brandon would
give her a job.

A bell sounded when she opened the door and she thought of
a few positive affirmations to get her attitude heading in the right
direction. *You're a capable woman. You look great. No one can make
you feel less than you are if you don't let them. You're good enough, you're
smart enough, and doggone-it, people like you!*

Within a few seconds Brandon came out of his office. She'd
worn a sports bra and a high-necked blouse in hopes Brandon

would look her in the eye. And he did. For almost five full seconds. Pathetic.

"Chrissy," he said brightly. "What brings you slumming down here?"

His voice was like sand between her teeth, but she forced a smile and got right to the point. "Well, I'm wondering if you guys could use additional help for a little while."

"Te reemplazamos," he said—*We replaced you.*

She'd forgotten how he loved to speak Spanish to her. Maybe being a hotel housekeeper wouldn't be so bad. If she were willing to try, she knew she could get hooked up with some people who helped illegals find jobs. But she wasn't an illegal and shouldn't have to work outside the boundaries of the law to get work. "I know, and if you're fully staffed, no big deal, I just thought I'd check."

He tilted his head and gave her a cocky grin, his gray-blue eyes shimmering. *"¿Nos extrañaste verdad?"*—*You missed us, didn't you?*

"Something like that," she answered with a smile most people would recognize as fake, but didn't even register with Brandon. "Where's Carla?"

Thankfully Brandon switched back to English. "She's had some problems with her daycare so she doesn't come in until one o'clock on Tuesdays and Thursdays, and actually, we've fallen behind on our filing system because of it. I don't know how long it would take to catch it up. Maybe by the time you finished, we'd have more work for you to do. I'm sure Carla would appreciate the help."

Filing, perfect. "That would be great," Chrissy said, relieved that this had worked. "I can start today, but I have some personal things I have to work on next week, so if you could be flexible with me, at least for now, I'd appreciate it."

Brandon smiled slowly, and Chrissy shifted her weight as his gaze traveled down. "I can be flexible," he said. The office phone rang, breaking whatever spell he was under. "You can use the extra desk and computer in the file room."

"Sure," Chrissy said, heading down the hall and beating down her reservations. She had found a job. She was going to be paid!

She opened the door to the file room and was startled at the disarray. When she had been here just over a month ago, everything had been in meticulous order. Now there were files stacked precariously on top of the large, metal cabinets and about a hundred Post-it notes stuck to the walls. She took one down. "Add the Ford truck back to the Pederson policy." It was dated over a week ago.

Brandon hadn't said that Carla was doing a *good* job managing the office, and if this note was any indication, perhaps Chrissy could get her old job back. Only, she didn't *want* her old job back. It was ironic that instead of having her normal life and a different job, she had her normal job and a different life. But there was no point thinking such dismal thoughts. She scanned the room again, not the least bit discouraged by the task before her.

"Soy bendecida por tener trabajo," she said to herself—*I am blessed with work.* It was something Abuelita had often said as she left for her second or third job. Chrissy put her purse on the only empty surface of the room—the top of the watercooler—kicked off the pink, kitty-heeled sandals she'd worn, and got to work.

CHAPTER 41

Idaho Falls, Idaho
Monday, May 26

I can't give you any information on that account."

"It's *my* account," Chrissy said into the phone. It was Memorial Day, so Almo was closed, but since credit never sleeps, she'd hit the phones. However, this was the second creditor today who was completely stonewalling her. Last week people had at least talked with her, but now she was getting nowhere. "How can you not give me information on my own account?"

"I'm sorry, ma'am, but it's policy that once an investigation has been opened we are no longer able to give information over the phone. You'll have to speak with your consultant."

Consultant? "So an investigation has been opened?" Chrissy asked. "When I called last week, I was told I needed a police report." Had they flagged it anyway? "I didn't know I had a consultant, can you give me the name?"

"I'm sorry, ma'am, I can't give you that information. It should have been given to you at the time you filed the official investigation."

"But it wasn't given to me!" Chrissy nearly screamed. "They told me they wouldn't start an investigation without a police report number."

"Which you must have given them."

"But I didn't! I can't get one until I get proof from you. I was hoping you would send it to me."

"We already did," the woman said, her own tone growing in annoyance. "I'm going to transfer you to my manager." The line clicked and Chrissy tapped her foot, trying to make sense of this new information. They told her they wouldn't start investigating, but now they were investigating and wouldn't talk to her? This made no sense at all. The phone clicked again before the line went dead as the transfer dropped her call.

"I'm going to lose my mind," Chrissy said to herself as she slammed the phone down, again. Covering her eyes with both hands, she tried to calm her frazzled thoughts. She'd thought that since she'd faxed and mailed all of the credit companies an explanation last week, she could make some progress today. But if anything, they were even harder to deal with now. Every creditor insisted on getting a fraud report from the police first. The police insisted on getting a fraud report from a creditor first. And this creditor had shut her down for a completely different reason.

Micah had warned her that the thief was a professional—he'd know all the loopholes, while she, Chrissy, was new to this, a complete novice. She hated feeling helpless in any situation, but even more so when it was her name—her life—on the line. Hot tears filled her eyes as she tried to think of what to do. It was like being trapped in a maze. She wasn't sure there *was* a way out.

Ninety thousand dollars!

The phone rang, making her jump. She hurried to grab it, thinking maybe one of the creditors she'd talked to had taken pity on her. The number was local, however, and one she didn't recognize.

"Hello?" she said.

"Chrissy?"

Her world paused for a minute, and she smiled. "Rosa?" she said into the phone. She gripped the phone with both hands and stood straighter. "Oh, how are you?"

Every time Chrissy saw the "For Sale" sign in Livvy's yard she felt like crying. The loneliness was overwhelming enough as it was, but to feel so alone amid all these other problems was truly the lowest Chrissy had ever felt in her life.

"We're okay," Rosa said.

Chrissy tried to scan her voice for the truth. She didn't detect anything and was a little disappointed that things weren't more miserable.

"Could you come pick us up?"

"Is something wrong?" Chrissy asked with alarm.

"No, but school's out and Mom's working. We're bored."

Chrissy looked at the statements and notes on the table and let her eyes drift to the notebook listing all the things she still needed to do. But there was no contest. She needed these kids today.

"You bet," she said, turning her back on the tasks waiting for her, grateful for a reprieve from all the stress. "Give me the address, and I'll be there in less than half an hour."

CHAPTER 42

~~~~

"Next week," Eduardo said, handing her the file. "I've got all the paperwork filed. We just need the final confirmation of the date and time."

Chressaidia took the file and opened it, scanning the papers inside. "And we're taking all the parts?" They'd originally planned to take two more trips to move the rest of the guns, but the problems with Chressaidia's identity made it seem wise to speed things up. She'd put as many safeguards in place as possible, but knew her time was limited.

"Yes, I ordered six pallets of formula. And I've arranged orders with stores in Mexico that will buy it, so the receipts will be legitimate."

It almost felt too easy, and that worried her, but she said nothing. "Who knows about this?" she asked. No way was he able to accomplish the arrangements all by himself.

He hesitated before answering. "Only two other people. A friend at the transportation company and another friend who helped me with the Mexico orders. They were asking too many questions, but I've already arranged for them to be paid."

Two more people? Chressaidia didn't like it. And payment? Without her authorization? Still, he'd done a great deal of work and she didn't want to react rashly. "How will you pay them?"

"After you leave and I take over the trade routes, I'll give them part of my profit. We couldn't do this without them."

"Too many people know," Chressaidia said, still looking at the papers. "I don't like it."

"There was no other way," Eduardo replied. "Especially since we need to do this so quickly. I think you should walk across again. I'll meet you at the racetrack. I'll drive. I'll take the risk."

"Good," she said, handing back the file. That's what she was looking for, his willingness to sacrifice himself. It was only fair, since he was the one who had made the arrangements. It validated his trust in himself. "Next week then," she said.

Chapter 43

*L*ivvy pulled up to the old farmhouse Doug had bought from his uncle a few years ago and turned off the car. She smiled as she got out and headed up the new steps Doug had built last month. They'd turned out really nice; Doug was good with his hands.

"I'm home," she called as she came through the front door. The smile on her face faded as she scanned the living room but didn't see anyone waiting for her. "Hello?" She put her purse on the table—also inherited from Doug's uncle. The farmhouse had some really nice furniture, but it had been a total mess when she moved in. However, it was nothing a little elbow grease, lemon oil, and Windex couldn't fix. Out of habit, her thoughts turned to how great Chrissy would think some of this furniture was—she had such an eye for character pieces. But immediately Livvy remembered their argument, the humiliation of having Chrissy say those things to her face.

"Guys?" she called as she moved farther into the house. No one answered. Maybe they were outside.

She found Doug in the old, run-down barn in the back and

greeted him with a long hello kiss. He made her feel so alive, so beautiful. Over the last few months she'd realized that she *had* to feel like she mattered, that someone loved her and wanted her. It was as necessary to her existence as air and water.

"Where are the kids?" she asked when the kiss finally faded.

"Don't know," Doug said, turning back to the stall he was mucking out. Livvy wrinkled her nose at the smell, but wouldn't complain about the pungent aroma of manure and sweat. Doug was really into his horses, and she was determined to get into them as well. It would be something they could share together. "They left around noon."

"Left?"

"Yeah, I thought you had it all figured out."

"They didn't tell you where they were going?"

"Nope," Doug said, throwing a pitchfork of used straw into a wheelbarrow. The physical labor made the muscles in his arms tighten, but Livvy looked away so as not to be distracted. He put the pitchfork into the ground and leaned against the handle, reaching out to pull her to him by the waistband of her pants. "Can't say I missed 'em though," he said, smiling at her. "Them kids make me crazy."

Livvy stiffened just a bit. He'd been saying things like that the last few days, and it made her uncomfortable, but she knew that in time he'd come to love them. He just wasn't used to having children around—his lived in Texas.

"It's after six o'clock," she said, putting her hands on his shoulders to keep some distance between them. "Maybe they left a note." But she could only think of one place they would go—Chrissy's. She wasn't sure whether to be relieved or even more annoyed by the idea.

He ignored her and tried to pull her closer. "Doug!" she said with sharpness, pulling away.

He glared at her, and she held his eyes, not sure what to do. He looked mad and she didn't like it. "Them kids is always coming between us. I gotta go to work in an hour, and all you care about is them."

"They're my kids," Livvy pleaded. "I have to figure out where they went. Then we can . . . spend some time together."

He didn't seem appeased, but he turned back to the horse stall. "It was some red car with a black hood that came for 'em."

Livvy was instantly relieved, but only for a moment. "Chrissy," she said out loud as anger raced through her veins at the confirmation that she'd taken the kids without Livvy's okay. She turned on her heel, intending to call Chrissy and give her another piece of her mind.

"Whatcha gonna do?" Doug called after her.

"Call her and make her bring 'em back." Livvy turned to face him again. "She can't do this. She is not their mother, and I'm so sick of her wanting to dominate things all the time. I told you what she said about us. Who knows what she'll tell them."

Doug regarded her for a moment and she began feeling foolish for reacting so strongly. She took a breath. "I'm so tired of her trying to run my life."

"If that's so, you ought to call the cops," he said.

The cops? On Chrissy? Livvy dismissed the idea as fast as it came and shook her head. "I can't do that."

"Then she'll just keep thinking she can do whatever she wants. You said you wanted your own life. This is your chance to prove it."

She held his eyes. This wasn't just about proving things to Chrissy; it was about proving things to Doug, too. She bit her bottom lip, debating her options. Things were so new with Doug; she didn't want to disappoint him. And he was right—she did want her own life. She took another breath, hoping to gain some confidence, and let it out slowly, allowing the anger to settle in. Doug was right. Chrissy couldn't do this anymore.

CHAPTER 44

The kids were exactly what Chrissy needed. They took a picnic lunch to the park and played soccer for more than an hour. After returning home, the boys played some computer games while Chrissy and Rosa worked on cleaning the guest room that Chrissy planned to repaint as soon as she had money to actually buy some paint. She and Rosa chatted about Rosa's new neighborhood and the school she'd be going to next year. Chrissy was careful to bite her tongue every time she wanted to say anything negative. That Livvy would let them come over was a step in the right direction, and she didn't want to mess anything up.

"I could pick you up for church on Sunday if you want."

"That would be cool," Rosa said with a nod.

Her answer went a long way to calming even more of Chrissy's stress and worry. She'd made it through her own difficult adolescence because of the Church, and if Rosa was willing to stay involved, then it could bless her, too, and perhaps soften the harsh choices Livvy was making.

"What time do you need to be home?" Chrissy asked when

dinner was looming. Rosa just shrugged and went back to putting away the odds and ends. "Because I can make some chili eggs for dinner if you want."

Rosa smiled. "I love chili eggs!"

Chrissy returned her smile. Chili eggs were simply scrambled eggs with a can of green chilies and some mayo. Chrissy had whipped it up one day for a quick dinner and wrapped it in a flour tortilla. The kids had loved it and it was one of the few dishes Chrissy always had the ingredients on hand for.

"Will you go check on the boys?" Chrissy asked when they were nearly done. She'd moved the computer to the living room last weekend, but hadn't heard much from the boys who were playing games on it. Who knew what they could be into.

"Sure," Rosa said, throwing an empty shoebox on the bed before leaving.

Chrissy plugged the vacuum into the wall and started making lines in the thick carpet. She was vacuuming under the bed when the sound of loud voices caught her attention. Thinking the kids were fighting over something, she turned off the vacuum only to realize she was hearing adult voices. Men. She reached the living room in less than two seconds, then froze in the doorway as two police officers looked up at her. She took an automatic step backward and looked around the men to see Rosa and the boys on the porch. One officer went outside and herded the kids off the porch toward a squad car.

"Are you Chressaidia Salazar?" the other officer asked.

Chrissy nodded. "That's right. What's going on?"

"We got a call from Silvaria Menendez. Did you take her children without her consent?"

She tried to look past the officer blocking the front door and thought she caught a glimpse of Rosa's red shirt but wasn't sure.

"Ma'am, did you take her children?"

Chrissy's heart was in her throat and pounding wildly. "I picked them up," she said, making eye contact firmly. "They called me and asked me to come get them—their mother was at work. I assumed she gave permission." She strained to look out the doorway while putting things together in her mind. Livvy had called the police? The kids hadn't told their mother they were coming to visit?

"Why don't we sit down," the officer said, indicating Chrissy's own living room. "So we can figure this out."

Chrissy swallowed and did as he said, sitting on the edge of her wicker love seat while he sat down on the couch beside it and opened his notebook. "You say your niece and nephews called you?"

Chrissy nodded, trying to wet the inside of her mouth which had gone dry.

"What time did they call you?" the officer asked.

"Around eleven-thirty this morning," she said.

"Did they say they had their mother's permission?"

"No," Chrissy said as the rage began building. "But I assumed they did. It's ridiculous that my sister called you. She knew they'd be okay with me. I watch them almost every day."

"Your sister said there were some problems between the two of you. That you took the kids away from her."

"That's crazy!" Chrissy said, her voice hot.

Suddenly the second officer came back into the house, moving fast toward his partner. The officer Chrissy had been talking to stood up and conversed with his partner in careful whispers for a moment. Chrissy saw the officer turn toward her, as if in slow motion, a very different look on his face.

He stepped toward her but she jumped up and took a step around the love seat toward her room.

"Were you aware of a warrant for your arrest?" the cop asked.

"Warrant?" Chrissy said, shaking her head fiercely and continuing stepping backward. "I don't have any warrants."

"Okay," the officer said in a tone she felt sure was supposed to be soothing, but had the opposite effect. "Why don't we sit back down and talk about this then."

"No," Chrissy said. Her back hit the door frame and she reached out to steady herself with one hand. "I don't have a warrant and I didn't kidnap my sister's kids. I don't understand what's happening here but I want you out of my house, now!"

The officer reached for the handcuffs at his belt. Her panic shot through the roof.

"What are you doing?" she asked, her breathing cut short and her heart speeding up.

"I need to talk to you, but if you won't sit down and discuss it—"

"You're arresting me for bringing my niece and nephews to my house for an afternoon? Let me talk to my sister, and Rosa—Rosa's the one who called me."

"And you have outstanding warrants—" He acted as if he were going to say more but instead lunged forward and grabbed her arm.

She yanked it away, taking another step to the left. But he grabbed her other arm and twisted her around, pressing her face against the wall in the hallway. Her head hit a picture of a Mexican village. It fell to the ground, the glass cracking. Rather than submitting, her anger peaked.

"Aren't you listening to me? This is insane! I don't have any warrants!" Chrissy's brain was buzzing.

The officer ignored her. "Chressaidia Josefina Salazar, you are hereby under arrest for kidnapping and outstanding warrants of possession and failure to appear. You have the right to remain silent—"

CHAPTER 45

I have never been arrested for drugs!" Chrissy said, too loud and too angry to sound reasonable. She watched TV; she knew what police officers thought of irate defendants . . . or prisoners . . . or whatever she was. The gray-green room they'd put her in at the police station had bars on the window, and one wall was covered in a mirror. She sat in a metal chair on one side of a metal table. A white man who'd introduced himself as Detective Ross sat across from her, watching every movement of her face. She hoped she spit a little when she yelled at him. "There's been all kinds of weird things happening to me. Someone got a second mortgage on my house. They maxed-out credit cards in my name, bought a car, drained my account. I've been working to fix it and—"

"And your niece and nephews were helping you with that?"

"No, they called me. They said that Livvy was at work, and they wanted to come over. They come over all the time."

"They said they hadn't been to your house in weeks."

Chrissy groaned and put her elbows on the dented metal table between them. She took a deep breath and prayed for calmness. "It's been about a week and a half, yes—their mother moved away. But she used to live right up the street and I used to watch them every day when their mom was at work."

"She said you two had a fight."

"Yes, we did," Chrissy said with forced evenness. "She was moving in with some guy she barely knows and took her kids with her. I thought it was horrible."

"So horrible that you'd want to save the kids from it, right? You were only trying to help, right?"

Chrissy glared at his attempts to play Good Cop. "Rosa called and asked if they could come over. I assumed it was fine with their mother. I missed them and so I picked them up. Please, just let me talk to my sister. I'm sure we can get this all cleared up."

"You're currently unemployed, is that correct?"

The calmness began retreating far more quickly than it had arrived. "Not like that," Chrissy hissed. "Not like 'irresponsible and a drain on society' unemployed. I'm not even getting unemployment. I'm just . . . between jobs, but I'm doing some work at my old job right now." In fact, they were expecting her to be there tomorrow morning—in twelve hours.

"And you're having financial problems?"

"Since someone emptied my account, yes."

"Why were you in California?"

"California?" Chrissy asked, backing up a couple inches as she considered this new piece of information.

"Well, I lived there for awhile, but that was a long time ago."

"April," he said, meeting her eyes again. "That doesn't seem too long ago."

Chrissy pulled her eyebrows together, wishing she dared grab the document from his hands. "I wasn't in California in April. Is that where the drug charges are from?"

"Two weeks ago you also failed to appear for your court date, which revokes your bond and adds another felony to your record."

"What!" Chrissy screamed. She couldn't help herself from lunging toward the paper.

He pulled it away sharply, and the other detective stepped up behind her chair. She imagined he had a gun pointed at her head and forced herself to clasp her hands back on the disgusting tabletop. There were coffee stains and who knew what else stuck to the surface. Her lap was a safer place for her hands. Digging deep inside herself, she prayed for the Lord to help her do this. She had to get beyond the panic; she had to come across as reasonable.

"Look," she said. "I don't know what's happening here. But I was in Idaho Falls in April. I was working for Almo Insurance. My last day was on April sixteenth. I just went back this last Thursday for some part-time work. I haven't been to California for years, I've *never* had anything to do with drugs, and I picked up my niece and nephews because they are my family and I missed them. I'm sorry. I won't do it again. I'll apologize to my sister. But please, something is wrong here. I tried to file a fraud report last week because some credit has been used in my name. The officer said I had to have a fraud report from a credit company first. Whoever charged all this stuff must have been arrested too—the warrant is for *her,* not me. She's the one you need to talk to."

Detective Ross looked at her as if she were telling him the sky was falling. She wished it was. Surely that would be easier to explain than this.

"Don't you see?" Chrissy said, leaning forward, trying to make him understand. "This isn't me. There is someone else pretending to be me."

"And let me guess," he said, leaning toward her so that their faces were only a few inches apart. His eyes narrowed. "This other

Chressaidia is the one who kidnapped your niece and nephews today?"

Inside her head Chrissy screamed at the top of her lungs.

The door opened, and they both turned to look as a young woman came in and handed the detective another sheet of paper. Chrissy's stomach dropped. *Please don't let it be something else.*

The detective scanned the information as the woman left the room and Chrissy watched his eyes.

"Hmmm," he said in a tone that gave her no reason to let her guard down. "You say you tried to file a fraud report last week?"

"Yes," Chrissy said. Had they found something that proved her story? "The officer wouldn't let me do it, though. He said I had to get proof from a creditor but none of them will give me proof without a police report."

The detective leaned back. "That's really weird, since Chressaidia Josefina Salazar recently filed a fraud report in San Diego County."

"What?" Chrissy breathed.

"However, *she* had proof that allowed an investigation to begin."

The room spun for almost a second and Chrissy used every bit of strength she had to look this man in the eye. She felt emotion rising in her face but had lost the ability to hold it back. "Please," she said, her voice choking. "Please help me. Someone has stolen my identity, and they are slowly ruining my life. I don't know what to do, but maybe you do."

His eyes showed the smallest amount of softening, and she sniffed and raised her hands to wipe at her eyes, looking away from him.

"If you came into the police station, there would be a number associated with it. What day did you come in?"

"Um, a week ago today," Chrissy said, shuffling through her

memory to find the date. "I spoke to an officer, and he said all he could do was file a complaint until I had proof."

"A complaint *is* a police report. You only needed the creditor proof for us to start the actual investigation."

Chrissy was confused. "You mean, the number I had all this time was what I needed to get the information from the people that say I owe them money?" She was going to lose her mind!

The detective stood up. "Hold on a few minutes, okay?"

Chrissy nodded numbly and tried to make sense of everything. The idea that she'd had the number she needed all along was almost too much to bear.

It was fifteen minutes before Detective Ross came back to the room. His expression was different, softer, but Chrissy still watched him warily.

"I have good news and bad news," he said as he sat down, some papers in his hand. She hoped he would let her choose which news to hear first, but he didn't.

"The good news is that I spoke to your sister and she's not filing charges."

Chrissy had all but forgotten about that issue.

"I also called to confirm the warrant and there is no mandatory extradition attached, so I don't have to send you to California if I don't want to, and I've found enough information to make me suspicious about you being the same woman California is looking for anyway."

Chrissy didn't know how to react. This was hope; hope was a good thing—but she wasn't sure she could believe it. "What's the bad news?"

"We still have to process you," Detective Ross said, hurrying to continue as the idea hit her in the chest like a two-by-four. "But it's for your own protection. We'll take your prints and your photo and compare those to the ones on the warrant. They can help eliminate you from being the woman they want, but you will be officially charged."

"That doesn't make sense," Chrissy said as her emotions rose up again. "If you believe me, then I shouldn't be charged at all."

"That's not how the justice system works," Detective Ross said. "We have two women calling themselves Chressaidia Salazar; what I think doesn't mean anything. The system will have to figure it out and that means you have to be put into it."

"But that means I'll have a criminal record," Chrissy said. "I'll go to jail."

"I've already called a bondsman," Ross said. "And I'm going to help you any way I can. We'll also do all we can to clear up the charges once things are figured out, but that's the best we can do."

Chrissy hung her head and wiped at her eyes again. Finally she nodded and lifted her head, unable to come up with any other solution except the one he'd offered. She'd tried to do so much on her own and was out of options. "Okay," she said. "What do I have to do?"

CHAPTER 46

<img>~~~~/</img>

Idaho Falls, Idaho
Wednesday, May 28

Chrissy blinked her eyes open Wednesday morning and stared at the ceiling dappled with broken sunlight. The light moved with the swaying of the overgrown lilac tree outside her window. She watched the patterns move and shift, grateful to be home, but still feeling overwhelmed and insignificant.

She'd had to stay at the police station overnight and although everyone had been very nice to her, even giving her a private cell, it had still been a jail cell. The next morning she had gone before a judge with a public defender by her side, told her story, and was ordered to come back in two weeks for a court date. Her attorney had given her his card while Chrissy waited for Amanda to pick her up. It had all been so surreal and despite Amanda wanting to somehow take care of her, Chrissy had to get to work. She'd been glad to spend the day alone in the file room with something to do. When she'd returned home she'd had a bowl of cereal and gone straight to bed. Now it was a new day—Wednesday—and she felt as despondent as ever, despite the sunlight streaming through her window.

"It's a beautiful day," she said to the sunshine—right before she pulled the pillow out from behind her head and put it over her face, screaming as loud as she could. She'd barely slept. The last thing she wanted was to face her life again. At least at night she had an excuse to do nothing. It had been nearly 4:00 A.M. when she last looked at the clock. She'd hoped to sleep at least until eight since she hadn't gotten any sleep in jail the night before. *Jail!* It was such a nightmare.

She traded in the pillow for her bedspread, pulling it over her face.

Twenty minutes passed as she tried to make a plan for the day.

Thirty minutes passed while she tried to fantasize that it really was all a bad dream.

Forty minutes passed without her succeeding at either attempt to get control of her thoughts.

She stayed under the covers, but was beginning to wonder why it had always seemed like such an escape. Having her head covered with the bedspread didn't protect her from her problems and her back was beginning to hurt from being in bed so long. Finally, in one movement, she threw the bedspread back and sat up.

When Amanda had dropped Chrissy off yesterday, her friend had turned to her and said, "You'll be okay. You're the strongest woman I know." The words mocked her today. She didn't feel strong, and she had little hope that she would be okay. Amanda must not know many people.

Chrissy grunted as she swung her feet over the bed and went about pulling the covers up.

"Eight, nine, ten, eleven," she counted to herself as she put her pillows in place. A magazine had once said eleven pillows was the magic number for a perfect bed arrangement. So Chrissy had kept her eyes open for shades of green and purple that would match the quilt she'd made last summer. Once she had them all, she realized the magazine was right. Eleven pillows made the bed look like something right out of *Better Homes and Gardens.*

Once done with the bed, she straightened her bedroom, then stared at her scriptures on the bedside table. It was only 7:30; she had plenty of time to read her scriptures, but there was a reluctance to turn to them since she knew there were no instructions on how to clear your name should you be falsely accused. It was tempting to think that nothing within those pages had any relevance to what she was facing. Amanda had said Chrissy had beaten the odds over and over again, and she was right. Chrissy had overcome having not one, but two deadbeat parents, withstood a lifetime of prejudice and discrimination, and still developed a strong testimony of the gospel. She'd survived a few broken hearts, made a life, and loved the people in it with her whole heart.

But I feel so lost right now.

As soon as the thought passed through her mind, she was reminded that there was One who knew her, knew everything about her, and she hadn't even given Him a chance to help—other than the begging, pleading prayers that only made her more angry when they weren't answered. She kept reminding herself that there was truth here. And Detective Ross was helping her prove herself now.

She picked up her scriptures, moving her thumb over her name imprinted on the cover. Amanda's parents had given her these scriptures on her baptism day. She'd treasured them ever since. With her legs crossed on her bed, she put on her glasses from the bedside table and opened to 1 Nephi 3:7, when Nephi tells his father that he knows the Lord gives no commandments without preparing a way for His children to accomplish those things. It was likely the most oft-quoted scripture from the Book of Mormon and it had always held great power for Chrissy. Many times she'd drawn strength from the fact that she'd been sent to Earth with a purpose and a plan, which meant every trial she encountered was part of that plan. And with the Lord, she could figure it out and be stronger for it.

Right?

She closed her eyes and tried to push past the despair. She had always been an optimist—looking for the good in any situation. Even though she didn't feel it, she had to find a way to believe that way again. She took a deep breath and let it out slowly. *There is a plan,* she told herself. *There is a reason.* So how did all *this* factor in? What part of the plan was this?

And then the anger came through again. She'd heard once that wishing for understanding in life was the booby prize. Did it matter if she understood? Would she go crazy before she ever got what she was after? There were plenty of other things in life she didn't understand, why should this be any different?

What she needed was momentum, accomplishment, and the satisfaction of knowing she'd done everything she could do to make the result of this nightmare as positive as it could be. If she sat back and simply waited for understanding, nothing would happen.

She read the scripture again, then listed in her mind all the things in her favor—including her arrest last night. Like Detective Ross had said, she was in the system now, her picture and fingerprints would soon be on the national database. She was making progress, and that's where her focus needed to be.

With that in mind, she knelt down, offered her morning prayer, and proceeded to get ready for work.

CHAPTER 47

*Livvy nibbled on her fingernail Wednesday afternoon, trying not to think about what she'd done, trying to convince herself it had been the right thing. *I didn't press charges,* she reminded herself, but she still felt sick to her stomach. She didn't understand why things had happened the way they did, but it wasn't her fault that Chrissy got arrested, was it?

The kids were outside playing with Doug's mangy dog while she watched TV, waiting for Doug to come home and give her reasons to stop thinking at all. That was the only good part of this— Doug had been proud of her. He'd said she was finally standing on her own two feet. It felt good.

The phone rang, and she looked at it, hoping it wasn't Doug's family. They weren't happy with his decision to bring his new girl-friend and her three children into his house full-time. Doug swore they'd come around, and Livvy hoped so, especially now that a rec-onciliation between her and Chrissy was impossible. It made her feel strangely vulnerable to have no family around, but those thoughts led her to feeling ungrateful. She had Doug after all.

Oh, and the kids too.

The phone rang again, snapping Livvy out of her introspection. She ran to it and answered on the fourth ring.

"Hello, this is Livvy." Twice now someone had thought she was Anna, Doug's former girlfriend, so she made it a point to introduce herself right away.

"Uh, yes—I'm looking for Silvaria Salazar Menendez. The listed phone number gave this as a forwarding—"

"Yes, I'm Livvy."

"Silvaria Salazar Menen—"

"Yes, that's me." How many times did she need to say this?

The man on the other end of the line let out a breath. "Oh, good. Um . . . my name is Jon Nasagi and I'm a psychologist at the University Hospital in San Diego. Do you have a sister by the name of Chressaidia Josefina Salazar?"

Nathan came running inside, and he let the dog in as well. Livvy pulled up against the wall. She hated that dog—one more thing she hoped would get better in time.

"Yes," Livvy said, her stomach tight again. Was this something about last night? She didn't want to talk about it to anyone. But why would they be calling from San Diego?

The man continued. "I'm not looking for your sister, but I am looking for her family, perhaps someone we can talk to about her son. I got your information from her insurance company."

"Her son?" Livvy asked, pressing herself even closer to the wall as Nathan ran past her and the dog followed. She covered up the receiver. "Nathan, get that dog out of here. *Vamos.*"

"Yes, her son. Didn't you know she had a son?"

"Chrissy doesn't have a son." She yelped as the dog ran to her and started licking her hand. She turned away sharply, holding the receiver with both hands. Abuelita had hated animals in the house, and Livvy and Chrissy both inherited her dislike. They were dirty and smelly—especially this one.

"Nathan!" she yelled, trying to push the dog away with her foot.

"Nathan?" the man on the phone said. "Is that what she wanted to name him?"

"You've got the wrong person. Chrissy doesn't have any kids," she said again, watching the dog carefully. Nathan finally headed for the door, but he didn't shut it all the way, which meant that the dumb dog could run in at any time.

"No, she does," the man said, his voice sounding excited. "She gave birth four weeks ago, but she abandoned the child at the hospital. When did you last see your sister?"

Livvy tried to reach the door with her foot so she could kick it shut, but the phone cord was too short. "I saw my sister a couple weeks ago."

"In Idaho?"

"Of course," Livvy said. *Where else would she be?* Nathan and Carlos were squealing, chasing the dog around the patchy back lawn. "But like I said, you've got the wrong Chrissy anyway. She didn't have a baby a month ago." Chrissy had never even had sex—another thing Livvy didn't understand.

"She did have a baby, and we need to find placement for him."

"She didn't," Livvy said, then she tensed as the kids headed toward the back door again. "Look, I've got to go, but you've got the wrong Chressaidia," she said. She hung up and lunged for the door, managing to slam it shut just seconds before the dog's scratching, dirty paws could hit the floor.

CHAPTER 48

$\mathscr{C}$hrissy knocked, and as soon as Micah opened the door she walked past him. It was hot today, and her car didn't have air-conditioning. Her eyeliner was melting. She'd worked at Almo until 4:00, but on her lunch break she made a few phone calls and took advantage of having a computer and fax machine so close by. Finally she had some success.

"How are you doing?" Micah asked with concern.

Chrissy waved it away. He knew she'd been arrested—Amanda had called him—but Chrissy was way past that and didn't want to risk getting hung up on it again. "I'm fine," she said. "In fact, I'm great!"

Micah lifted his eyebrows. "Really? You ought to get arrested more often."

Chrissy smiled. "It does have a way of putting things in perspective, and apparently it solidifies one's motivations—I highly recommend it."

Micah chuckled.

"So I got some statements," she said, holding the faxed papers out to him and beaming with her triumph. She'd done *something!* "You wouldn't believe what I had to do to get them."

"Sell your firstborn?" Micah asked, taking the papers and giving her a half-smile. "It seems that was the going rate when I was trying to do it."

"Worse—since I don't have a firstborn," Chrissy said, trying not to let the fact sting. "I had to send over my birth certificate, most recent bank statement, a letter from the bank regarding my claim, my Social Security card, my father's proof of citizenship, *and* a copy of my most recent police report."

"You have a copy of your father's citizenship papers?"

"I'm Mexican. It's a good thing to have on hand—proves I'm legal. Turns out this chick filed a fraud report in San Diego and then filed complaints with the creditors, which has made this huge mess all the messier. Oh, and she bought a gun in my name. Can you believe that? A two-shot pistol."

Chrissy caught movement out of the corner of her eye and looked over to see a teenage girl looking at her. She had yet to be formally introduced to Mallory and finally realized she was the girl at the water fight at Amanda's house several weeks ago. "Oh, hi. It's Mallory, right?"

Mallory nodded, but regarded Chrissy in a stiff, polite way. "Hi," she said evenly, not meeting Chrissy's eyes.

Chrissy noticed a jar of nail polish on the coffee table and thought maybe she could open a dialogue. Mallory had been a pretty easygoing kid when they'd met at Amanda's. In fact, Mallory had dumped a bucket of water over Chrissy's head. "You doin' nails today?"

Mallory looked up at her, confused, and Chrissy pointed to the polish. "Is that yours?"

"Yeah."

Another one-word answer. Chrissy was trying to think of something else to say when Mallory looked at her dad, then at Chrissy. Her eyes narrowed ever so slightly, but enough that Chrissy's next comment died before it reached her lips.

"So," Micah said after a few awkward moments. "Should we take a look at your statements?"

"Oh, right," Chrissy said, turning toward him. She glanced once more at Mallory, who continued to regard her with a cold look. Chrissy tried not to dwell on it and smiled at her.

"This is great work," Micah said, scanning the top page before flipping it to the back. "We can go back to the office."

Chrissy nodded and followed him down the hall, taking in the tack strips lined up along the edges of the sub-flooring. Peeking into the bedrooms, it seemed they had met the same floor-stripping fate.

"New carpet?" she asked, anxious to get away from Mallory's less than warm welcome.

"Tomorrow morning," Micah said. "I found a remnant that will cover the hallway and two bedrooms, but not the living room, so I'm thinking of doing laminate there instead." As the last word left his mouth, he stopped in the middle of the hallway, a fact Chrissy didn't notice until she ran right into the back of him. He was completely solid so she bounced backward and caught herself on the wall. She apologized and looked up at him, wondering what had caused him to stop in the first place. His eyebrows were pulled together under the brim of his hat as he stared at the paper in his hand.

"What?" she said, stepping forward until she could see what he was looking at . . . and smell his cologne. She took a deep breath and forgot for a minute what they were doing. Their arms touched briefly, and it felt strangely intimate.

"Compuline," Micah said.

Chrissy was brought back to earth. She looked at the paper. There were a few different purchases made from a company with that name on the statement.

His eyes moved farther up the page. "And it's a Providian account."

"And?" Chrissy said, waiting for the punch line.

Micah turned his head so he could look at her. "One of the cards opened in my name was a Providian card, and they also made several purchases from Compuline. It's an online company that sells laptop computers. I think they resell them on eBay or someplace like that."

"That's weird," Chrissy said slowly. "What are the chances we'd both have the same card with purchases from the same company?"

"Pretty high if the same person took both our IDs." He started moving again and was soon in the study, Chrissy right behind him.

She put her purse on one of the chairs and walked to the desk where he had just sat down, toggling through his computer. He also pulled open a drawer and fished through a file, finally pulling out a paper that looked a lot like Chrissy's statement.

"Look at this," he said, moving over so she could join him at the desk. "Both our cards were opened within a week of one another. And the purchases are really close, too—these ones were made on the exact same day." He pointed to the address. "Different addresses, but both of them in San Diego. The same place where the fraud report was filed, right?"

"But what are the chances of the same person getting our information at the same time?" Chrissy asked, trying to catch up with his thought process as she leaned over his shoulder so she could see what he was doing . . . and smell him some more.

"I don't know," Micah said slowly. Then he paused and turned in his chair so he was looking up at her. "That date we went on, at that café—what did you use to pay for your dinner?"

Chrissy searched her brain. "My debit card," she finally said as the evening and all its splendor came back to her. "I'm really sorry about leaving like I did that night, by the way. I never told you about that. See, I had just—"

"Did the gal take it to the back?"

"She said the front machine was broken."

"Did she take your license back with her as well?"

Chrissy skewed up her face and thought about it. "I don't know . . . wait." She remembered the girl had asked for it. "Yeah, she did."

Micah slapped the desk and met her gaze with a triumphant, yet angry, look on his face. "That's it."

"What?"

"They got our cards and copies of our license numbers that night," Micah said. He put his hands on the sides of his head and leaned back as if he were holding in his excitement. "I've been racking my brain for months to figure out when it could have happened. That girl made copies and either used them or sold them." He shook his head and then laughed. "That's when it happened!"

"How can you be so sure?"

"You and I are very different people, right?"

Chrissy nodded. "Right."

"And both of our thefts occurred after that night, right?"

"Right, but the thefts are so different. You didn't have a fraction of the amount of money stolen that I did."

"That's true, but there are still a lot of similarities."

"Sounds like a long shot," Chrissy said. "You said yourself this is the fastest-growing crime in America. Maybe we just get gas at the same station."

"I have a Chevron card and it's all I use for gas—Techron, ya know."

"Well, then the grocery store. I usually go to Albertsons or the Mexican markets."

"Never go there," Micah said, shaking his head. "I've got my Fresh Values card linked to the kids' schools at Smith's, and it's just down the block." He stopped and looked at her. "Why don't you want to even consider it?"

Good question, Chrissy thought as she settled into a chair and tried to come to grips with this turn of events. "Maybe it's just hard to accept that the evening was even worse than I thought."

CHAPTER 49

$\sim$

*D*on't you see?" Chrissy said to the cop. "We know who took our identities!" She'd caught on to Micah's excitement by now.

"And we'll follow-up," the officer said. He was tall, but portly, his belly straining against the buttons of his shirt when he leaned back. "You've filed your report, we've got copies of your statement, and I've put a note in the report of the possible link."

"Can't you follow-up right now? I mean, I know that you're really busy." She cast a glance at Micah, who gave her an encouraging smile. He said most people, but cops especially, responded better to people they didn't think were certifiably insane. Chrissy was scared to death being back at the police station, so that kept her on alert as well. "But we know when the theft occurred, and we know who took it. That's got to be better than pretty much every other ID theft case around."

"Yes, it's wonderful," the officer said. "And I've got it all here in the file." He tapped the manila folder that looked like the approximately 300 other manila folders stacked on his desk. Was hers going to go into the stack too? She wanted sirens and those APB things.

Would a K-9 unit do any good? "I'll give it to Detective Ross as soon as he gets back."

"Where is he?" Chrissy asked. "Could we wait for him?"

"Uh, no," the officer said as if she were an idiot for asking. "He's on vacation with his family. He'll be back next week."

Chrissy blinked. *He was on vacation?* Her court date was next week, would he be back in time?

She kept smiling politely all the way out of the police station, but scowled as soon as the doors shut behind them. "Ross is on vacation and no one else cares," she said as they headed toward Micah's truck. "Why would they assign my case to someone who was just about to go out of town?"

It was a beautiful day, bright and sunny, and the early evening had cooled enough that the earlier heat was no longer sticking to her skin and threatening her eye makeup. If not for all the chaos in her life she'd take off her shoes, walk down to the riverbank and watch the Snake River roil and tumble in the summer sun. But instead, she barely had the energy to notice something as infinitesimally important as the weather, or the world at large. "They're not going to do a dang thing. I can't believe I pay taxes for this kind of service."

"It's not a dry cleaner," Micah said, hurrying to open the door of the truck for her. He held out his hand so she could step onto the sidestep and slide into the passenger seat. She paused and looked at him, smiling at the chivalry.

"Thank you," she said, her voice much softer now. He nodded and closed the door after she'd climbed in. When he slid into his seat, she asked, "What's next?"

"Well," Micah said as he turned the key. The truck was a diesel and the engine growled and rumbled, a perfect accompaniment to how she felt. "They had to have gotten some of your identification in order to get a mortgage."

"Couldn't the documents have been forged?"

"Maybe," Micah said as he pulled out of the parking stall. "But maybe not. We know the theft originated here in Idaho Falls, wouldn't it be worth their time to try to get an original? Besides, title companies are trained to spot fakes."

"Even stupid online title companies that trust criminals they never even meet in person?" They turned onto the street and she realized the truck was high enough off the ground that she could look across the tops of almost every other car on the road.

Micah laughed. "Yep, even them. If they loan someone forty thousand dollars, they have to be somewhat careful." He turned right, then half a block later he turned right again and pulled up to a large, ugly, brown building.

"Vital records," he said, putting the car into park. "Let's see if anyone's requested a copy of your birth certificate lately."

"You think they'll tell me?" Chrissy asked as they made their way up to the front doors.

"If you're nice."

She gave him a dirty look. "Why do you have to make everything so hard?"

CHAPTER 50

It was nearly seven when Micah and Chrissy pulled up to his house. They had arrived at vital records just before closing and had only been able to leave a note for the department supervisor who'd already left for the day. "Um, do you want to come in?" Micah asked. He wasn't sure why he was inviting her in, but after spending the afternoon with her, he was hesitant to let her leave.

Chrissy looked toward the house and her car parked in front of it, and seemed to consider it, but in the end she shook her head. "I'd better not. I need to get home. Thursday is mopping day."

Micah tried not to be offended about losing to a mop.

"Besides, I don't want to interfere with your time with Mallory. I've had your attention all day. Thanks for your help though—I couldn't have done it without you." She turned toward him and smiled in that way that made his stomach flip-flop again. She was wearing a lime sherbet kind of green printed top with a white skirt and silver heels. Silver! It was disconcerting the way he noticed the things she wore, even more so that he noticed the way they fit, the way the fabric moved and stretched and—

"Micah?" Chrissy asked, bringing him back to the cab of his truck and meeting her eyes. Beautiful eyes. Dark, wide, and tapered at the sides, framed by high eyebrows and smooth, mocha skin. He wondered if her face felt as soft as it looked.

"Sorry," Micah said. "I was just thinking that . . . uh, maybe I'll go through my other statements now that I have yours. Maybe something else will match up."

"Good idea," Chrissy said. "I don't know how I'll ever pay you back for all you're doing for me."

"Go to dinner with me," Micah suddenly blurted out too loud and too fast, causing Chrissy to jolt back slightly. Micah rushed on, "We could go back to that same place. Maybe ask about the gothic girl who took our cards that night. And, well, ya know, try again."

She regarded him speculatively for what felt like a long time, and he wished he knew what she was thinking. After a few moments her lips pulled into a smile. "I would love to," she said, almost in a whisper, holding his eyes and sending a tingle down his back. She must see something of worth in him. The idea gave him a bit of a high.

Micah grinned back, feeling like the high school kid who'd finally worked up the nerve to ask a girl to Homecoming. "Tomorrow night?"

"Perfect," she said.

"I'll pick you up at six-thirty?"

"I'll be there with bells on."

She wore bells too?

CHAPTER 51

Micah might have been humming when he came inside; he couldn't be sure. Chrissy's car made its way down the street behind him as he shut the door and headed for the kitchen. What to make for dinner? Mallory was on the phone. She didn't respond when he came in, instead turning her back toward him, deftly replacing all Micah's happy feelings with those of concern. He thought back to her not-so-warm welcome of Chrissy and wondered why she'd reacted that way. When he watched the water fight, Mallory had seemed to like Chrissy well enough.

"He just walked in," Mallory said into the phone. "Here he is."

"Who is it?" he asked quietly as he took the phone.

"Mom," Mallory said before disappearing into her room down the hall. It was fun to have her around more often, but demanding. One more kid to keep track of, but this one didn't have a car or many friends in the area. He'd been working from home more often, so she wasn't entirely on her own, but he knew she wished she were somewhere else more often than not.

Micah took a breath and prepared himself. "Hello?"

"Micah?" Natalie asked.

"Yeah," he said.

She was quiet for a few seconds, then sniffled on the other end of the line. "What time does Blake get off work tonight?"

"Eight," Micah said. "Why?"

"I need to come over and talk to you guys. If I come at eight-thirty, will he be home?"

"Yes," Micah said slowly. "What's going on?" He looked down the hall. Mallory's door was open, so he turned away and kept his voice down.

"Dennis moved out," Natalie said, her voice shaking. "I guess he met with an attorney months ago; he's just been waiting for the right time." She started crying openly. "I've done everything I can, Micah, really—I'm a size-six for heaven's sake! And all the while he's just been biding his time, setting up his own accounts, sending out resumes all over the country. He's moving to Omaha in July and leaving me with these kids all by myself. I just—I can't believe this is happening to me again."

Micah took a deep breath, wishing he could ignore that she was lumping him in with Dennis. Yes, he'd left, but he'd never abandoned her or the kids. The fact that she said this was "happening to her" showed that for the second time, she couldn't see her own contribution to a failing marriage. But he knew that now wasn't the right time to bring that up. "I'm really sorry, Natalie," he said, meaning every word.

"Yeah, well maybe it's good riddance," she said, bitterness replacing her sorrow. "The last couple years haven't been any fun at all."

Since that's why you got married—for fun, Micah thought.

Natalie continued. "I wanted to come over tonight and tell the kids. I thought it would be best to tell them together."

"I think that's a good idea," Micah said. "I'll call Blake and make sure he comes right home after work."

He hung up the phone and looked down the hall toward Mallory's room. His stomach tightened and he shook his head, not looking forward to tonight at all.

Chapter 52

"*H*i, Dad."

"Kayla," Micah said in surprise, pulling his oldest daughter into a hug. She lived eight hours away. He hadn't seen her since she'd come home for Christmas vacation and hadn't expected her to be here since she'd decided to stay at her job in Utah until the study abroad program started in August. He looked over her shoulder and raised his eyebrows at Natalie, who stood behind their daughter on the front porch.

"I asked her to drive up," she said once Kayla had gone inside. "I thought they should all be together. But she already knows." That explained her somewhat withdrawn welcome, and Micah dreaded what was coming more than ever.

Micah nodded and waved Natalie inside. Mallory and Blake were on the couch. Kayla perched on the armrest, asking if they'd had a fun week of summer vacation and teasing Blake about having a girl-friend now that he was old enough to date. She was acting upbeat and bubbly, which had always been her style, but she fidgeted with the hem of her T-shirt.

Micah didn't know whether he should sit or stand. For the first time he wondered if he should really be here at all. Kayla asked Blake to move over so she could sit in the middle. In the next instant Micah relived the night almost twelve years ago when five-year-old Blake and seven-year-old Kayla had looked up at their parents with scared eyes and confused expressions. Two-year-old Mallory had lived out the moment on Natalie's hip. Micah had moved out two months before, and it had been strange to be back in the house he and Natalie had lived in.

"What's divorce?" Kayla had asked after they explained what was happening.

"It's when people don't love each other anymore and can't live together anymore." It had seemed like a good explanation at the time, one he'd practiced on a few friends who agreed it was the best way to say it. The kids, however, didn't hear it the same way.

"You don't love us anymore?" Blake had said, his eyes big and scared.

"No," Natalie hurried to say, shooting Micah a dirty look. "We love you guys so much, but we don't love each other anymore. Your dad and I aren't going to be married anymore."

The rest of the attempted discussion had been awkward and painful, both of them trying very hard to justify what they were doing and yet reassure the kids that they would always love them. Even then Micah could see how hard that was for the kids to understand. If Mom and Dad could stop loving each other, it didn't seem so far-fetched that one day they'd stop loving the children they made together. But he'd wanted out so badly back then that he hadn't dwelled on that. Instead, he kept reminding himself that he and Natalie *didn't* love each other anymore. It wasn't fair for the kids to grow up watching a marriage like that. That night had haunted Micah for years.

He tried to shake the memory from his mind, but he couldn't ignore that his children were facing it again. He finally sat down in the recliner—ironically one of the only pieces of furniture he was awarded in the divorce. He wondered what Dennis would walk away with.

"What's going on?" Blake finally asked. He looked braced, as if he were on a turbulent flight.

Natalie sat on the edge of the coffee table a few feet in front of Micah, crossing one foot over the other, then uncrossing them, and crossing the other leg instead. She was dressed in jeans made for a woman fifteen years younger, a snug-fitting top, with her hair and nails perfect. He knew she'd likely spent an hour getting ready and yet it gave her a manufactured look. Chrissy, on the other hand, pulled off her own style of dress, makeup, and hair with such ease.

"Your mother has something she needs to tell you guys," Micah finally said, when the tense silence had stretched to its breaking point and Natalie made no move to explain why she was there. Three faces stared back at him. Kayla's expression reflected that she would be strong for her little brother and sister. Blake's face was guarded, but Mallory looked terrified. Micah felt a lump rise in his throat. How would they ever believe in marriage if the only ones they ever saw ended this way?

Natalie took a breath and then in a long—and arguably subjective—explanation, told them what was happening. During her monologue, Kayla took Mallory's hand in her own and put her other hand on Blake's arm.

"I tried to get Dennis to go to marital counseling, but he wouldn't go. That was months ago. Since then I've just done my best, but I guess my best wasn't good enough. Dennis wants a new life, and I have no choice but to give it to him." She smiled as if determined to keep things light and cheery. Micah tried to ignore his frustration, unsure how he should feel, but not liking the way she was laying this out.

When Natalie finished talking, the room was silent. Mallory stared at her lap, Kayla tried to smile encouragingly at her mother, and Blake's face had gone hard.

"What about Pat and Andy?" Blake asked.

"Well, I'll have full custody, like I do with you guys, and they'll visit Dennis for holidays and summer. It will be a lot like what you guys do with your dad."

"I *live* with Dad," Blake said.

"Well, for now," Natalie said. "But that's only temporary."

Micah felt his eyebrows rise. When Blake looked at him, shocked, Micah hurried to jump in. "It's as temporary or permanent as Blake wants it to be," he said, holding Blake's eyes and hoping it gave his son confidence. "It's been great having him here." Mallory looked up at Micah then too. "And Mal too, of course." He winked, and she seemed to soften a little bit, but it didn't hide that she seemed to be doing everything she could to hold back tears.

Natalie turned around to look at Micah. "But he's not staying, especially now that Dennis is gone. That's why he came, you know; he and Dennis just couldn't get along. After summer visitation is over, he'll come back home with me."

Again, the room was quiet until Micah tried to save the moment, thinking only about Blake. It was hard to form statements without making Blake feel obligated to choose either option. "If he's happy here come the end of the summer, I'm happy to have him stay."

She glared at him and he held her eyes, trying to communicate that right now was not the time to argue about this. "When will the divorce be final?" he asked tightly, trying to keep the discussion on point.

It seemed to get her back to the original subject. "July, I think. He's moving to Omaha next week." She turned to look at the kids again, and when she spoke her voice was higher, sweeter—as if she were talking to little kids, not two teenagers, and in Kayla's case, an adult. "Are you guys okay with this?" she asked—an impossible question. What did it matter if they were okay with it or not? "Do you have any questions?"

Kayla asked if Natalie would be moving to a new house. "Not a chance," she said, the first hint of bitterness in her voice. "I've got the best lawyer there is. He'll get me the house just like he did last ti—" She stopped and Micah clenched his teeth together.

Silence fell again.

"Can I go to Nick's?" Blake suddenly said.

"We need to finish talking about this," Natalie said.

"I'm finished," Blake said strongly, standing up and looking down at his mother. He shifted his stance, looking at Micah for permission. "Can I go, Dad?"

"Yes," Micah said even though it was almost nine o'clock. Natalie whipped around, but he didn't meet her eyes, still looking at his son. "But when you get home, we'll talk some more, okay? Be home by ten-thirty."

Blake looked annoyed, yet relieved, to be off the hook, at least for now. "Okay." Without another word he headed for the front door and shut it with a thud.

Kayla was still holding Mallory's hand.

"Mal," Natalie said, turning to their youngest daughter and leaning forward. "This doesn't change anything for us."

Micah furrowed his brows toward the back of Natalie's head. *It doesn't change anything?*

Natalie continued, "Everything will be just the way it was."

"No," Micah said. Kayla and Mallory both looked up at him.

Natalie's back straightened. "This changes a lot of things." He held Mallory's eyes. "Divorce is horrible." He looked at Kayla, who was now the one staring at her lap. He imagined that despite her tough and "everything will be all right" façade, this was very hard for her to face again. She'd had the hardest time when Micah and Natalie had divorced. This had to resurrect some of those feelings for her. "But you know it's horrible, Mal, and so do all of us. When families break up, it's never okay, and it's never easy. But sometimes, even when we don't want it to happen, it happens anyway. This *isn't* going to be easy, but your mom is going to do everything she can to take care of your brothers, and take care of you. Your mom loves you. I love you, and so does Dennis. Things will be different, and they will be really hard sometimes, but we're still a family."

"And Pat and Andy are still our family too," Kayla said, turning to Mallory and putting her big-sister-face back on. "I remember when Mom and Dad split up—it was hard, but it all turned out, and ya know, it's important for people to do what makes them happy. If Mom and Dennis aren't happy, then it's not good to be married anymore."

The simplistic response just made Micah sicker. Was that what Kayla thought? That as soon as you were unhappy, you jumped ship?

Isn't that what he'd done?

They talked for another twenty minutes and then Natalie said she needed to pick up Pat and Andy from a neighbor. Mallory still seemed unable to make peace with the myriad emotions that continued to play across her face, but she was keeping them tightly reined in. How could a fourteen-year-old girl make sense of this? She could clearly tell how big it was, despite Natalie's insistence that life wouldn't change too much. Natalie hugged Mallory and she and

Kayla left, leaving Mallory and Micah in the living room. He turned to his daughter. She was already heading toward her room.

"Mal," Micah said, reaching out. She pulled her arm from his reach and kept walking. He took a few steps to catch up. "Mal," he said again, grabbing her arm and holding it, though she didn't seem to resist, leading him to believe she was as desperate for some reassurance as he was to give it. But he couldn't think of anything to say, so he pulled her into a hug, resting his chin on the top of her head and taking a deep breath. "I'm so sorry, Mal," he whispered. "You've lived your whole life with the mistakes your mom and I made, and now you're having to face it all over again. I'm sorry."

For a moment he thought she might resist, pull out the *I'm-too-old-and-too-cool-to-care* card and refuse his attempts to comfort her, but she didn't. Instead she burrowed her face into his chest and started to cry.

CHAPTER 53

*M*icah closed the door to Mallory's bedroom and wandered into the kitchen, rinsed some dishes, and contemplated doing more than the absolute basics. His glance took in the Tupperware container on the counter, overflowing with screws, hinges, and other miscellaneous hardware items. There was a spool of twine and half a dozen tools piled next to a teetering stack of bills and other papers. He really ought to straighten up and at least take the tools and hardware to his workbench in the garage. But then . . . what was the point? No one saw his countertops other than him and the kids, and the kids didn't care. He started the dishwasher and thought about Chrissy's praise of his study when she'd seen it last week. Not many people had seen that room; the compliments were very nice to hear.

The enjoyment of the memory didn't last long, however. Vague realizations filtered into his mind. Did he have time for a woman? The answer was no. Was it fair to his kids for him to even entertain the idea of a relationship? Again, the answer was no, and it made his stomach roll. This was not fair, and yet even before Natalie's announcement, he'd been hesitant to pursue a relationship. Her divorce was just one more reason added to the list. But it was a big reason. A final reason. It all came back to the kids and doing what was right by them.

The satellite TV had been reconnected a few days ago, and after he spent thirty minutes grunting through some curls, presses, and push-ups, he decided to see what was on. His hope was that maybe he could escape from his thoughts while he waited up for Blake. A channel caught his attention. Two women laughing and talking in Spanish. Neither of them looked like Chrissy aside from the dark hair and brown skin, but they reminded him of her anyway. One woman was holding up two shirts—a plain one and a colorful one—and the other woman was pointing to one and then the other. Chrissy would wear the colorful one, he was sure of it. In the times he'd seen her she was always dressed in something bright. Had he ever known a woman so . . . feminine?

"Dad, what are you watching?"

Startled, Micah turned partway to see Blake standing behind the couch, looking at him strangely. Micah turned back to the TV where the woman had put both shirts on over the one she'd already been wearing. Both women laughed and spoke in Spanish. Micah changed the station as if he'd been caught watching something of a questionable nature.

"Uh, nothing," he said, settling on ESPN before remembering he needed to talk to his son. He turned off the TV. "Come have a seat," he said, patting the area of couch beside him. Blake's expression fell as if he'd been hoping his dad would forget about the promised heart-to-heart. For one last instant, Micah thought about Chrissy. In the next instant, he knew what he had to do. But it could wait until tomorrow. Tonight, he needed to talk to his son. Blake sat down, and Micah pled in his heart he could say the right thing.

CHAPTER 54

Idaho Falls, Idaho
Thursday, May 29

As with every other night for the last few weeks, Chrissy didn't sleep well. Everything loomed so big in her mind all night. Every hour or so she found herself staring at the ceiling. She got up for a drink, then spent a little time working on a Quinceniara dress order from Lupe. The only thing that seemed to calm her tumultuous thoughts was Micah. Thinking about him reminded her that *everything* wasn't horrible and managed to silence her raging fears. She considered what she would wear tomorrow night, how she'd do her hair and makeup. She wondered what his favorite color was. Having another chance to get to know the man was exciting enough to push past her fears and frustrations, at least for a little while, each time they got the best of her.

Around 3:00 AM she finally fell asleep, and didn't feel she'd been asleep long enough when she was awakened by someone knocking. She sat straight up, realized it was daylight, then ran for the door as the second round of knocking ended. When she pulled the door open with a whoosh, she saw Micah, his hand raised to knock again.

He froze, staring at her as she squinted into the early morning sunlight that framed his broad shoulders on the front porch.

"Micah?" she asked, barely able to see who he was and definitely wanting a better look. She ushered him inside, where it wasn't so bright. How did he know where she lived?

The door had been shut barely a second when her hands went to her hair. She always pulled it up in a knot on top of her head when she slept, but a restless night had left it a mangled mess. "What are you doing here?" she asked as she tried to press her hair down, then realized that was impossible. She instead began tugging at the elastic holding it up.

"I'm sorry to have come so early, and . . ." He looked at her, his neck and face pink in the sunlight streaming through the living room window. "I didn't mean to wake you up."

"No big deal," Chrissy said, still fumbling with her hair. "What's up?"

Micah put his hands in his pockets and rocked back on his heels. He looked as if he were dressed for the office: khaki pants and a light green button-down shirt. He still wore a hat, however, though this one was light tan and without a logo. His sunglasses rested above the brim and she found herself even more curious about why he always wore a hat, though she was pretty sure she knew. One of these days she was going to swipe it off his head to prove she was right. She wondered if there was a casual way for her to tell him she had no issues with bald men.

"I need to talk to you," Micah said.

"Sure," she said as her hair finally fell free of the elastic and tumbled down her back in crumpled waves. Yikes. "Do you mind if I put my hair up while we talk?"

She turned and headed for the bathroom a few yards away without waiting for a response. After putting on her glasses, she quickly gathered her hair into her hands and wrapped it with the elastic once again. Much better. Her eyes settled on the T-shirt and flannel pants she'd worn to bed and she scowled.

What time was it?

"I can't go out tonight," Micah said.

She left the bathroom and made a mental note to make herself some nice pajamas as soon as possible. She stopped a few feet away and looked at him, feeling a smile pull at the corners of her mouth. He was more attractive every time she saw him. That shade of green was beautiful with his coloring.

"Okay," she said, a little disappointed that he'd break their date. "We can do it another time," she said, taking a step forward, narrowing the space between them and feeling the air start to sparkle.

Micah let out a breath and looked at the ground, signaling that she'd missed something. He was stiff, formal—something was wrong. She felt her smile fading.

"Chrissy," he said. "I've really enjoyed spending time with you and getting to know you and I think you're a really remarkable woman, but right now my life is really complicated and . . ."

He kept talking but she'd tuned out. She'd been here before, heard all of this a dozen times, it seemed. But it felt like the first time, and she fell back to earth as if she'd been thrown from a hot air balloon. In the next instant, she felt so incredibly foolish for thinking of him the way she had, of having any expectations at all. When would she learn? When would she grow up and stop expecting . . . anything?

"Okay," she finally said, cutting him off.

He stopped talking and finally met her eyes. She forced a smile, though she knew it had no warmth. Inside, she was devastated, but she knew better than to show any of that. It would only seem like manipulation to him, and though she was lonely, she wasn't stupid enough to force something that he didn't want.

"Okay?" he repeated.

Chrissy shrugged, moving a few feet away to organize some bills on the little table by the phone. "Sure," she said, her tone careful and even. "No big deal."

He just stood there, as if her interrupting his monologue had broken his chain of thought completely. She made the mistake of looking up and meeting his eyes. They were so soft, so . . . apologetic?

"I'm sorry," he said.

"You could have just called, ya know." Tears were growing in her eyes and she blinked them away as fast as she could. The feelings were rising up and if he didn't leave soon, she'd either throw a plate at his head or start crying relentlessly. She wasn't sure which option would be worse.

"I felt like I should tell you in person since we've been together so much the last couple of weeks. And I brought you this." He held up a book and stepped forward to put it on the table. "It's about identity theft—what to do, how to fix things. I found it very helpful. Now that my stuff is mostly resolved, I don't need it anymore. Just remember, no one will fight for you harder than you will."

A book? That was his offering to make this not sting so badly? It was also a not-so-subtle way for him to step out of her life completely. After all, his stuff was *resolved.* He'd seemed to emphasize that word. He wasn't pursuing things with her anymore. Their connections didn't matter. His life was too complicated.

"Thanks." She went back to organizing the bills, stacking them perfectly as if it made any difference at all. "I gotta get ready for work," she continued, moving a few steps further into the kitchen so she could organize the magnets on the fridge, anything to avoid his eyes.

"Right," he said, nodding.

"Yeah," she said, turning to face him, trying to look casual while holding tight to her feelings. "So. You'd better go."

He held her eyes again. She looked away first. He didn't say another word, and she waited to look back until he pulled the door shut behind him. *What just happened?* Things had been going so well. Was she that stupid, to see things that weren't there? To feel things so completely one-sided? And now what? They'd just discovered a connection with their ID theft problems. Was she supposed to keep following it up by herself? Did she even know how?

Oh, yeah, he'd given her the freaking book!

Tears rose up. One more dream out the door, moving down the sidewalk, getting into his truck. She tried to tell herself they hadn't started anything, that having hurt feelings now was ridiculous. But she couldn't quite convince herself of it. He was leaving.

In the next instant, she darted for the door, pulled it open, and ran down the steps. "Micah!"

He was just stepping into his truck, but turned toward her. The crumbling sidewalk cut into her feet, but she didn't stop, she didn't think. She just had to test a theory, and besides, what did she have to lose? What was the worst that could happen? He was already leaving.

She stopped a few inches away from him and tilted her head back so she could look in his eyes, really look. All that potential she'd felt between them screamed at her, and before she could talk herself out of it, she reached around his neck and stood on her tiptoes—since the lack of her usual heels made him seem even taller—pulling his mouth toward her until their lips met. She fully expected him to push her away, but once she realized he wasn't going to, she extended her fingers on the back of his head, dislodging his hat, and turned her face to deepen the kiss.

He hadn't pushed her away, but he didn't respond—at least not at first. But then, she felt his arms come around her back, pulling her closer. Her whole body ignited and relaxed at the same time, her heart racing as the strength of those arms held the two of them together, lifting her feet off the ground. The thrill of being touched at all was amazing. The thrill of being touched like *this,* kissed like this, responded to like this, was beyond what even she had imagined. This was what she'd wondered—whether she'd only imagined their chemistry would mix this way. And now she knew—too late.

A car honked as it passed and she pulled her mouth away from his, but she didn't ease out of the embrace, and he didn't put her down. She could hear his shallow breathing as he tried to reel himself in. She looked at his lips and tried to get herself under control as well.

"I just had to know," she said breathlessly, her hand still at the back of his neck. She could feel the heat of his skin, smell that cologne she loved, feel his body pressed against hers.

The first kiss.

The last kiss.

The only kiss.

He finally released her enough so their eyes could meet. "Chrissy," he said in a breathy voice. It was still laced with regret, and she realized that he had his reasons for stopping what they hadn't started yet, and one stupid kiss wouldn't change it. But she hadn't expected it would. Not really.

She pushed against his shoulders, tight from holding her up, and he lowered her to the ground where she turned away, heading into the house without looking back. What was the point? Once inside, she shut the door and leaned against it, closing her eyes and letting the tears truly fall. She listened to his engine start, and then fade away as he left. She dropped her head and gave in to the regret that was slowly taking her over.

One more failure. One more loss to add to the others. Why had she even allowed herself to expect anything different?

Trust me.

She snorted, swallowed the lump attempting to form in her throat, and headed for the bathroom. She had to get to work.

CHAPTER 55

Vamos a almorzar," Brandon said, startling her—*We're going to lunch.* She turned and faced him where he was standing in the doorway. *"¿Cómo va?"* he asked—*How is it going?*

"Fine," Chrissy said. Her back ached, and she had a couple killer paper cuts. But she'd only been here for—she had to look at the clock hanging above the door—four and a half hours. Once Micah left this morning she'd gotten ready in a hurry, eager to take her mind off the morning—well, most of the morning. She continued to play the kiss over and over in her head. It might be the last one she'd ever have. She wanted to remember it.

"¿Quieres acompañarnos?"—*Want to come with us?* Brandon asked.

"No, thanks," she said. "I'm not very hungry."

"You know, we've missed you around here," Brandon said. "It's nice having you again."

Chrissy picked up another stack of files she'd already sorted. "I really appreciate you having me back."

"I've been wondering if you'd be interested in getting your old job back, taking over the office management again. As you can see, Carla hasn't done a great job."

Chrissy's eyebrows went up and she met his eyes. "Really?" she asked, visions of her old paychecks dancing in her head. No background check, full-time employment, a job she knew and was good at. "What about Carla?"

Brandon nodded. "I'd offer Carla the option of staying on as your assistant, of course. But the office hasn't been the same without you." As he spoke, his tone dipped down to a level that hinted at intimacy and secrets.

Chrissy took a mental step back. There seemed to be more than a reference to her job performance. But a full-time job again? She needed it so badly. "I'll need to think it over," she said. "Can I tell you on Monday?"

"Of course," he said, grinning, watching her too closely. "You sure you don't want to join us for lunch?"

"No, thanks," she said again, smiling politely. "But I appreciate the offer."

"Anytime," he said. As he turned for the door, he winked. Her stomach tightened but she immediately raised argument with the part of herself determined to see the worst in him. *I need this job,* she told herself, wanting to talk herself out of having seen the wink at all.

CHAPTER 56

Idaho Falls, Idaho
Friday, May 30

Chrissy thumbed through one file at a time, making sure they were in alphabetical order. Tiek, Tielmann, Tilly, Timmons, Timmonson, Timothy, Tepori . . . aha! She pulled the offending file from the rack and moved it back about six inches, again thumbing through the files until she found its home between Tenbrook and Terry. The filing had gone much faster than she'd expected it to today—possibly fueled by her disappointment and frustration with every part of her life right now. It was after seven and everyone else had cleared out an hour earlier, ready for the weekend. Chrissy had chosen to stay and finish up a project so she'd be ready to start new tasks on Monday.

Monday—the day she needed to give Brandon an answer to his job offer. *It's obvious,* she told herself. *You need this job; you know this job. Taking it is the right thing to do. It's an answer to your prayers.* But what about taking the job away from Carla? And could she work with Brandon on an ongoing basis?

"You're still here."

She jumped and spun around, the expectation of being alone

heightening the fear of discovering she wasn't. Brandon stood a few feet away. He'd gone home, changed his clothes, and was dressed in a T-shirt and long gym shorts. It was weird to see him in something other than Dockers and button-downs.

"You scared me," Chrissy said, letting out a breath but remaining very much on guard.

He didn't apologize; he just smiled at her as if to say that had been his point. "I brought you something to eat."

Chrissy looked at the Subway bag he held in his left hand, then back at his face. "Thank you. That's very nice, but I'm not hungry." She was starving. Other than a Snickers bar and some almonds she'd gotten from the vending machine at the Laundromat next door, she'd eaten nothing all day. But as far as Brandon was concerned, she wasn't hungry at all.

"Nonsense," he said, walking to the desk and pulling out the sandwich. "Just take a break. Eat with me."

Chrissy didn't move. "Didn't you eat with your *family?*" She emphasized the word in hopes that it would remind him he had no right to be alone with her like this. He'd been married for at least six years and had two children.

"Marni took the kids to her parents' place in Salt Lake for the weekend. Her cousin is getting married. You wouldn't want me to eat alone, would you?"

Chrissy said nothing and returned to her filing, anxiously considering her options. She could leave—tell him he was a jerk and smash the blasted sandwich in his face. But that option ended with her going home jobless and hopeless. But would she really take advances from a married man in order to keep her job? Part of her would. She needed this job—*badly*—and she wasn't afraid of him. She was pretty sure that if it came to punches, she could take him.

In the next moment, however, she was angry. Why did he have to be such a weasel?

She took a breath and turned around. He hadn't opened his sandwich; instead, he was leaning back in a chair with his arms behind his head, leering at her. For an instant she pictured Micah, the way *he* always watched her too. But that was different. Micah looked at her in a way that made her think he wanted to see inside her, know what she was thinking, how she felt. A very different kind of wanting. Or, at least she'd thought that's what it was, or thought it could be. She still hadn't gotten over his pronouncement, no matter how hard she tried to push it into the corner of her mind.

"Um, would it be possible for me to get paid tonight for the time I've put in these last couple weeks?" She turned to face him and tried to look casual in her request.

"I thought we could just pay you on payday. Carla added you to the payroll already."

"Right," Chrissy said as if this was an acceptable option, which it wasn't. "And that's okay, but I'm in a bit of a financial bind and could really use an advance. I'd be very grateful."

Brandon raised an eyebrow. She fantasized hitting him in the head with a cinder block. He reached into his pocket. "I could give you a personal advance," he said, pulling out his wallet. "I have no problem paying for services rendered."

Chrissy pretended not to notice the implication. "Thanks."

He pulled out almost three hundred dollars and handed it to her. She took it, trying not to smile at her triumph, and rolled it into her palm. "Thanks again," she said, before taking a breath. She was paid up and could now vocalize her concerns without fear of getting ripped off. "If I'm going to come back full-time, we need to establish some professional boundaries."

Brandon managed to look surprised. "Boundaries?" he said, chuckling. "Have I crossed some boundaries?"

"Yes, you have." She waved toward the sandwiches on the desk. "Like bringing me dinner."

"I just thought you'd be hungry. I certainly won't do it again." He was still smirking at her. "Anything else?"

She closed her hand around the bills. "I don't appreciate the way you look at me and—"

"How do I look at you?"

Chrissy felt like a child having to point this out but she wasn't going to dance around it. "You look at my breasts. A lot."

"I apologize," he said in a patronizing tone. He still wore that slick little smile on his face. "Is that all?"

"And I don't like you to speak Spanish to me. It's not professional."

"Oh, okay, no more Spanish."

This was not working. He was simply letting her talk, and none of her words were making an impact. She turned back to the files and tried to gather her thoughts and words together. If he'd listened to her, maybe there would be a chance she could stay on, but she was simply some kind of entertainment to him. Her stomach dropped and she let her head fall forward, letting herself mourn for just a minute. If she didn't work here, where would she find a job?

"You have to admit though—" He was right behind her. She jumped and spun around to face him, pressing her back against the files and trying to swallow. His face was only inches from her own. "You do have very nice—"

In one motion she brought up her knee, hard, and as soon as he grunted, she pushed against both his shoulders and ran for the door. Brandon fell against a filing cabinet and was still moaning as she grabbed her shoes and purse on the way out, the bills he'd given her still tightly gripped in her hand. She didn't stop running until she reached her car and as she pulled out of the parking lot, she knew she'd never be back.

CHAPTER 57

The rest of the evening Chrissy tried to tell herself she was okay, that nothing had happened, but she could still feel Brandon's breath on her neck, and it made her shiver. She locked all her doors, even though she knew it was silly, and she worked on the dress for Lupe—first while playing her Shakira CD at full blast, and then switching to Josh Groban, in need of something peaceful. She'd done nothing wrong, and Brandon hadn't even touched her, yet she still felt dirty and vulnerable to have even been the object involved. Had she somehow sent out signals that she would be open to that kind of thing? Had she been a precursor to his action? The idea made her sick. Should she tell his wife? That made her even more sick. What would she say? What would his wife do? Would she blame Chrissy?

She considered talking to Amanda about it, but she'd probably tell Cam, and Chrissy didn't want that kind of advertising. She'd called Livvy, hoping she'd answer, needing to talk to someone. She was even ready to apologize, forgive everything, just to have a connection to someone who could tell her she'd done the right thing today. But the call went straight to voice mail, and she didn't leave a message.

At ten, the sun was down, the evening shadows having been sucked into the night. The CD had come to the end, and she was finishing the zipper on the Quinceañera dress, glad that she could take it to Lupe tomorrow and get some money. The bank had sent a letter; for now, they were refunding her five hundred dollars but were still working on the rest. She was grateful they'd restored some of her money, but it wouldn't pay the mortgage that was due next week.

The silence bouncing between the walls and furniture was suffocating. When she finished cleaning the kitchen, there were no more distractions to keep everything from falling in on her. She stood in the middle of her living room and felt herself giving in to despair. "I'm not weak," she said out loud, wanting to believe it was true, yet overwhelmed with feeling so *affected* by the things happening around her.

How did she shake off the fact that someone else was living life in her name, while, piece by piece, the edges of her own life were crumbling? How did she confront a married man making advances on her? How did she make sense of the connection to Micah she felt, even though his life was apparently too "complicated" for him to feel the same way toward her?

She shook her head, wanting to clear out the thoughts, tear away the chains that seemed to have snaked their way around her ankles and wrists. Where would she find a job now? How would she pay her bills? Was this other Chressaidia still posing as her, still complicating her life and sinking her further into a pit she could not claw her way out of? And what of Livvy? What of the kids? Would they ever be a part of her life again? Had she lost the only family she would ever have? She had a court date in a week. Had she made any progress? Would the judge believe her? Could she go to jail again? She clenched her eyes shut and balled her fists.

"This is not fair," she said to no one. Never in her life had she felt so powerless, and she hated it. It was not the way life was supposed to be. Life was about choices, about agency, and she felt denied, trapped by the choices of others. A few days ago she'd turned to her scriptures and they'd empowered her enough to get her going again, but she'd lost that drive somewhere.

"This is not what it's supposed to be," she said again. She paused. She went very still and then lifted her head as thoughts came together in her mind. This *wasn't* how it was supposed to be, and waiting it out, enduring consequences of poor choices she had not made wouldn't make it better. She'd done *nothing* wrong.

Then do something, a voice said in her mind. A voice she recognized. In the next instant, an electric current seemed to travel through her body before resting in her head, making her brain buzz and her thoughts connect. *I am not alone,* she thought to herself. *And I am not insignificant.*

"And *I* am Chressaidia Josefina Salazar," she said out loud. This other woman, for all her clever tactics and brilliant scheming, was not Chrissy, and until Chrissy could prove that to everyone else, she would be trapped in the world this other woman was creating for her. That was not the plan of her Father in Heaven, to be forced into an existence over which Chrissy had no control. Perhaps she couldn't fix everything. But she could do something. She took a deep breath, expanding her lungs, filling her body with new breath and fresh convictions.

Something Micah had said to her the other day came to mind and she said it out loud, knowing it was the truth: "No one will fight for me as hard as I will fight for myself."

CHAPTER 58

Idaho Falls, Idaho
Saturday, May 31

Livvy spent Saturday running errands and straightening the farmhouse. Doug was working that weekend, and she was glad to have some private time with the kids.

She shut the door to her car and went to get the mail as the kids ran inside. The post office was forwarding her bills now, but she and Doug weren't sharing money yet. Maybe in a few more months. She'd been working full-time since Marius had left four years ago, and she wanted more time at home with the kids. In fact, they'd talked about Livvy cutting down to part-time once her house sold and they could refinance Doug's farmhouse to a lower payment— they were expecting an offer on Livvy's house sometime today. Livvy was looking forward to the future.

Right on top of the stack of mail was a purple envelope without a stamp, meaning it had been put there by someone other than the mailman. Livvy knew right away it was from Chrissy. Her sister's flowery handwriting was scrawled across the front. If Doug were home, he wouldn't want her to open it. He'd had a lot to say about how he felt about Chrissy. But Livvy missed her older sister, despite still being mad, and frustrated, and tired of being judged. But besides all of that, Chrissy was the only person who had always been there for her. And now, even with Doug and the kids, she couldn't overcome her feelings of loneliness. She and Chrissy had never gone this long without speaking.

She hurried to open the letter while walking toward the garbage can on the south side of the house. She'd read it and throw it away immediately so Doug wouldn't know.

Inside the purple envelope was a simple card with tulips on the front. Tulips were Livvy's favorite flower. The fact that Chrissy knew that, and found a card that reflected it, made Livvy miss her even more. Why did things have to be so complicated between them? If only Chrissy hadn't become a Mormon. If only she had even once loved a man so much that she was willing to make sacrifices to be with him.

Why did they have to be so different?

Livvy,

I'm so sorry for taking the kids. I thought they had worked it out with you or I never would have brought them over. I worry about you—probably too much—but I love you, and I love your kids. I'm leaving for California for a few days. Trying to clear up some bank and credit things that have turned into quite a bear. When I get back, if you feel up to it, I'd like to meet you somewhere. Maybe I could come to your work? I have some things of the kids' that I've found around the house, and I miss you. I hope things are going well for you and Doug. Please hug the kids for me.

Love you,
Chrissy

CHAPTER 59

~~~~~

San Diego, California

$\mathcal{H}$ere is all the information on the southern drug line," she said to Eduardo, handing him a stack of files. They were in the small office she'd rented last week after Frederico had confronted her. She didn't want to take any chances of him finding out what she was doing—stealing her power, taking her glory. "You will start taking over my communications with our dealers immediately. Remember, we are running a business, not simply a drug trade."

"Right," he said, taking the folder.

The sound of a door opening caused both of them to snap their heads to the side and stare. Frederico stood in the doorway, glaring.

"Get out of here," Chressaidia said, standing up from the cheap desk she'd been using. How had he found her in the first place? Her heart was racing with the dual emotions of anger and fear. She didn't want him involved, didn't want him to have any part in this.

"Go," Frederico said to Eduardo. He turned to look at Chressaidia and she nodded at him. Should she need to, she could defend herself. Her two-shot pistol was with her all the time now; and she was no longer simply Frederico's subservient wife. She had power all her own and had done in a month what he hadn't accomplished in almost a year. She'd more than proven herself worthy of her hire.

Eduardo left, and Frederico shut the door, locking it, before approaching her. She didn't flinch, holding his eyes without blinking.

"You think you can do this to me?" he said, his voice low and angry. "You think you can just take over?"

"I already have," she replied, lifting her chin. "Your work here is done."

"No," Frederico said and he launched himself at her, grabbing her arm. She pulled back hard, trying to free herself from his grasp, but he tightened his large fingers and yanked her closer toward him. With his other hand, he grabbed her hair and pulled her head back. "You will not do this to me," he hissed through his teeth.

Chressaidia sucked in a lungful of air, but said nothing as her free hand reached slowly into the pocket of her jeans.

He pulled on her hair again, yanking her head back even farther. "You are only a woman," he said into her ear.

"And you are an addict," she shot back, her nostrils flaring as she took deep breaths. Her entire skull was burning. "Which is why these lines were failing. You cannot use the product and rule effectively. If not for me, everyone would know this already. I've protected you."

He growled deep in his throat and tightened his hold on her. "You've ruined me!" he said. "I'll kill you before I'll let you dishonor me this way."

It took less than a second to pull the pistol from her pocket, press it against his stomach, and pull the trigger. The popping sound it made was deceiving in its muted execution. It was only a .22 so the damage was minimal, but she still had another bullet and she was well-trained enough to know how to use it to her best advantage.

Frederico released her and staggered backward, clutching his stomach, his eyes wide as he stared at her. She walked toward him as his back hit the wall.

"I have always known," she said with perfect calmness, "that one day I would find my place within the ranks of my father's army."

Frederico slid to the floor, his face confused. The drugs had made him too weak to fight her. Chressaidia stood over him, looking down at him with contempt. He narrowed his eyes and reached toward her, but she kicked him in the stomach, making him scream in pain and crumble even more.

She crouched down and placed the gun beneath his chin, pointing the barrel toward the back of his skull. Her aim would need to be perfect. He swallowed against the barrel and looked her in the eye, pleading with her through his pain. His fingers clenched and unclenched against his stomach, his hand slick with the blood he could not stop.

She cocked her head to the side and stared at him, wanting to remember every detail of the look on his face. "I suppose I still have you to thank for the reward I will be given when the army learns the truth." She pulled the trigger. His head snapped back with the impact and his eyes were instantly vacant. She lowered her hand and turned away, checking her clothes to see if she'd gotten any blood on them.

Three small knocks sounded at the door and she went to it, unlocked the bolt, and let Eduardo back in. He looked at Frederico's body and then at her with surprise and a little bit of fear.

"We need to pack up," she said, returning the pistol to her pocket and basking in the power she felt radiating through her whole body. This was what it felt like to be a warrior, a soldier in her father's army, fighting the war for her country. "We won't be able to use this office anymore."

CHAPTER 60

Idaho Falls, Idaho
Sunday, June 1

$\mathscr{I}$s your brother awake?" Micah called to Mallory as he hurried down the hall Sunday morning, his tie, unknotted and loose around his neck. By the smell of things, his toast was burning.

"I don't know," Mallory countered from her room. The door stood open and she was putting on her makeup in front of the mirror. The new carpet looked great; he only wished the remnant had been big enough for the living room too.

Micah turned around and went back to Blake's room, pounding on the door for the third time. "Blake, get up!"

"I'm up," Blake called from inside, and by the sound of things he was at least vertical. "Gosh," he muttered as Micah headed back toward the kitchen. They'd all slept in this morning, and church started in ten minutes. Micah hated the nine o'clock block.

He pulled his toast from the toaster and buttered it, trying to keep the ends of his tie from getting in the butter. Mallory came into the kitchen and started working on her own toast. She was dressed in a long black skirt, flip-flops, and a bright-pink top that was too tight for church. But they were already late, and Micah

220

didn't have time for the argument they'd have if he told her to change.

Blake came around the corner of the kitchen and looked at the two of them. "It's Fast Sunday, you heathens."

Micah looked at his toast at the exact moment his stomach rumbled and someone knocked on the front door.

"I got it," Blake called, turning toward the living room.

Micah wondered who on earth would be visiting them right before church.

"Oh, hi," Blake said. "You looking for my dad?"

"Um, yeah, just for a minute."

Micah froze at the sound of Chrissy's voice. In a split second, he relived their kiss. He'd already relived it a hundred times, but now she was here, a few yards away. He went to put his toast down on the counter but it fell from his fingers and left a trail of butter and crumbs on his shirt and slacks as it tumbled to the floor.

"Shoot," he said under his breath, reaching for a napkin and trying to dab at the spots on his shirt while stalling having to go into the living room. His heart was pounding. *What is she doing here?* Mallory was watching him when he looked up, an accusation on her face. He threw the napkin on the counter and avoided her eyes on his way to the door. Should he be mad Chrissy had come here after he told her they couldn't see each other? In the next instant he found himself wondering if there was anything he could do that would make her kiss him again.

"Um, hi," he said, striding quickly to the door. She hadn't come inside; the screen door stood between them. Blake stood to the side as if waiting to see what would happen, but Micah gave him a look as he passed and Blake retreated to the kitchen.

"Hi," Chrissy said. "I'm really sorry to bug you and I know

you've got church, but I need those statements I left here. I've got copies of everything but the Providian and the Chase."

It took Micah a minute to catch up. He tried to ignore the disappointment that she hadn't come to see him. But he didn't want her to do that anyway, right? "Um, sure," he said. He stepped forward and pushed open the screen door. "Come on in, I'll get them."

"I'll just wait here," she said, taking a step backward. She was dressed in white, knee-length shorts, that red polka-dot top he liked so much, and red-heeled sandals—in a word, stunning. But her tone was formal, and her expression guarded, like it had been on Friday—before the kiss. He knew she was hiding her feelings from him and felt horrible. He liked the out-there Chrissy, who was intense, who had plenty to say because she always said what she thought. But she was keeping that Chrissy away from him now. It was no less than he deserved, but he wished he could explain things better to her. However, she didn't have kids. She'd never even been married. She wouldn't understand and he couldn't think of any way to say it that didn't sound as if he were searching for forgiveness. There was no answer. It was what it was—two people with strong feelings for one another, and two kids who rendered those feelings inconsequential.

"You can come in," he said again. *Please come in,* he thought. *Let me feel a little bit redeemed.*

"I'll wait out here."

He finally gave in and headed to the office. He pulled the file he'd labeled *Chrissy* out of the desk drawer. Why hadn't he given the statements back when he dropped off the book? Was he subconsciously hoping to see her again? He wouldn't put it past his rebellious heart that had not yet made peace with what he'd done.

He started thumbing through the file, looking for the copies of what she needed, then realized he ought to give her everything. His stomach sank. He wasn't a part of this anymore. He'd made that perfectly clear to her, so why was he still holding on to the file that would surely bring her back?

"Here's everything I've got," he said when he returned a minute later, opening the screen door and handing the file to her. "Sorry I forgot to give them back." He kept the screen door open and looked at her, visualizing her the last time he'd seen her in this shirt— soaking wet and running after kids with a hose. That day, he'd thought about how much had changed since their first date. Now he thought about how much had changed since that water fight. Where was a rewind button when you needed it?

"No big deal," she said, holding the file in front of her.

"Can I ask why you need them today?"

Her eyes flashed briefly, as if to say, "It's none of your business anymore, remember?" but she looked away before he could be sure. "I'm going to California," she said, tucking some of her thick, dark hair behind her ear.

Micah stepped forward, "Are you kidding?"

Chrissy raised her chin. "No," she said bluntly.

"What about your bond? You can't leave the state, can you?"

Chrissy shrugged as if she didn't know the answer, but he suspected she did.

"You're going alone?" he asked.

"I lived in California for almost ten years and I know how to take care of myself."

"But—"

"Micah," she said, cutting him off. "You're the one who said no one would fight harder for me than I would. I've got a PO Box where the statements were mailed. I've got a copy of the original police report and the complaint I filed. I've left half a dozen messages for my new attorney and he's not calling me back. Detective

Ross won't be back until Tuesday. I've got my original birth certificate, my dad's papers, and a copy of my high school yearbook. I'm out to prove who I am, to get this taken care of so I can get on with my life. Who knows, maybe I'll run into the other Chrissy while I'm down there and give her a piece of my mind."

"But . . ." Micah said, trying not to sound like a parent, and not doing a very good job of it. "I just don't think that's a good idea."

She held his eyes for a moment, but then turned without saying another word and headed for her car, her heels tapping on the sidewalk. He glanced over his shoulder to see both Blake and Mallory watching him from the kitchen. Blake looked curious; Mallory looked suspicious. He hesitated another minute, then hurried after Chrissy, catching up a few feet away from her car.

"Chrissy," he said.

She turned and looked at him with exasperation but said nothing, making him do the talking.

Micah racked his brain for what he could say to her, what he *should* say to her. "Can you afford it?"

"Can I afford not to?" she replied. "I'll be fine." She started to move toward her car again.

"But you don't have a credit card," he added. "How will you get a rental car or hotel room? You're not leaving now are you?"

"I'm driving my own car so I'll get there by nightfall," she said. "And . . ." She paused and her face closed off again. "This isn't your problem." She reached for the door handle.

"Wait," Micah said, still searching for something he could do. Maybe he couldn't stop her, but he wanted to help. Whether it was inflated chivalry or some kind of gut instinct, he didn't know, but he didn't feel good about this. "Let me get you some money."

"I don't want your money," she said as if disgusted with the offer.

"It's okay," Micah said, smiling and putting his hands out to indicate that he wanted her to wait. "I've got some cash. It'll help." He turned toward the house.

"No," Chrissy said strongly. "I don't want—"

"I'll be right back," he called as he ran in the front door. Chrissy mumbled something under her breath, but it was in Spanish so he couldn't know what she'd said even if he'd heard it well.

"We're late for church," Mallory said when he got inside. He ignored her and passed both kids who were now in the living room, watching. He hurried to his bedroom. He grabbed his wallet from the dresser and opened it, counting out just over two hundred dollars. It was almost his full month of spending money, but it wasn't much to help with a road trip of a thousand miles. Maybe he could run to an ATM real fast. He held the bills in one hand and ran back to the front door . . . just in time to see Chrissy's car disappear down the street. He pushed the screen open and walked outside slowly, staring at the corner.

"She said to tell you thanks anyway," Blake said from behind him. Micah felt his shoulders fall.

"Um, is she going to be okay?" Mallory asked.

Micah didn't know how to answer that and turned to face his kids. Blake looked worried, Mallory looked confused as to how she should feel—Micah could relate to both. He absolutely hated that Chrissy was going alone, hated that helping her would go against the boundaries he'd set.

"You heard her," he said, trying to put on a brave face. "She can take care of herself."

Oh, please, help her take care of herself.

Chapter 61

~~~~~~

Idaho Falls, Idaho
Monday, June 2

When Monday came, and Micah's alarm clock woke him up, the very first thing he thought of was Chrissy. He hadn't been able to get her out of his head all day yesterday, either. He'd talked briefly to Cam about her at church but didn't want to make a big deal about how worried he was. Cam agreed that it was crazy, but, like Chrissy, brought up the fact that she was very familiar with California.

"What does she have to lose?" he'd asked, looking at Micah in a way that made Micah feel responsible for her decision.

And yet, what *did* she have to lose? The thought made him feel even worse. Had he done the right thing when he called off their date? He immediately told himself he'd done what he had to do. He couldn't take the chance of making things more complicated for his children. His breaking their date was not the reason she left.

When he got out of bed, he looked at the clock. Chrissy would be in San Diego by now. *Where did she sleep?* he wondered. *Is she okay?* He could only hope she'd go directly to the police when she got there and not try to do anything on her own.

What does she have to lose? he repeated as he headed for the shower. If he'd done the right thing, if pulling away and not pursuing a relationship with her was the right course, then why did he feel so horrible about it? Thank goodness he was going into the office and had plenty of work to do. If he were sentenced to only his own thoughts he'd lose his mind.

Mallory and Blake were already up, something that surprised him since this was the second week of summer vacation. Mallory was stirring her bowl of cereal that seemed to have gone soggy long ago.

"Mal?" Micah asked, wondering at her mood. "You okay?"

He noticed a look pass between his children, then Blake went back to his breakfast. Micah waited for someone to say something. Neither of them did.

"Mal?" he asked again, moving closer to the table.

Mallory pressed her lips together, as if that would keep her from saying anything.

Blake looked up, watched his sister for a moment, then turned his eyes to his dad. "She's feeling guilty."

"For what?" Micah asked.

Mallory kept stirring.

Micah pulled a chair out from the table and sat down. "What are you feeling guilty for?" He licked his lips that had suddenly gone dry—he did not feel up to whatever was coming next. It was moments like this that made his inadequacies as a parent rise to the surface.

"'Cause you won't help Chrissy because of her," Blake said.

Mallory rounded her shoulders, seeming to shrink a little.

Micah raised his eyebrows. "Is that what you think?"

She wouldn't look at him, so he reached out and directed her chin up until she met his eyes. "Is that what you think?" he asked again in a tone that was soft and hopefully trustworthy.

"She doesn't like her," Blake said.

Micah shot him a look.

"Well, she doesn't."

"You're not helping—finish your breakfast." He turned back to his daughter. "Do you feel guilty about not liking her?"

Mallory just shrugged, but Micah thought he understood. "Mal, you haven't done anything wrong. And I would help Chrissy if there was a reason I should, but there isn't. She's doing what she thinks is best, and I'm doing what I think is best."

"What do you think is best?" Mallory asked in a quiet, little-girl voice.

Micah paused, then smiled. "Staying here with you guys and praying that everything goes well with Chrissy."

Blake cut in. "But don't you think you should have gone with her or something? I mean, the people she's after are the same people who messed up your stuff, right? So wouldn't it be good to be there, too, helping her, making sure she's okay?"

"I don't know," Micah said, leaning back in his chair and crossing his arms over his chest. "But I do know that you guys are out of school, I've got a loan that's closing on Thursday, and that although Chrissy's and my situations are connected, we don't know how and my stuff isn't active anymore."

"Oh," Blake said, almost seeming disappointed.

"And it's not my fault you're not helping her?" Mallory asked.

"Actually," Micah said. "I've been helping her all along and she was very grateful for that. I think I did the right thing, and now she's doing what she feels is right."

"I don't hate her," Mallory said.

Micah smiled and stood up from the table. "I'm glad to hear

that, Mal. She's a very nice lady." *Even if she is nuts to be doing this on her own.* Despite his reassurances to the contrary, he hated that he wasn't helping her somehow, that she was doing this alone. He hoped she wouldn't do anything stupid.

"None of this is your fault, okay?"

Mallory smiled. "Okay—but if you need to help her, you can, I won't be mad."

Micah laughed, stood up, and kissed her on the top of the head. "I'll keep that in mind." *If only there was something he* could *do.*

CHAPTER 62

Imperial Beach, California

"Hi," Chrissy said, putting her purse on the counter of The Box Stop and smiling at the woman behind the register. Three walls of PO Boxes surrounded her but she tried not to look for the number listed on the statement. She also tried not to look nervous.

"Can I help you?" the woman asked in a bored tone. She was white, though it was hard to tell from her over-tanned and weathered skin. She smelled like stale cigarettes and had rolled up the sleeves of her T-shirt, presumably to show off her flabby upper arms that swung back and forth when she moved. Sometimes Chrissy believed people bought magic mirrors that spared them from reality. She wondered where she could buy one, even as she hoped she would never let herself go enough to need one.

Chrissy had already taken out her driver's license and now laid it on the counter. "I opened a PO Box here a few months ago, and I'm having trouble with UPS. They want a physical address from me, but I'm never home and can't have them leave boxes on my doorstep, ya know? So I need a copy of my original application to prove to them that I do have a legitimate physical address, but that they can send packages here and—"

"I can fill out a shipping verification for you," the woman said, grabbing a slick-looking paper from a stack without looking and putting it on the counter. "This will be what they need to send packages directly to us. So long as they get the package here between seven AM and six PM we can hold it for you."

Shoot. Chrissy dug deep to find another reason. "That's what I thought," Chrissy said. "And I told them that, but they keep insisting that they need the original application. Something about comparing signatures and stuff like that. I've been working on this for weeks, so if I can just get a copy of the original application I can finally be done with the address confirmation."

The woman's expression didn't change. "Well, I'm not supposed to—"

"And I know there's a fee." Chrissy pulled out a twenty-dollar bill and put it next to her license on the countertop. The woman looked at her and Chrissy held her eyes, smiling in a way she hoped made her look incredibly honest. "I guess that's what I get for not keeping better track of the copy I got when I filled it out, right?"

The woman looked from Chrissy to the money and back again. Chrissy held her breath. *Please, please, please,* she thought. *I just need a few more dishonest people so that I can get my life back.* She knew she needed to go to the police—and that had been her original goal—but during her fourteen-hour drive, every time a police car came into view her heart leapt to her throat. What if she got pulled over? There was still a warrant out for the other Chressaidia. Was she not supposed to leave the state like Micah said? Would they put Chrissy in jail again? By the time she arrived in San Diego, she'd decided to wait to go to the police until she had as much proof as possible that the Chressaidia they had on record was not her.

"I think it's a forty-dollar fee," the woman said.

Chrissy felt herself relax and tried not to wince as she pulled out another twenty-dollar bill. She remembered Micah offering her money, and her chest burned. She'd known he'd done it to ease his conscience and she had found it horribly insulting, even if she could have used a few extra dollars. She did not want to feel indebted to him.

The woman smiled, revealing horrendous teeth that made Chrissy grateful for dental insurance. After putting the forty dollars in her pocket, the woman headed for the back office. A minute later she returned and handed Chrissy a piece of paper, still warm from the copy machine.

Chrissy scanned the information as she walked away, then she turned back. "Oh, and I forgot my key." She smiled sweetly. "Could you get my mail for me, too?"

"We're not supposed to do that," the woman said, pointing to a sign that said "Attendant cannot retrieve mail if you forget your key."

"However," the woman continued. "For a forgot-my-key fee I can make an exception."

CHAPTER 63

Idaho Falls, Idaho

Around 11:00 Micah was doing a final check on the Jeffsen refinance when his cell phone rang. He picked it up from where it lay on his desk. The number was unfamiliar.

"This is Micah," he said, still scanning the computer screen.

"Micah Heet?" the nasally voice said.

"Yes," he said absently, looking closely at the property assessment to make sure it was the most recent version. There had been some discrepancies in the original plat so the land had been resurveyed last week.

"This is Marsha from Personal Protect. Can ya'll please verify your account name and access code? The contact code is J as in John, T as in Tom, 34781."

Micah straightened in his chair, then reached for his planner. "Just a minute," he said, flipping to the very back of his planner where the contact code—a sequence they would use when contacting him—and a name and access code were written. There was no heading or company name, just the information that only he would know how to find and what it pertained to.

"Can you repeat that?" he asked.

She repeated the contact code, which matched the one given to him by Personal Protect when he enrolled. She then asked him three security questions that he answered correctly. Only then did he read off the letters of the account name, HMEIECTAH—his first and last name scrambled—and the access number, 945593217, a completely random number he'd made up based on no personal dates of importance.

Micah had subscribed to Personal Protect back in March, after everything had happened. For a yearly fee, they monitored his credit report and would notify him whenever someone ran a credit check. This was the first time he'd heard from them.

"Perfect," Marsha said. "I'm calling you because there has been a credit check run against your name and Social Security number. I'm just calling to verify that you were aware of it."

"I'm not aware of it," Micah said, grabbing a pen. "What's the name of the company running the check?"

"Dover Haciendas," Marsha said. "They are a rental agency out of southern California. You're absolutely certain they would have no reason to run a credit check? You haven't co-signed a lease or made vacation plans to that area?"

"None," Micah said. *Southern California,* he repeated in his mind. "Can I get their contact information?"

"I can give you that information," the woman said. "I'll also issue a non-verification to the company so credit is not extended. Here's their number . . ."

When Micah hung up a minute later, he stared at the address and phone number, unsure what to do with it, but realizing he had a lead. Was he going to ignore it? And, even if he did ignore it, would he withhold it from Chrissy when it might be connected to her situation as well?

He picked up the phone again, dialed the number he'd just written down, and easily slipped into the introduction he'd perfected when he was fighting the credit card companies. "Yes, hello. My name is Micah Heet, and I understand you ran a credit check in my name. I have recently been the victim of identity theft, and I did not file an application with you, but I need information on who did. I can fax you my criminal fraud report if that would be of assistance in resolving this."

Ten minutes and two faxes later, he hung up the phone and stared at the page of notes in front of him. He thought back to the conversation he'd had with his children that morning. They were both worried about Chrissy, but he'd assured them there was no reason for him to be involved. But things were different now.

He had a choice to make, and he could only hope he'd make the right one for everybody.

CHAPTER 64

Imperial Beach, California

I've double-checked everything," Eduardo said.

Chressaidia looked up from the stack of paperwork she'd been studying. They'd abandoned the beach house after clearing the office of everything but Frederico's body, and found this rental that would let them move in right away. She'd used the name of one of the IDs she'd found in Frederico's file and the apartment had instantly become their new headquarters. Since then, she'd spent nearly every minute poring over Frederico's files, overwhelmed by how much she knew nothing about, trying to shore up her planning and put everything in place. "When can we move the guns?"

"Thursday at noon," Eduardo answered.

She wished it were sooner. "When will we pack the truck?"

"Wednesday night, after dark. Everything is ready."

"Nothing can go wrong," Chressaidia ordered, but there were still so many variables. Eduardo didn't yet have the truck in his possession; Frederico's body was still at the old office. And yet, she'd planned well. She'd worked hard for this. "We have no room for mistakes."

"I know," Eduardo said. "It's only a few more days. Everything will be fine."

There was a pounding at the door and they both turned to look at it. Who could be here? Chressaidia met Eduardo's eyes. He nodded while she went to the back bedroom, closing the door enough so she was not seen, but could still hear the exchange. They'd only filed the application in a man's name and said no one else would be living with him.

Eduardo opened the front door.

"Hello," he said as if the person on the other side of the door was someone he knew.

"There's a problem with your application," a man said. "You've got a choice—either leave the deposit with me and get out of here, or I call the police and tell them anything they want to know."

CHAPTER 65

Chressaidia pulled into The Box Stop parking lot and hurried inside. She'd been so busy with other things that it had been five days since she'd checked the box. She'd soon be abandoning it forever, but she had some cards in the name of Angelina Rodriquez that should be arriving any day, and she needed the funds now that the real Chressaidia's finances were tapped out. She hurried inside, barely looking at the employee behind the counter.

She fished her key out of her purse and turned it in the lock, pulling the metal door open, fully expecting the box to be stuffed full. Instead, she stared into emptiness. Nothing? How was that possible?

After a few seconds she went to the counter. "Has there been a problem with the mail?" she asked the woman who was doing something on the computer.

"Nope," the woman said without looking up.

"I have no mail."

The woman shrugged. "I don't know what to tell you, lady."

"Well, check the back, look around. I have some very important things coming."

"The mail's already gone out today," the woman said with impatience. "Come back tomorrow after nine."

"Maybe someone put a forward on my box," Chressaidia said, her heart racing. Who would have done that? Frederico? "Surely you can check that."

The woman sighed and finally got off her chair. She went to a small card file and opened it up. "What's the box number?"

"Four-eight-three."

The woman's eyes jumped to Chressaidia's face, then went back to the file. Something was wrong in that look.

"Um, nope, no forward," the woman said. Her demeanor was now light and friendly, with none of her earlier annoyance showing through, though she looked nervous.

Chressaidia stared at her, trying to understand the change. The woman shifted from one foot to another. "Why are you lying to me?" she asked simply. The other woman swallowed but said nothing. "Give me that box," she said, pointing to the card file.

"I can't do that," the woman said. "It's confidential."

Chressaidia reached into her purse and wrapped her fingers around the pistol. She continued to stare at the woman, letting her eyes bore into her when the door chime sounded. The sound of voices immediately followed, and she turned her head to see a woman and two young girls walk inside. Another car pulled into the parking lot and she had no choice but to release the gun. She looked back at the employee and leaned forward so as not to be overheard. "I'll be back, and you will have answers for me."

CHAPTER 66

$\mathscr{C}$hrissy looked at the map again, then leaned forward to double-check the numbers on the side of the building. This was it—the address on both the police report and the PO Box application. Her heart hammered in her chest. What now? Should she just walk up to the door and ring the bell? What would she say? She glanced at the stack of mail on the passenger seat and felt her stomach flip. She'd planned to open the mail immediately but was now working up to it. Seeing her name on those strange envelopes had made everything so real.

Her palms were sweating when she climbed out of her car, papers in hand. The smell of salt water and wet sand from the nearby beach was strong and not necessarily pleasant. She knew most people loved the smell of the sea, but it must be something they grew into. As she walked up the flower-adorned walkway, she surveyed the area. It was a nice complex, right on the beach, well tended. It had the seaside look of rusted railings and chipping stucco, but she knew those were typical maintenance issues associated with the sea air rather than signs of neglect. A Hispanic man was standing in the middle of a flower bed, cutting off the dying blossoms with a pair of clippers attached to an extended rod that kept him from having to bend over.

"*Hola, Señor,*" she said, smiling as she approached him.

He looked up at her. "*Hola,*" he said, then went back to his work.

"I'm looking for . . . a friend who lives here. She's in unit two-thirty-two." She didn't know what she'd do if she found her, but she had to try.

He looked up at her again. "*Latina?*"

"*Sí, sí,*" she said, and repeated her request in Spanish.

He started to shrug but Chrissy pushed on. "*Chressaidia Salazar.*"

"*Ah, bonita,*" he said.

It was a bit shocking to hear someone describe her thief as pretty, but Chrissy went along with it. "*Sí,*" Chrissy said. "*Muy bonita. ¿La ha visto?*"—*Have you seen her?*

"*Se fue,*" he said—*She's gone.* He then went on to say she'd moved out two days earlier; he'd seen her packing her things out. Chrissy tried not to show her disappointment as she looked back toward the doors of the apartments. All this and she hit a dead end? Already?

"*¿No sabe a dónde fue?*"—*You don't know where she went?*

"*No,*" he said, shaking his head. He pointed to the left. "*El dueño.*"

Chrissy nodded and headed toward the manager's office. "*Gracias,*" she said, even though she wasn't sure she wanted to see the manager. However, the groundskeeper was watching her. She looked over her shoulder and smiled at him one last time before turning a corner. He smiled too.

When she reached the door marked "Office" she took a quick

peek at the emergency evacuation plan screwed into the wall. It showed the different floors of the complex and how they were oriented. Relief settled into her stomach and she indulged in a brief feeling of success as a plan began to formulate.

CHAPTER 67

*W*as this the view you wanted?" the manager asked, a white woman who looked as if she'd been meant to have a normal height and weight, but had somehow gotten stretched an extra foot. She had to be at least six foot two and was painfully thin. Chrissy could only imagine the pair they presented—the manager Gaylynn, tall and shapeless; Chrissy, short and squat. What a picture.

Chrissy walked to the windows that lined the front of unit 232. This is where *she* had lived, where she had orchestrated the events that had sent Chrissy's life circling the bowl. She swept over the floors with her eyes, looking for something, anything. In the movies people always seemed to find matchbooks or business cards. Was that so much to ask—one stinkin' matchbook for all her efforts?

"It's perfect," Chrissy said, looking at the waves roll onto the shore and feeling her anger rise even more. The other Chressaidia had really lived it up, hadn't she?

"I'm really sorry it's not cleaned yet. Like I said, the previous owners only left a couple days ago. The other apartments I was telling you about are ready to go."

"But this is exactly what I wanted," Chrissy said, continuing the explanation that she had started in the office where she had half a dozen reasons to narrow down her interest to only one apartment—232.

"Well, it's just over eleven hundred square feet," the woman explained. "With a gas stove and central air conditioning. You have beach and pool access, as well as wireless Internet capabilities."

"Oh, wow, a pool," Chrissy said. "What's the pool like?"

As the woman went on and on, Chrissy walked the perimeter of the room, still scanning, still looking for something, anything.

"Could I use the bathroom?" Chrissy asked, interrupting a fascinating relay of how the pool had been retiled last summer.

"Oh, sure," the woman said.

Chrissy went into the bathroom and turned on the fan to mask any noise she might make, then she opened every cabinet and drawer. Nothing but some hair.

Hair! That meant DNA.

Feeling foolish, yet driven, she dug in her purse for something she could put the hair in. She found a piece of gum at the very bottom and she unwrapped it, folding the piece into her mouth while smoothing out the wrapper. Very carefully she picked up each strand of hair she could see and put them in the gum wrapper, then folded it up neatly and put it back in her purse. She was heading over to flush the toilet when she thought of the shower drain. She always had hair in the drain after a shower, and sure enough, this Chressaidia did, too. She dug in her purse and found a travel pack of tissue. She unwrapped the gum wrapper and put the other hair inside it as well, layering the hair between two sheets of tissue. Gross!

And yet, she exited the bathroom feeling very triumphant. CSI, eat your heart out!

Chapter 68

Chrissy had just settled into the car when her cell phone rang. She lifted it and immediately recognized the number. They'd only traded calls for a little over a week, but she'd saved his number in her phone as Mmmmmm and had smiled each time he'd called. She wasn't smiling right now, though, and wondered why he was calling at all. Had he forgotten an insult and wanted to make sure to work it in? She hit the *end* button, sending him to voice mail. She was a rock. She needed no one. A minute later her phone beeped that a message had been left. She fumbled to call her voice mail, disgusted with her need to hear what he had to say.

"Uh, Chrissy, this is Micah. I just talked to Amanda. I'm on my way to Salt Lake to catch a flight to San Diego. Call me. I have some information."

"What?" she said out loud, pressing the *repeat* button and hearing him again. He was coming here? What the heck for? She hung up from voice mail and immediately dialed another number she knew by heart.

"What on earth are you doing to me?" she yelled as soon as Amanda picked up.

"Calm down," Amanda said. "Did you talk to him?"

Chrissy took a breath and explained the voice mail. "You set this up. I know you did, and it was a horrible thing to do. He doesn't want to be with me, okay? I've accepted it. You need to accept it as well."

"You don't understand," Amanda said. "Someone's using his name again. They tried to rent a house in San Diego. He's going out there to figure it out, just like you did."

Chrissy paused. "So this has nothing to do with me?"

"It has everything to do with you," Amanda said. "He was really worried about you on Sunday and now his name has been pulled into it again. Face it—your paths are connected. He's realized that."

"This doesn't sound like the Micah I know," Chrissy said, fumbling for something to say.

"You don't know him as well as you think you do. Be grateful for his help and try not to be too big a pain in the neck, okay?"

"Amaaaaaanda," Chrissy whined. "How am I supposed to act, huh? As if this isn't hard enough."

"Why don't you ask him how you should act. You guys have some stuff to work out, and this will be a perfect opportunity."

Stuff.

She made it sound so easy.

CHAPTER 69

*W*here are you?" Micah asked when she answered her phone around 8:20 that evening. Chrissy's heart thudded a little at the sound of his voice, and she berated it for its treachery. She'd argued with Amanda for almost twenty minutes, getting most of the irritation out of her system. Then she'd sent Micah a text message saying she'd come to the airport to pick him up. He texted back that he'd be in the Delta terminal at 8:00. Texting instead of calling meant she could put off the *stuff* a little longer.

"I'm on the freeway," Chrissy said, scowling at the other cars around her, all of them moving slower than she could walk. "There's road construction."

"How far away are you?"

Chrissy looked ahead. "The good news is I can see the airport," she said. "The bad news is that doesn't mean much. I haven't moved a full block in the last fifteen minutes."

"Okay, call me when you get here."

Another half hour passed before she pulled up to the curb. Micah opened the back door, threw in his bags, and got into the passenger side. He didn't say anything. Chrissy was at a loss, so she just focused on her driving and tried not to think about the toe-curling kiss and him holding her so tight she could barely breathe. They were quiet for at least five minutes, the discomfort not the least bit appeased by their silence.

"Amanda said you slept in your car last night," Micah said, lifting his hat for just a moment before repositioning it on his head. She'd known she'd been right about him hiding his receding hairline under his hats when she saw him on Sunday, but hadn't thought that was a good time to mention it. Right now didn't seem like such a great time either.

"If this had taken place in LA or further north, I'd have a dozen people I could stay with. Unfortunately, I could never afford the southern California lifestyle, and my friends here haven't yet won the lottery or invented the newest must-have push-up bra. It wasn't so bad, though."

"I'm not a car-sleeping kind of guy," Micah said. "If we can find a hotel, I'll get us some rooms."

"I'm down to just over three hundred dollars," Chrissy said. "I can't afford a hotel room."

"Don't worry about it," Micah said, looking out the passenger side window.

For whatever reason his statement lit her fire of frustration all over again. "I don't want your money, Micah, and I don't need your charity."

He turned toward her and she saw his jaw clench. "Will you stop being so dang stubborn!"

"Will you stop being so dang dominating!" She dropped her voice and muttered in Spanish about how ridiculous this was and how she'd be a lot better off on her own.

He softened his voice when he spoke again. "Look, they're using my name again. They tried to rent an apartment. We have a common interest, and working together will bring it to a closure sooner than if either of us were doing this alone."

"Fine," Chrissy said, taking a right onto the I-5 south freeway, still looking for a way to get an upper hand in the conversation and privately making plans to egg Amanda's house when she got back. "But don't kiss me again."

He turned to look at her. "Me?" he said, reminding her of the fact that she had been the one who had not only initiated the kiss, but had run after him to do so.

This wasn't going well and yet she couldn't turn her mouth off. "We'll be alone together, and I've still got some virtue to protect."

"I'm flattered you think so well of me," Micah said in a flat tone, looking forward again and shaking his head slightly. "But your virtue is not what I'm after."

"I was teasing you," Chrissy said without humor, now wishing she'd said nothing at all. "You made yourself perfectly clear that your interest lies elsewhere." How petty of her to have brought that up, but she couldn't help it. She was a very petty person.

"Can I be completely honest with you?" Micah said after a few more awkward seconds. He wasn't looking at her. Instead he was turned toward the passenger window. He looked very uncomfortable, and she found herself not wanting to hear the *stuff* after all.

"Does the fact that you need to ask permission to tell me the truth mean that you've been lying to me up to this point?"

He turned to look at her, but she kept her eyes on the road. "I'm trying to be serious and get some things settled, okay?"

"Okay," she said, feeling reprimanded. She changed lanes, but they were still in the construction zone, so the freeway was a crush of cars.

"My ex-wife just got a legal separation from her second husband.

I need to be there for my kids—*all there*. I can't afford to be distracted by anything—anyone—else, no matter how much I might enjoy their company. Does that make sense?"

Chrissy was quiet, absorbing what he'd said as her righteous indignation fractured into a very different array of emotions. "That's why you broke our date?" she asked after digesting his words.

"Yeah," Micah said, then let out a breath. "I don't know if this will make sense, but when Natalie and I got a divorce, I felt so free. It was as if I could live my life all over again. But these last few years have been different. My kids are growing up. In five years they'll all be adults and I wonder—what have I given them? I've thought that at least with Natalie in a stable marriage, they'd have that example, but now it's messier than ever, and I feel . . . almost *consumed* by the responsibility to make the years left with them important ones. To make sure they know they matter, to be honest with them about the mistakes their mom and I made, to have a good enough relationship with their mom that they don't feel pulled between us. And then you happened and—"

"I *happened?*" Chrissy cut in. "Yikes, I sound like an earthquake or a traffic accident."

"Well, that's kind of what it was like," Micah said.

Chrissy looked at him, deeply offended. "What?"

"Not something bad," Micah said quickly, meeting her eyes for the first time. The traffic was practically at a standstill. "Just that you're like . . . I don't know, intense. After that first date I couldn't stop thinking about you. That had mostly faded until I saw you at Amanda's one day and then it started all over again. I kept thinking I saw you at the grocery store, and I'd wonder when I might run into you again. And then you were suddenly *there* again, in my life, and I had this opportunity to pursue it, and I thought maybe . . ." He paused and let out a breath. His voice was softer when he continued and he straightened in his seat. "Maybe I could do both—be a dad and spend time with you. It was exciting to have someone I wanted to be with, and a little scary. The next thing I knew, Natalie was telling me her marriage was over, and my kids were stuck between trying to convince themselves it wasn't a big deal and knowing that it really was. And I was in the middle of it, knowing I couldn't give them my all if I was dividing my time between them and you."

He looked out the window again, seemingly absorbed in a Hummer that was parallel to them in the next lane. He shifted away in his bucket seat as if afraid he'd said too much. "Sorry," he said quietly after a few seconds had passed. "That was the long story. I didn't mean to get into all of that."

Chrissy took a breath and let what he'd said settle. He did feel something for her. It wasn't only in her head and her heart. Even all the roadblocks he'd just mentioned didn't rob her of the thrill of knowing she was not alone in her feelings. However, the relief didn't move the roadblocks out of the way, and that was depressing. She couldn't help but remember her own childhood and the changes Livvy's kids were dealing with. If she could take herself and her own feelings out of the equation, there was no question of whether he'd done the right thing. Dang it anyway!

"You made the right choice, Micah."

He glanced at her quickly, his eyes questioning.

She checked her mirrors and moved into the left lane, where the traffic was moving faster.

A few minutes passed without any words, but the traffic compressed once again and they made very little progress. Chrissy wondered if it wasn't meant to be that they have this conversation. A celestial traffic jam of sorts.

Chrissy cleared her throat. "My mom remarried a year after my folks divorced. She shipped us to my dad who had moved in with a woman with four kids of her own. For the next few years, our parents were always arguing about whose turn it was to have Livvy and me. Finally, Abuelita gave us a stable home. She took us to the Catholic church, introduced God into our lives, taught us the beauty of our Mexican heritage. She changed my world, and I'm so very grateful to her for the sacrifices she made for us, but it didn't disguise how unimportant we were to our parents."

"She did a good job," Micah said.

Chrissy shrugged and changed lanes again. "She's remarkable, but we still suffered for the choices our parents made. I think Livvy answered her insecurity with boys, and then men. She is so hungry to belong somewhere that she'll do anything to be important to someone else. She has a good heart. She's not evil or selfish—she's just terrified of not mattering. I, on the other hand, seem to have defined myself with needing no one. So here I am, thirty-five with no one to show for it." She smiled at her own joke, then wondered if Micah thought she was taking some kind of jab at him.

She swallowed the lump rising in her throat before she continued. "I wonder, if either one of my parents had put us first, had done what it took to ensure us a stable place where we felt important—where would Livvy and I be? Would I have a family, despite the risks of being hurt sometimes? Would Livvy be comfortable by herself? Or would she have found a healthier relationship to make a life with?" She shrugged. There were no answers. "You're a father, Micah," she said. "I would never in a million years expect you to make a decision that might somehow hurt your kids. But I appreciate you explaining it to me. You didn't have to."

Micah was silent, and now Chrissy was the one shifting uncomfortably in her seat. She might not like playing games, but being so blatantly honest wasn't easy, either.

Micah cleared his throat and spoke again. "I enjoyed your company, Chrissy," he said. Hearing him say her name made the lump in her throat a little thicker. "It just seemed best to end what hadn't started yet so I could do what I knew was the right thing."

Chrissy reviewed those moments of listening to him explain why they couldn't go out, how much they had hurt, how many expectations they had shattered. It would have helped if he'd told her his true reasons. Then she remembered what she'd done next. "And then I chased you down and . . ." She relived the kiss yet again and wondered if he was doing the same. "Sorry about that."

Micah grunted and nodded, half his mouth pulling into a smile as he looked over and met her eye. "That's when I knew you were the devil."

CHAPTER 70

~~~~~

San Diego, California

*W*ho is he?" Detective Long asked after staring at the body and getting a feel for the trajectory of the bullets and placement of the shooter. Execution style, but not in the typical fashion. The smell wasn't too bad yet, though the beginnings of decomposition were definitely there.

"Frederico Ramirez. Guatemalan-born, but legally immigrated nine years ago. Alone."

"Record?"

"Nothing serious. However, we received a tip several months ago that he's part of a militant faction in Guatemala. We're pretty sure he's running drugs—but we've poked around and haven't found anything substantial."

"Looks like he was using," Long said, taking in the graying fingernails and dark fingers. Meth rotted its users from the inside out, turning their eyes and skin gray and ashy-looking once it really had its hooks in a person.

"Yeah," the officer said. "Tox will likely verify it."

"How long do you think he's been here?"

"At least forty-eight hours, maybe longer. Landlord said a lady rented the office a few weeks back. He said the last time he saw her was Friday, but he wasn't here over the weekend." The officer shrugged. "Of course, he's managed to lose all the paperwork the renter filled out at the time of rental and she paid in cash. So far we haven't found any prints. The whole office seems to have been wiped down."

"Of course," Long said. It was often the case in slum buildings like this one for the owner to rent out space without any background checks. He'd charge a premium for his accommodations, only take cash payments, and there would be no paper trail if someone came looking.

Detective Long scanned the office. "Doesn't look like anyone plans on using it anymore." There was a cheap desk and two folding chairs, but nothing else. "Anything else about the victim? Does he work, does he have a girlfriend, an address?"

"No job that we can find, but he's likely supported by the faction he's part of. However, he is married."

Detective Long looked up at the officer. "Good. Who is she?"

"Chressaidia Josefina Salazar—she didn't seem to take on his last name—American-born Mexican. Lived in Idaho Falls until showing up here back in March. They married a few days later."

Detective Long furrowed his brow. If their victim was here as an appendage to a militant group, why marry? Typically people like him didn't want connections in America. "Find her. See what she knows."

CHAPTER 71

Idaho Falls, Idaho

"Sorry I'm late," Livvy said to the kids as she came inside. "They started the quarterly audit today and the computer went down because of the overload." She put her purse on the table and looked up with a smile. "Hey, don't you look nice," she said to Rosa who was finishing dinner preparations—quesadillas, by the smell of it.

"Do you like it?" Rosa asked, turning from side to side to show off her new shirt. "I asked Doug if I could use the sewing machine downstairs and he said I could, so I took one of those old shirts of yours you gave me and took it in. I changed the neckline too."

Livvy stepped back and looked at the way the shirt fit her daughter's blossoming figure. "I love it," Livvy said.

"Chrissy taught me how," Rosa said, still smiling. "But I've never done it by myself."

"You did a great job," Livvy said, ignoring the reference to Chrissy. She hadn't made a decision since getting the letter, but she had admitted to herself that she wanted to clear things up with her sister. If only she knew how to do it without somehow admitting she'd made a mistake or making Doug angry. She let out a breath and focused on her daughter. "Look at the woman you're growing into. Wow, but you're a beautiful girl."

"Isn't she, though?"

They both turned to see Doug coming out of the bathroom. He zipped up his pants as he walked toward them and Livvy cringed and looked back at Rosa, smiling as if that would keep her from noticing. But Rosa's face had gone slack, her expression guarded as it usually was when Doug was around. The boys had warmed up to Doug pretty well, but Rosa was still hesitant.

"She's one hot little number, that girl of yours," Doug said.

Livvy's eyebrows went up, and she took a protective step toward Rosa, turning to face Doug. "She is very pretty," Livvy said, hating the nervous feeling that washed over her.

"I'd say." He looked past Livvy and winked at Rosa. Livvy swallowed. *He doesn't mean anything by it,* she said to herself. *It's just his way of giving her a compliment.*

"Um, Rosa made dinner. Where are the boys?"

"Outside," Rosa said softly from behind her mother. "I'll go get them."

The meal was filled with chatter, mostly the boys telling about their day, finishing each other's sentences and being entertaining enough that Livvy stopped worrying for awhile. At least until she looked at Doug. Each time she looked across the table, he was watching Rosa. She noticed, too, and would only stare at her plate and pull up on the neckline of her shirt, which was rather low now that Livvy really paid attention.

By the end of the meal, Livvy was sick to her stomach and fighting tears. She spent the rest of the evening trying to keep Doug out of the same room Rosa was in. Chrissy's words came back to her: *What kind of man is he? How do you know he won't hurt your kids?*

When it was time for bed, Livvy tucked each of the kids in while

Doug watched TV and finished off his sixth beer of the evening. On her way out of Rosa's room, she turned the lock on the doorknob.

She pulled the door shut and leaned against it, testing the doorknob to make sure it was secure. She felt disgusted. She was locking her daughter's door. Why? Her mind wouldn't let her admit the reasons. She dropped her head and tried to swallow the tears as humiliation battled with regret and even . . . *jealousy* inside herself.

Maybe it will be better tomorrow, she tried to tell herself. *Surely, Doug would never* . . . but her mind couldn't form the words. She thought of Rosa on the other side of the door. Had she noticed Livvy locking it? What did she think of that?

Dear Lord, Livvy said, though the prayer sounded foreign to herself. *What do I do now?*

Leave, a voice said, making her jump and press her back to the door. She looked around the hallway, but no one was there. She immediately crossed herself against the evil spirits Abuelita had convinced her were very real. But she realized the feeling wasn't one of darkness. It was urgent, it was strong, but it wasn't frightening. The voice came again, and the urgency increased.

Leave now.

CHAPTER 72

꩜

Imperial Beach, California

O h, and will you grab that mail on the backseat?" Chrissy asked, positioning her bag over one shoulder and shutting her door. Micah had gotten them two rooms at the El Venturo Motel in Imperial Beach—just a few blocks from the new address Micah had found. "I appreciate this," Chrissy said, wanting to be sure he knew she was grateful for the room.

"No problem," he said as he reached into the backseat. "Where'd you get this?" Micah asked a few moments later when he closed the back door and looked at the mail in his hand. The intimacy of their confessions had lingered for awhile but eventually a sense of discomfort returned. He'd explained why they couldn't be together and she'd agreed. Now what? How were they supposed to act? What were they supposed to do? So they both tried to ignore it. So far, so good.

"The place that rents out her PO Box," Chrissy said, using the key to open her room. She put her foot in the door to keep it open and turned, holding her hand out for the mail.

"What are you going to do with it?" Micah asked.

"Look through it—well, the stuff that has my name on it, anyway. I figured I'd turn the rest of it over to the police at some point, along with the hair."

Micah looked up at her. "Hair?" He handed her the stack of mail.

"Yeah, I got some hair samples from the shower drain in her old apartment."

"You've been busy," Micah said, his expression showing concern.

"Yup," she said, moving inside. "We're running out of daylight, so I thought I'd go through this stuff and make a plan for tomorrow." She was also looking forward to having a bed to sleep in. Though she certainly could sleep in her car again, she was very grateful for a room tonight.

Micah nodded. "Good idea. I'd rather not be knocking on her door after dark."

"Right," Chrissy said. "Thanks again for springing for the rooms."

"Sure," he said, shrugging it off. They both stood there. "Well, I guess I'll see you in the morning," Micah said. He looked as if he wanted to say something else. She understood. For a moment she imagined them watching a movie together, eating popcorn, and going over the mail. But that would cross the invisible and unspoken line they'd agreed to draw between them. They were partners in this, and friends, but the attraction they both felt made more than those two roles off-limits.

"Yeah, I guess so," she said. "Thanks again."

"No problem," Micah said, smiling slightly. "I'll come get you at nine?"

"Perfect."

CHAPTER 73

$\mathcal{M}$icah flipped from one TV station to another, trying to find something of interest, trying to keep his thoughts from straying to the woman three rooms down. Was coming here a completely stupid thing to do? It had made so much sense at the time. Not leaving Chrissy to do this herself, and making an attempt to find whoever was doing this to his own life seemed like a good idea. But now, a few hours later, he worried about leaving the kids. Natalie had been happy to have them, though just a teensy bit arrogant at having him ask. Blake had urged him to go, and Mallory had given a non-committal shrug that was wearing on him. After Natalie's announcement, and his decision to break it off with Chrissy, he was here? With her? What was he thinking?

When he got to the local news, he finally stopped flipping channels. With voices in the background to drown out his thoughts, he sat at the small table by the window and opened his laptop. Might as well check his e-mail before he went to bed. He had a loan he was supposed to have done by Thursday and began coming up with the reasons he could give on why that wouldn't happen. The motel was cheap and smelled like stale beer and mildew, but at least it had wireless Internet—a staple in California, apparently.

The weather woman was giving tomorrow's forecast, briefly explaining the fog that had covered San Diego most of the day. The weather woman called it June Gloom and expected a few more days of it before it moved off. Wasn't California supposed to be sunny?

He read and replied to several e-mails, including one from Mallory asking if he'd take her shopping for summer clothes when he got back. He smiled as he replied, realizing how much he missed his kids. Having them around so much made it harder than it had ever been to be away. Hopefully, he'd be home by the end of the week. He'd take potato fields and freshly mowed hay over the beaches and billboards of California any day.

" . . . ressaida Salazar—with the married name of Chressaidia Ramirez—please call the following number."

Micah spun around and stared at the TV, but the anchorwoman had moved on to a report about a car fire in Chula Vista. Was he hearing things, or did they just say Chrissy's name on the news?

He looked at the logo in the bottom corner of the TV screen and went back to his computer. After opening a browser window, he went to Google and typed in the call letters.

CHAPTER 74

$\mathscr{C}$hressaidia watched the news without flinching. She'd hoped it would be a few more days before they discovered his body. Perhaps she should have moved it, but that would have presented another complication. Where would she put it? What if someone saw her?

She stood and walked to the window of the high-rise hotel she and Eduardo had checked into, keeping her anxiety at bay by watching the lights reflect off the incoming waves. She was so close and she had already accomplished so much. A few more days and she'd be gone forever, heralded as a hero, finally finding the place she deserved amid the hierarchy of the People's Army for Freedom. The police finding Frederico before she'd determined how to explain it to her father was a complication she did not have time for.

She grabbed her keys and headed for the door of the hotel, calling to Eduardo on her way out the door. "Meet me at the storage unit," she said. "We have work to do."

The best thing to do to keep from falling victim to fear was to get busy doing something else. They'd been so careful, keeping everyone else involved with the transport at arm's length, dealing with the details on their own. It meant there would be less chance of betrayal. It meant that she would be in charge. It meant she could claim ultimate victory when she succeeded.

She closed the door of the hotel, taking note, as she always did, of every face she passed on her way to the parking garage. It paid to be cautious.

When she got in the car, she made another call. "Father," she said when he answered, preparing in her mind the story she would tell him, blaming the murder on one of his dealers. "Something has happened. Frederico has been killed."

CHAPTER 75

～ᗡᕑᓮ～

*C*hrissy had her hair up, her scrubby lounge pants on, and was just starting to paint the middle toenail on her right foot when someone knocked at the door of her motel room. She looked at the glowing red numbers of the alarm clock on the nightstand between the two queen beds. It was after 10:00. She hoped it was Micah. Who else would it be?

She put the bottle of polish carefully on the dinged-up veneer nightstand and walked to the door, her toes spread and lifted so as not to mess up the polish. She looked out the peephole.

She'd been right, it was Micah. "Hi," she said as she opened the door.

"Did you watch the news?" he asked as he strode past her and put his laptop on the small table. He pulled out a chair and sat down.

"I hate the news," Chrissy said, closing the door. "What are you doing here?"

"You're *on* the news," Micah said, clicking his mouse and then

265

turning the screen to face her. She leaned forward, forced to squint without her glasses or contacts.

"What are you talking about?" she asked, sitting down in the other chair.

"Look," he said, pointing at the screen. "Police are looking for a Chressaidia Salazar Ramirez in regards to a shooting that occurred in a downtown office building. Though not considered a suspect, police would like to confirm her whereabouts and see if she has any more information."

Chrissy sat back. "Oh, my gosh," she said, making a face. "That is so creepy. She's married?"

Micah nodded and looked back at the computer. "I have a feeling we're in over our heads here."

"Well, I've known that all along," Chrissy said, giving a dismissive wave to his discovery. "But what are we supposed to do with this?" She motioned toward his computer. "All it really says is that, more than ever, I need to prove I'm not *this* woman."

"Then let's go to the police," Micah said. "Show them what we have, explain the situation."

Chrissy considered this, but remembered too well the night she'd spent in the Idaho Falls jail. That was Idaho, and it was freaky. How much worse would it be in southern Cal? The Idaho police had charged her, even though they seemed to believe that she wasn't the woman who committed the original crime. Plus, she'd left the state. How would that look when she walked into a police station with the same name as a woman being looked for by their department.

"I think we need something more than my documents. What about that address you got from that rental agency?" She remembered the mail and stood up too fast, feeling her wet toes brush against the bedspread. She looked down at her ruined nail polish and scowled, but moved past it in the spirit of sharing her finds.

"Look at this," she said, grabbing a stack of papers and handing them to him.

"Apparently, the key to all this is to simply pretend to be the woman who's pretending to be me instead of trying to explain to everyone that I'm Chressaidia, but not the Chressaidia they think I am."

Micah took the papers, looking confused. She sat back down in her chair again, resting her feet on the edge of the bed to see if she could repair the mangled polish. "Look at that top one—the storage unit bill."

Micah sifted through the papers until he found the one she'd indicated. He read it over.

"I wonder what she keeps in there," Chrissy mused.

Micah looked up at her with an incredulous expression. "You're not going."

"Of course I am," Chrissy replied, as if he had asked a question instead of making a statement. "It's the best lead we've got. We go to the storage unit, see if there's anything of interest, and who knows, maybe we'll find something we can take to the police—something that irrefutably proves I'm not her."

Micah kept reading, then nodded and let out a breath. "This whole thing is crazy, ya know?"

Chrissy shrugged. She could tell he was just as curious as she was. She leaned forward to punch him in the arm. "Hey, you came out here too."

CHAPTER 76

~~~~~~

Imperial Beach, California
Tuesday, June 3

"Good morning," Chrissy said when she answered his knock the next morning. She was still formulating what else she could do to put off going to the police a little longer, but for now, she was just focusing on one step at a time, and Micah had agreed to go to the storage unit first.

She left the door open and waved him in as she returned to the mirror bolted to the wall above the dresser. He followed slowly, as if uncomfortable to be in a girl's room—as if he hadn't come barging in the night before. He was dressed in jeans, a red T-shirt, untucked, and his Boise State hat. She wondered if men ever matched their hats to their clothes the way women matched their purses to their shoes. She'd never thought about it and Micah didn't seem to.

She returned to the mirror and leaned forward so she could put the last of her accents on her eyes. She was wearing lavender today, one of her favorite colors, so she'd chosen pink and purple eye shadows to coordinate. The knit top fit snug, but not obscenely so, and the skirt, with angled pink, purple, green, and yellow stripes helped to slim her hips. She'd put on an eyelet-trimmed slip that peeked out from beneath the hem, and topped it all with a pastel-themed necklace and matching bracelet. The cheery shades helped her ignore the seriousness of what she was doing today—tracking down the person who had become her. Trying to imagine what might happen today caused a shiver to run down her spine.

She sought Micah's reflection in the mirror and found him, not surprisingly, watching her. She stood a little straighter, but still leaned forward. "I like your hat," she said. She put down her eye shadow brush and blinked, opening her eyes wide as she compared both lids to make sure they matched. They did.

"Thanks," Micah said, still uncomfortable, still watching her.

She stood back up, and turned to make sure the lines of the skirt hung smooth. Thank goodness the room had come with an iron. Transporting cotton blends was always tricky business. She walked to where five pairs of shoes were lined up against the wall.

"You brought five pair?" Micah asked, as she kicked her silver ankle-strap, kitten-heeled sandals away from their sisters.

She sat on the bed, only a few inches from him, trying to pretend she wasn't completely aware of the distance, or lack of it, between them. She leaned forward and slid her right foot into the shoe, then bent down to fasten the buckle. "Well, I never know what I'll want to wear."

"They all look the same," Micah said. "Except for the color."

She flipped her hair over one shoulder and looked at him incredulously. "They all look the same?" she repeated as if he'd announced he had a bomb under his hat. She looked back at the four other pairs of shoes, each of them completely different—overall style, height of the heel, color, clasp. *But he is a man,* she reminded herself. Even most women couldn't put into words the difference between a stiletto and a spool heel.

"Well," Chrissy said, keeping her ire in check and fastening her other sandal. "These I'm wearing today are a Manolo Blahnik. They retail for about five hundred dollars, but I found them at a consignment shop for thirty. They were missing the clasp." She pointed to the clasp on the right shoe. "I took it to a cobbler and they repaired it for eight bucks." She stood up to make sure the ankle strap was tight, but not constricting. Her foot practically melted into the lines of the shoe, and she looked at him in time to see his eyes travel slowly from shoe to shoulder. It was as if he were scanning her with a laser, for the heat that slowly filled her body.

"How can you even walk in those?" he asked.

Chrissy shrugged. "I guess years of practice have given me very strong ankles. I love heels."

Micah stood, but looked back at her shoes. "You must, you wear them all the time."

They lapsed into silence, until Micah met her eye and smiled. "So, you ready for today?"

"Why not?" she said, walking past him to get her purse. "Most things in life simply take a little work, a little faith, and a sturdy pair of heels."

"I'll take my sneakers, thank you very much," Micah said as he followed her to the door.

"Suit yourself," Chrissy said. "You won't mind if I keep my stilettos?" She couldn't help but cock her head coyly to the side as she awaited his answer. Feminine wiles—outside of her control sometimes.

The right side of Micah's mouth pulled into a grin. "Oh, I don't mind a bit."

CHAPTER 77

Micah stood a couple of feet behind Chrissy as she put her hands on the countertop and smiled at the woman behind the desk. The other woman was Hispanic—Colombian, Chrissy guessed from the fact that she was very beautiful and rather tall and slim for a Latina. A dark-skinned, dark-eyed toddler sat in the corner playing with blocks.

Based on the open doorway behind the desk, Chrissy guessed the woman and the child lived on the premises. Chrissy could only hope this woman didn't watch the news or read the morning paper. On their way here they'd picked up a copy and found an article about the police looking for Chressaidia.

"Hi," Chrissy said. "I need to get into my unit but can't remember the number." They'd searched the statement to see if the number was on there somewhere, but couldn't find it. However, she'd managed to intercept the first bill and learned that the unit had been opened only a month ago.

"Here's my statement and ID." She kept her tone light and innocent-sounding . . . she hoped. She dug into her purse and pulled out her statement. The woman looked at it, looked at Chrissy, and looked back at the statement. She went to her computer and typed, then looked at the license again. Chrissy still held her breath.

"This isn't the address on the application."

"I know. I moved to Idaho after it was opened. I'm ready for all my stuff sooner than I expected I'd be. I must have misplaced the paperwork in the move."

The woman eyed her with continued caution. Chrissy smiled, hoping the woman wouldn't notice the license had been issued two years ago. "I'm assuming you also forgot the entry code to get into the storage area."

There's an entry code? She grimaced. "I'm afraid so."

"There's a thirty-five dollar fee for me to give you the code again," the woman finally said, and Chrissy felt like she could breathe again. San Diego and their fees! No wonder the cost of living was so high.

"No problem," Chrissy said, fishing out two more twenty-dollar bills. Maybe she'd find a suitcase full of cash in the storage bay. One could only hope.

CHAPTER 78

Idaho Falls, Idaho

"But where's Chrissy?" Rosa asked after Livvy opened the front door of Chrissy's house and ushered Rosa and the boys inside. Around one o'clock in the morning, she'd remembered her spare key to Chrissy's house.

"She's in California for a few days, but you'll be fine here, okay?"

"Why can't we stay at Doug's?" Nathan asked, throwing himself on the couch and letting one leg dangle over the edge. "We can play with the dog there."

"Well, here you've got Chrissy's computer," Livvy said, checking the doors and windows to make sure they were locked. "And Chrissy's not here to make you set the timer."

"Oh, yeah," Carlos said with a grin. Nathan scrambled to his feet to follow his brother. They were soon contentedly bickering with one another over who got to be Mew and who would be Mewtoo.

"Aren't you already late for work?" Rosa asked once the boys had cleared out. She hadn't asked a lot of questions when Livvy told her they weren't staying at Doug's today. Livvy was grateful; she really didn't want to put words to her fears right now. It didn't help that she missed Doug, that she still wanted to be with him. It confused and disgusted her to feel so torn. Knowing she was doing the right thing, despite her feelings, gave her confidence. And for now, that was enough.

"I actually called in sick today," she said, keeping to herself that she might not go back. She liked her job, but Doug worked at the hospital too, and she didn't know that she was up to seeing him again. She could only imagine how he'd react when he got home and found that she'd left. She loved him and would miss him, but that didn't mean she wasn't afraid of him as well. "We're moving out of Doug's place."

"We are?" Rosa said, her whole face brightening. "Are we moving back to our house?"

Her house was already under contract—something Livvy had thought to be an incredible stroke of luck, but now seemed a bitter irony. Livvy didn't know if she could break the sale. That was another issue she needed to deal with. It would all be so much easier if she hadn't heard that voice last night, if the impression had at least faded so she could talk herself out of it. But instead it had grown until the fear that something would happen was not some vague possibility, but a fact.

"I don't know, but for now we'll stay at Chrissy's."

"She isn't mad anymore about you calling the police?"

"No," Livvy said, her voice choking just a little bit. Yes, Chrissy could be dominating and judgmental, but hadn't she been right? Livvy had failed . . . again, and yet she knew Chrissy would be there to catch her. "She's not still mad at me."

"Good," Rosa said, smiling. "She's going to be so happy to see us."

"Yes, she will," Livvy assured her, but her stomach flipped. She did not look forward to making the call to her sister and admitting she'd been wrong.

CHAPTER 79

Imperial Beach, California

The door to the storage bay rolled up its track, grinding and squeaking as it went. Micah held the new bolt cutters in one hand and the cut-through lock in the other. He'd been silent since they'd left the office of the storage unit complex.

"Would you rather wait in the car?" Chrissy asked, feeling guilty for him being involved in all this, yet reminding herself that he was the one who had followed her here. And she could never have done this without him. She'd have never thought of the bolt cutters, and now that she was in the thick of things, she couldn't imagine doing any of this by herself. The door stuck about three feet off the ground.

"And let you go in there alone?" Micah said, putting down the cutters and the lock before stepping forward and wrenching the door upward with those oh-so-nice arms of his. The door flew up, and Chrissy watched it come to a stop a few feet above their heads. She turned to her knight-in-the-Boise-State-cap and smiled.

"Nice," she said admiringly, putting a hand on his arm and squeezing for just a moment.

He looked embarrassed and stepped ahead of her, pulling on the string of the single bulb hanging from the ceiling.

Chrissy turned her attention to the storage bay. "This is it?" she said, looking at the twelve or so moving boxes lining the back wall.

"What were you expecting?" Micah asked, stepping toward the boxes and seeming to read the content descriptions written on the outside.

"I don't know," Chrissy said, moving to join him at the boxes. "Gothic skulls and a big, fat address book, I guess. Maybe a few crates of limited-edition Beanie Babies I could sell on eBay."

Micah snorted and pulled back the flap of one of the boxes. He stepped back to read the box again. "This isn't kitchen stuff," he said, pulling out a round, plastic object.

"What is it?" Chrissy asked, taking it from him and turning it over in her hand. It was round and hollow, like a pipe, but with detailed grooves and notches.

"I don't know—looks kinda like sprinkler parts. This box is full of 'em."

"Sprinkler parts?" Chrissy repeated, looking into another box. This one had a lot of black plastic things wrapped in heavy plastic and the number 50 written on each bundle. She moved onto another box with loose parts. "My ijacker is a sprinkler distributor?"

Micah was digging into another box.

Chrissy threw the part she was holding into the box full of its brothers and sisters and moved to another box. "So what part of a sprinkler is this?" she asked, holding up a long, narrow tube. "It's metal." She turned it over, then squinted and looked through the small hole that ran from end to end. Suddenly, Micah grabbed it from her, causing her to jump and pull back. She'd have said something about his rudeness if his face hadn't looked so scared.

"No way," he said under his breath as he looked the piece over, then moved to another unopened box.

"No way, what?" Chrissy asked, watching him move at a more frantic pace.

In answer, Micah pulled something out of the most recent box and turned to face her. "What does this look like to you?"

"A handle of some kind," Chrissy said, looking at the slightly-curved piece of black plastic. "Looks like part of a water gun," she finally said. She looked up and met his eye. "So my ijacker is a sprinkler and water gun distributor? Is that what my ninety thousand has gone toward?"

There were some papers on top of a closed box, and she picked them up. They said something about an order for baby formula. She flipped to the next paper that had all kinds of official-looking stamps. At the top was written "Border Crossing Agreement."

Micah had been still for a moment, looking at the two parts he held. In the next instant he threw them back in the box, grabbed Chrissy by the hand, and dragged her out of the storage unit. The papers in her hand fluttered to the floor.

"Hey!" she said, stumbling in her heels and barely catching herself as Micah turned, pulled the door back down, and cursed the lock they'd cut off. "What?" she demanded as he turned to face her again.

He grabbed her arm this time and began leading her to the car.

"Wait a minute," she said, wrenching her arm out of his grip and stopping. "What's going on?"

"Those weren't water guns or sprinkler parts, Chrissy," Micah said, turning to face her. "Whatever this is, it's way too big for us. We need to go to the police."

"The police who want to question me about a murder?" Chrissy reminded him. "We don't have enough proof yet. I'm not going near a police station until I'm sure I can prove I'm not the woman they want."

Micah paused for a moment, then stepped toward her, his voice low and intense. "Better the police find you than the gun dealers who rented this storage bay. We need to get out of here . . . now." He leaned down to snatch the bolt cutters off the ground.

"Guns?" Chrissy said, looking over his shoulder toward the moving boxes. *Why would someone take guns apart like that?* she wondered.

"Yes. Let's go."

"No, wait," Chrissy said, turning around and heading back to the door. She pulled up on the door, and it stopped at three feet again, but she bent down and headed back inside, picking up the papers as she went. Her heart rate increased. A storage bay full of guns and permission to cross the border? Holy cow! With a box in her arms, she ducked back under the door to get out and then headed for the car. Micah was still standing where she'd left him.

"What are you doing?" he asked, running up behind her and attempting to take the box from her arms.

"It's proof," she said, holding it as tight as she could.

"We don't need this kind of proof," Micah said, looking to the right and left, as if waiting for a car to turn the corner and some thug to open fire on them. "We'll just tell the police where they are."

She pulled hard, yanking the box from his hands. "No," she said strongly, and balanced the box with one arm as she opened the trunk of the car. "I'm not taking any chances. We can't fit them all in here, but we can fit some of them."

Micah stood there. "This is insane, Chrissy," he said. "We need to get some help with this. It's too big for us."

"It's always been bigger than us," she said. "And these documents show that in a few days these guns are crossing the border into Mexico. You really want to leave these here and let it happen?"

Micah groaned as Chrissy put the box into the trunk and headed back for another one.

"Hurry," Chrissy said, passing him. "Or are you going to make me do this all by myself?"

Chapter 80

I'm not driving around with these things in the car," Micah said. His already white skin was completely blanched around his knuckles as he clenched the steering wheel. She'd made him take her to the PO Box again, but there wasn't any mail today.

"Fine, we can take them to the motel," Chrissy said. "We couldn't just leave them there, Micah. If they are guns, then we need to get them away from the bad guys."

"This is not a video game!" he yelled.

"Don't yell at me!" she yelled back. They both went silent.

After nearly a minute, Micah cleared his throat. "They are going to notice they're missing half their stuff. And it's not like we just took some dishes."

"Maybe they don't go there very often." She kept to herself that the border crossing papers were dated June 5—two days away.

"She's wanted for murder, Chrissy, and I don't think people put illegal gun parts in a storage unit and forget about them. She's a totally freaky woman, and we're messing with her."

Chrissy threw her hands up. "Well, I don't know what to do.

But it just seemed wrong to leave them there, waiting for them to come back and ship them over the border. In fact, isn't that aiding and abetting? To do nothing is as bad as helping it along. Besides, she doesn't know we're here."

"She will now."

"She doesn't know it's us," Chrissy said.

"We don't *think* she does." He let out a breath. "Look, I'm not keeping those boxes in the car and no way are they coming to the motel with us."

"Well, those are about the only two choices we have. So, do you want to drive with them in the trunk—where no one can see them—or take them to the motel and wait for a curious house-keeper to figure out what they are?"

"I want to take them to the police."

Chrissy groaned.

"What more do you want before you ask for their help?"

She crossed her arms over her chest and looked out the win-dow. "A guarantee," she finally said. "I want some way to guarantee I'm not going to end up in jail."

"And if there is no such thing? Are you going to keep driving around San Diego with illegal weapons in your car?"

She threw her arms up. "I don't know," she said, turning to look at him; challenging him. "I don't know, okay! Just . . . give me a minute. I didn't plan on this whole illegal weapon thing this morn-ing, ya know."

Micah glowered at her and clenched his teeth.

Chrissy was about to tell him if he couldn't handle it, he should go home when her cell phone began ringing. She pulled it from her pocket and looked at the number, her heart skipping a beat.

"What?" Micah asked. "Who is it?"

Chrissy looked up at him. "It's Livvy."

CHAPTER 81

～✦～

"We can't load yet," Eduardo said as Chressaidia put the last of her items in her suitcases. She wasn't taking them with her over the border because that would look too suspicious, but she couldn't leave anything here. The household items had been left at the last rental—the one where the man had told them to leave before he called the police; her clothing would go to the Salvation Army. Most of the documents would be shredded. She would fill one bag with necessities, and just as she'd done on their first trip, she'd cross the border on foot.

Eduardo kept talking. "We need to wait for tomorrow night to load, like we planned."

"We don't have that long," Chressaidia said, whipping around. "You've got the truck. Let's load it now. We can keep it on the street until we get to the warehouse and pick up the formula." The morning paper had talked about Frederico, mentioning his ties to a militant group in South America and giving a detailed description of his wife, whom the police were still looking for. Having that kind of attention changed everything.

"You're overreacting," Eduardo said with an uncharacteristic dominance in his voice.

Chressaidia came and stopped directly in front of him. "Do not question me," she said. "Too much has changed. They've found Frederico. Someone went to my PO Box. We need to get out of here."

"I've spent weeks working out these details. Changing them now is not an option. We need to stick to the original plan, and we can't show up to receive the formula with boxes of gun parts already in the truck."

"Maybe you should ask Frederico about whether plans sometimes have to change."

Eduardo made no reaction.

"We're moving the product," she said in slow, calculated words. After holding his eyes for a few more moments, she turned away and went back to clearing out the hotel room. "Do not get in my way, Eduardo."

CHAPTER 82

Idaho Falls, Idaho

Livvy finished explaining and braced herself for an "I told you so" from her older sister. Chrissy was silent on the other end of the phone.

"Livvy," she finally said. "I am so glad you thought to go to the house. I'm only sorry I'm not there."

Livvy felt herself relax a little bit more. "I've got most of our stuff packed—well, not the furniture, I'm not sure what to do about that since I can't move it myself—but I've got our clothes and things. I have a call in to my real estate agent, to see if I can cancel the sale, but there's no furniture or food there anyway. Can we stay here, at your house, in the meantime?"

"Of course," Chrissy said. "As long as you need to."

Livvy let out a breath and threw the last garbage sack of clothes into the backseat of the car. The whole time she'd been packing she'd feared Doug would come home, wondering why she wasn't at work. She had no idea what she'd say to him, how she'd explain. But the fear motivated her to move faster, believing that because she was finally doing the right thing, it would turn out okay.

"Thank you, Chriss," she said quietly. They both paused. "Now, what are you doing in California?"

"Oh, it's been such a mess," she said and went on to explain a story that sounded almost unreal, it was so intense. "I'm trying to get things figured out. It's really weird to have someone living this whole other life in my name."

"Oh, hey," Livvy said, remembering the strange phone call she'd had a few days ago. "Maybe that's why that guy called me."

"What guy?"

"The one who called and asked me about the baby."

Chrissy was quiet for a moment. "What baby?"

CHAPTER 83

Imperial Beach, California

Eduardo was in the driver's seat of what used to be a moving van but that had been repainted white, though the paint was now dinged and scratched after years of use. The vinyl seats were cracked and the ride was bumpy, but it seemed like a luxury vehicle compared to the old trucks the army was using to move their war forward. It would be an added bonus to present the soldiers with this truck in addition to the guns.

Chressaidia had been thinking a lot about the reunion, about the honor she would receive for accomplishing this task. Even the death of Frederico could not mar the tribute they would show her when she arrived at the camp. She was so anxious to get there, so anxious to shed the life of Chressaidia Salazar and take her place among the generals—the men—and now a woman—who would change the world.

Eduardo pulled up to the number pad at the storage unit's gate and typed in the entry code, then sat back against the driver's seat as the big metal gate rolled open. "It's not safe to leave this on the street," he said. "We need to find somewhere else to store the truck and somewhere to put the guns while we load the formula."

"We will find somewhere," Chressaidia said. "We only need to keep it there for thirty-six hours."

Eduardo nodded and took the first right down a paved aisle wide enough for a large van, like theirs, and lined with storage bays. He took the next left, then another right. "What do you have left to do before we go?"

"I have two more dealers to meet with," she said. "I'm meeting them tonight. Then I only need to dispose of the documents."

The truck rolled to a stop, and Chressaidia opened the passenger door, fingering the small, gold key in her pocket. She reached the bay and lifted her hand to grab the lock. Her whole body froze as she looked at the empty latch. For a moment she couldn't compute what she was seeing. Was she at the wrong unit? Had she made a mistake? She looked up and confirmed the numbers as heat rushed through her. In the next instant she looked at the ground and saw the cut lock lying on the asphalt. Her heart was thumping as she pulled up the storage door and rushed inside.

Eduardo swore behind her. She turned on him, her eyes full of rage as she counted the boxes and came up half a dozen short. "What have you done to me?"

Eduardo's eyes went wide. "Me? I've done nothing."

"You are the only person who knows about this place. You are the only one left who can betray me."

"I'm the only one left who can make this work," Eduardo returned with anger and offense. "I did not—would not—do this. What good would a portion of gun parts be to me? And if I'd wanted to steal them, I'd have done it a long time ago."

CHAPTER 84

❧

San Diego, California

*L*ong?"

Detective Long looked up from his desk and made eye contact with the officer standing in the doorway of his office. "What?"

"I found something on that Salazar woman."

Long lifted his eyebrows, waiting to hear it.

"She was arrested on our warrant in Idaho Falls a week ago. She's been living in Idaho for almost five years."

"A week ago?" Long asked.

"Right," the desk officer said, coming into Long's office. "A few days after that, there was also a request for the Salazar fraud report that had been filed here. The request was from a public defender in Idaho Falls, and a fraud report was filed in Idaho as well—also by Salazar. I called and left a message for the attorney but talked to the receptionist. The Salazar they have been dealing with is appearing in court next week, and they're developing a case of mistaken identity. The receptionist is faxing me some information, including some statements showing local purchases made in Idaho on the day

Salazar was arrested here and fingerprints they took when they booked her for the failure to appear."

"So basically, there are two of them and the Idaho woman is probably the right one."

"Exactly."

"Which means we have no idea who we're looking for."

"Pretty much."

CHAPTER 85

⟨~~~⟩

$\mathcal{C}$hrissy and Micah walked side by side down the gleaming hallway of the San Diego hospital. Livvy had gone online to try to identify the hospital that had called her. They all hoped she'd found the right one.

"So, what do we do?" Micah asked, moving toward Chrissy so as to avoid a piece of equipment in the hallway.

"I don't know," she said. The nursing station came into view, and she shared a look with Micah as they approached the desk. They had to come. The idea of a baby being part of this upped the stakes to a whole different level and the hospital was the only lead they had.

"Can I help you?" a woman asked. Her sleek black hair was pulled into a twist and caught the fluorescent lighting overhead. Even when Chrissy straightened her hair it was never that straight, that shiny.

"Yes, I'm looking for some information," Chrissy said. "I'm looking for a woman who had a baby here sometime in the last month or so."

The woman's face lost some of its softness as Chrissy continued. "I'm just wondering if there were some nurses I could talk to? Maybe someone who worked when she was here and can give me some information?"

"We can't give out any information about a patient."

Duh, of course they wouldn't. "Well, see, she used my name," Chrissy tried to explain. "And she's in all kinds of trouble. I'm really worried about this baby. Isn't there someone I can talk to about it? Someone who could, you know, follow-up on the baby, make sure it's okay?"

"That's not what we do," the woman said.

"What do you mean that's not what you do? You take care of mothers and babies, and this baby is in trouble."

"Um," Micah broke in, using a calm and reasonable tone. "We're just trying to get some help for this child. Is there a social worker, or someone like that we can talk to? Really, we're not trying to pull anything."

The woman looked between the two of them. "I guess I could send a note to our social service director." She pulled out a notepad. "What's your name?"

"Chrissy Salazar. Chressaidia Josefina Salazar."

The woman's head whipped up, and another nurse at the station looked over at her. They shared a look and the other nurse picked up the phone. Chrissy took a step backward, but Micah grabbed her arm to keep her from going any further.

"You've done nothing wrong," Micah whispered, his breath making the hair around her ear move. "Let's play this out."

Two minutes later the sound of heavy footsteps caused Chrissy and Micah to turn and see two blue-clad security guards coming toward them. Her heart leapt in her chest, and only Micah's hand on her arm gave her any reason not to bolt.

CHAPTER 86

Imperial Beach, California

Teri turned the key in the outside lock of The Box Stop and tested the doorknob to make sure it was secure. It was two o'clock and since she was working alone—again—she locked up the store while she took her lunch break. She turned away from the building and headed for the burger joint on the corner, curious as to the smell of gasoline in the air. But there were often weird smells and weirder people in this part of town. Probably some teenage kids were huffing around the side of the building. It was of no concern to her; she had bigger problems to think about. Like what to do about her job.

If they didn't hire another person to help her run the desk, she was going to quit. Between the ten-hour shifts she'd been pulling all week and the scary Mexican chick who had threatened her yesterday, she'd had about enough. She pulled a crumpled pack of smokes from her pocket—the generic kind because they were cheaper—and paused to light up real fast. She was holding the lighter to the end of her cigarette when all of a sudden an arm circled around her neck, pulling her toward the back of the building.

"What the—" Another hand reached up and covered her

mouth. Panic shot through her arms, legs, and spine. She started screaming and kicking, but the arms that held her were strong, and despite her clawing and fighting, she couldn't gain any advantage. Within moments she was behind the building, shielded from the street.

Someone stood in front of her. A woman. She bent down and picked up Teri's lighter that had fallen to the ground. Teri stopped fighting and took sucking breaths through her nostrils. She stared at the woman. It was that scary Mexican chick from yesterday. *What is going on?*

The woman flicked the wheel on the lighter, igniting the flame, and started walking toward Teri, holding the lighter in front.

Teri pulled back as the lighter came within inches of her face, close enough to singe her hair. The man holding her from behind tightened his grip and pushed her forward, toward the flame. Smelling burnt hair and feeling her mascara melt with the intense heat of the little flame, Teri started screaming again behind the hand held over her mouth. She curled her body back against her captor, but he pushed her forward. It was the middle of the day, wasn't anyone around? Would anyone help her?

"Someone got my mail," the Mexican woman said in that deep monotone voice Teri remembered from yesterday. "And you are going to tell me who." She moved the lighter down to the sleeve of Teri's T-shirt and held it there until the fabric began to singe. Searing heat enveloped her arm, and Teri screamed again and struggled as her flesh burned.

Suddenly the woman hit her arm where the heat had been growing, putting out the flame, and sending a whole new level of pain through Teri. She thought she might pass out. Her eyes moved to the woman's face again, and she nodded quickly. She'd tell her everything she wanted to know.

"If you scream," the woman said as Teri felt the hand on her mouth relax, "we'll have to start over."

Teri shook her head. Once free, her breaths were hesitant and she had to hold herself back from crying. Her arm still felt as if it were on fire and in addition to the burning hair, the smell of cooked skin now filled the air as well. She was going to throw up.

"Who was it?" the woman asked.

"A woman," Teri choked.

"What was her name?"

"She had ID and everything."

"ID?"

"Yes, a driver's license. Her name matched the box."

"Salazar?" the woman asked abruptly.

Teri nodded. "Yes, she said it was her box. I swear, I didn't know. I—"

"Tell me everything."

Teri swallowed and proceeded to give her an exact account of every detail; even down to the red-and-black car she'd arrived in.

"What time was this?"

"In the morning, around eleven. Right before you came in."

"Has she come back?"

Teri nodded. "Yes, today, but I didn't give her anything. She brought a man with her, this time. She called him Michael or Mike or—"

"Micah," the woman said quickly, her eyebrows going up with surprise.

"Yes," Teri said, gaining confidence. She was giving this woman what she wanted. That was good. She'd be okay. "Maybe she'll come back tomorrow. If she does, I could keep her here till you come."

The woman nodded. Teri felt her first ray of hope. The woman wasn't a monster; she could be reasonable. Teri would get away. She'd go home and call the police.

"You could do that," the woman said as if she were considering it, then her eyes moved to the man behind Teri. She nodded and Teri let out a breath as the grip around her neck relaxed. But in the next instant something cold and wet poured over her head.

"What—?" She tried to figure out what was happening as she looked at the liquid dripping off her fingers. And then she smelled gasoline again. The last thing she saw was the woman flicking her lighter to life one last time.

CHAPTER 87

Idaho Falls, Idaho

The phone rang, making Livvy jump. She stared at it. Was it Doug? Had he figured out where she was? The kids were playing outside, and she was cleaning up the kitchen, trying to take confidence in what she'd done, but missing Doug like crazy, even though she felt sick about it. On the second ring she went to the phone. The caller ID read "Unknown number," and Livvy bit her lip, wrestling over whether she should answer or not. After six rings—and still no decision—the phone stopped, and she let out a breath. She didn't have to worry about it now. She was two steps away from the phone when it started ringing again.

It's not my house, she said to herself. There was no reason to answer and if Chrissy needed to talk to her, she'd call Livvy's cell. It stopped ringing again, but she stayed there, staring at it. What if it was Doug trying to call? What if he could explain himself? The idea both repulsed her and gave her hope. Maybe she had misunderstood, maybe she was overreacting.

The phone rang again, and she jumped.

Rosa's voice startled her even further. "Mom, aren't you going to answer the phone?"

"Oh, sorry," Livvy said, and she picked it up on the third ring.

"Chressaidia Salazar?" a crisp-sounding voice with a hint of a Latin accent asked before Livvy even said hello.

It wasn't Doug. Relief and disappointment flooded through Livvy. "No, she's not here."

"Where is she?" the woman on the line asked.

"Who is this?"

"This is Maria Vasquez from City Bank. Someone tried to use her debit card out of state, and I'm calling to verify it. There have been problems with her account lately."

"Oh," Livvy said, wishing she knew more about the situation. "Yeah, well, where was the charge made?"

"I'm afraid I cannot give out that information. Perhaps you could tell me where she went and I can see if that's the same location."

"She's in California. I don't know where exactly, but it's all part of the account problems you mentioned, I think. She won't be home for a few days. Could I have her call you?"

There was silence on the other end of the line. "And she's traveling with someone?" the woman asked. "We have another signature on a charge and wondered if she was with a companion. We can put him on the record and then let the charges go through. We believe his name is Micah Heet."

They can do that, over the phone? Livvy thought. "Um, who do you represent again?" The line clicked. "Hello?" she said as the line went dead. "Hello?"

CHAPTER 88

San Diego, California

*C*hrissy explained her situation to the security guard, who had kept Micah out in the hall. When the security guard left the room, she fell forward onto the table, letting her hair hang over her face and fantasizing that when she flipped it back up, she'd be on a beach somewhere, sipping fancy drinks with fresh fruit in them and watching the waves roll in and out.

"Ms. Salazar?" a voice asked, and it didn't sound like the bartender of her fantasy island. She flipped her hair up and looked at an Asian man with spiky hair and angular features. His name tag read "Dr. Jon Nasagi." As he looked at her, his face softened, something she hadn't expected. "Chressaidia Salazar?"

"Yes," she said slowly.

He pulled out a chair and sat down, looking at her. She waited a few seconds, assuming that he'd take the lead, but he didn't.

"Someone has stolen my identity," she explained, just as she had to the security guard. "And had a baby in this hospital."

He nodded. "You're from Idaho?"

Chrissy furrowed her brow and pulled back slightly. "How do you know that?"

"I was looking for family members." He shook his head. "I—I wondered if something like this had happened. You do know your insurance information on file is all relayed to California, right?"

Chrissy shook her head. "No," she said, in awe, once again, of the details her thief had thought to take care of. "You were . . . looking for me, I mean, the other Chressaidia?"

He shook his head. "Not her, just her family, for her baby."

Chrissy leaned forward and realized that maybe he could help her. "Yes, her baby. She's into something bad—really bad. That's why I'm here. That baby isn't safe, but you must know that if you were trying to find help for it." He didn't say anything so Chrissy continued. "This woman is involved in gun smuggling. I think she's also involved in the death of her husband, except I guess he wasn't really her husband because she used my name to marry him." Did that mean he was Chrissy's husband? "Anyway, to know there's a baby involved just makes me sick. Someone has to find her."

"I wish I could be of more help," he said. "However, I personally followed up every lead in her file and found nothing."

Chrissy leaned forward and tucked her hair behind her ear, staring at him, pleading in her mind that he could give her something she could use. "Can you tell me anything about her? Anything that can help me figure out who she is?"

"There are privacy issues."

"For a woman like her? Someone who's putting her baby in the middle of a situation like this?"

He leaned back in his chair and regarded her in a way that made her feel as if he could see right through her. "I don't think I have anything that would help you anyway," he said, letting out a breath. "She was here less than eight hours, and I only met her once."

"What did she look like?" Chrissy asked, leaning forward.

"Dark. Darker than you, smaller, pretty—one of the nurses thought she was Guatemalan."

"Guatemalan? Why did they think that?" Chrissy asked, feeling starved for this information.

"Well, it might not mean anything, but she also brought in a red-and-yellow woven blanket. This nurse I mentioned thought the designs were Guatemalan, where this nurse is from."

Chrissy looked down at the table. She knew very little about the country of Guatemala other than the fact that there was a great deal of fighting there and that sometimes tourists were attacked. Were the guns part of that? And the baby was born to a woman like this?

"She took the blanket with her when she left," he continued. "However, her son is here and is very safe."

Chrissy looked up and blinked in absolute shock. "He's here?" she breathed.

Why was he still here? Did he get sick? Why hadn't Social Services already taken him away? Relief washed over her and she let out a breath. "He's here," she repeated again. "He's safe?"

CHAPTER 89

*M*icah Heet has two rooms at the El Venturo Motel," Carbon said into the phone. He'd lived in this area most of his life, which was why he was such a valuable dealer to have on their line. He had also proved valuable when she needed information about details such as this. He knew everyone. "He checked in yesterday. Has the rooms for two more nights."

The woman on the phone had confirmed that the real Chressaidia was here, but it wasn't until she compared the Salazar and Heet files that she realized the connection. They were from the same town. Their information had been purchased around the same time. How stupid could Frederico be?

Chressaidia grabbed her keys and yelled for Eduardo as she headed out the door. He quickly appeared with only a towel around his waist, his dark chest still wet from the shower. She'd insisted he wash the smell of gasoline off him as soon as possible.

"We found them," she said. "Get dressed. We have work to do."

CHAPTER 90

~~~

"Cleft palate?" Chrissy repeated as the elevator doors opened to a long sterile hallway. Micah, still the strong, silent sentry, stood behind her and followed them out of the elevator. He placed his hand on the small of her back and she felt more support than she could have imagined from such a simple thing. It connected them, reminding her she wasn't alone. "That's when the top lip is kind of messed up, right?" she asked.

"That's what people see," Dr. Nasagi explained as they made their way down the sterile hallway. "But it's only one part of the condition. The palate, or bone across the top of the mouth, isn't fully formed during embryonic development. He has what we call a bilateral cleft, which means that the fissure in his lip is wide and the gap in his palate is severe. On a scale of one to ten, our maxofacial surgeon says Baby Salazar registers as a seven or eight. Several surgeries should be able to repair most of the defect over time."

"Baby Salazar," Chrissy whispered, a rush of wind traveling through her as Dr. Nasagi continued. No one else seemed to notice the way the floor shifted. Baby *Salazar?* Since learning the baby was here, she felt as if she were in the eye of the storm, as if everything else, all her other worries, had been put on hold.

"Since he's a ward of the state, there is no time line for his first surgery. For now, he can finally suction for bottle feeding, though it's intensive to feed him. Often we feed him through a syringe."

"And he's been here for five weeks?" Chrissy asked.

Dr. Nasagi nodded. "Once he'd been here for thirty days and his mother hadn't returned, he became what we call a Boarder Baby, and we reported him to Social Services. Unfortunately, it's not that rare. He was number ninety-two this year."

Chrissy let out a breath. "That's horrible."

"Typically, Social Services would find a foster or adoptive home for an abandoned child, but with his condition and circumstance, it's complicated. The nurses often stay late and hold him, and we have some volunteers who also make it a priority to spend time with him."

"He's living in a hospital," Micah said. His hand wasn't on her back anymore, but Chrissy could still feel it somehow. "It's still an institution."

Dr. Nasagi looked at Micah. "Yes, it's certainly not ideal. That's why I called your sister, to see if there was family available who could take him in. I guess . . . that's not really an option." He hurried forward with his words. "I should warn you that his appearance is shocking." His eyes moved past her and focused on the window.

Chrissy turned her head, following his gaze, and gasped. She heard Micah do the same. They all fell silent as they stared at the infant on the other side of the glass.

He was sleeping, but the peaceful picture was ruined by the large gap in the middle of his upper lip. One side extended up through his nose, and his left nostril was pulled out to the side. It looked as if someone had sculpted a perfect little boy, and then pinched a chunk of flesh from the middle of his face.

Chrissy had seen pictures of children like this, and known a few adults who'd had cleft lips as children and later had them repaired, but to see it up close, on a child this small, was different. She swallowed a lump in her throat and tried not to give in to her desire to look away.

"Are there any other problems?" Micah asked after a silent minute.

"He has a heart murmur," Dr. Nasagi said. "We've been watching it, and it seems to be okay. At first we thought it meant he had a more serious condition, but we've managed to rule that out. He was only five pounds when he was born, and has struggled to gain weight, but considering his circumstances, he's quite healthy. Healthy enough that the state will likely not consider surgery an absolute necessity, though several of us at the hospital are trying to convince them otherwise.

"If he's adopted, then I'm sure the parents will see to it that he gets the help he needs, but the chances of him being adopted are slim. At least his toxicology tests came back normal. His mother seemed healthy to those of us who met her, so that's a plus."

Chrissy was still staring at Baby Salazar. Would the other Chressaidia have kept him if not for his disfigured face? "She came to the U.S. to have him?" Chrissy asked even though the answer seemed obvious. Relief flooded through her and she wished she could communicate to the child how blessed he was to be free of this woman. This woman who may have killed this child's father, who was involved in something horrible. Thank goodness for his deformity. It may have saved his life.

"It's possible," Dr. Nasagi said. "And at least she came to the hospital, where he could get the help he needs. We're doing everything in our power to find a home for him, but his mother could help us a great deal. She still has parental rights. Taking them away from her, without her present, is a lengthy process."

Chrissy turned and he met her eyes as he continued. "If you find her—if the police find her—please don't forget this little guy." He waved toward the glass, and she followed his hand, looking at the baby again, feeling a lump in her throat.

"I won't forget him," she said, looking back at the baby behind the glass, the baby that shared her name.

CHAPTER 91

I know what you're thinking," Micah said from the driver's seat of her car.

Chrissy chuckled humorlessly and continued to stare out the window at the cement walls that paralleled the I-5. "I bet you don't." She wasn't even sure what she was thinking and she wasn't about to say it out loud.

"You'd make a good mother," Micah said, though the casual tone in his voice was forced and pointed.

"Said by the man whose daughter hates me." She turned to look at him long enough to see that he understood her point. She went back to the window.

"Mallory's feelings are much more about me, and her mother, and herself, than you. She's fourteen. She's been through a lot and I can't say I blame her for being hesitant to embrace new people in her parents' lives. I can tell you she was worried about you when you left on Sunday." He paused for a moment. "And I talked with both kids before coming out here, and they both agreed it was the right thing for me to do."

She was surprised by that and went back to the subject he'd originally brought up. "It would never work," she said, still thinking of the baby in the hospital. "Can you imagine the red tape? I'm single, I'm unemployed. I'm still considered a felon."

"You're the one who was looking for purpose in all this," Micah said. "I'm just saying—"

"Don't," Chrissy said. "I can't—I need to focus on this right now. I can't get caught up in daydreams." And yet, in a weird, cosmic—maybe happily-ever-after way—it made sense. Chrissy wanted a family and had none. Baby Salazar needed a family and was similarly without. But, sheesh, Chrissy wasn't a romantic. She lived in the real world and didn't believe in fairy tales anymore.

"So, where to now?" Micah said, effectively changing the subject away from the homeless, disfigured child in the isolette. "You ready to go to the police yet? Jon said he'd help out. He'll tell them it wasn't you."

Chrissy inhaled deeply and looked out the window. They weren't stuck in traffic tonight, it was too early for that. She found herself wishing for a traffic jam. The morning cloud cover—June Gloom—had lifted, opening the sky to the splendor of beach living. Micah had taken the Silver Strand highway south from San Diego this time. The road followed the coastline, allowing a view of the ocean nearly the entire way. It was lovely, and she kept watching the waves, waiting for a solution to rise up like King Triton from the depths of the sea and point her in the direction she should go. But other than the cresting water, some shore birds, and endless tourists, there were no underwater messengers to lead her.

"I know he'd vouch for me," Chrissy said. The very idea of going to the police was still as enticing as going back to work for Brandon. "I just wish we had more to give them."

"Chrissy," he said, in a please-be-reasonable tone. "What more do you want? You've got the documents, half the parts, a hair sample, and an eyewitness who can prove you are not the same Chressaidia Salazar everyone is looking for. How much more do we need?"

"Do you think we should check out that address you got?" Chrissy asked, knowing she was stalling. "Carefully, of course, but if we had a location to give them, they'd have somewhere to start looking for her and they would realize I'm trying to help."

"We'll give the address to them, let them know where she is— or where she was. It's not just about us anymore. The police need to find her so they can start proceedings on taking parental rights away from her. We don't want to hold that up."

Chrissy nodded, but her stomach was in knots. Going to the police was an overwhelming thought, but as Micah had pointed out, they *had* gathered a great deal of information. She deflated against the seat of the car and gave in. Maybe there was something someone else could do that she could not. But it was hard to let go—hard to trust another person with something this important. However, she felt the same thing he did, that they'd pushed this as far as they could—as far as they should.

"You're probably right."

"What?" Micah said, feigning shock. "Did you actually say I was right about something?" He patted his chest and pockets as if looking for something. "Gosh, where's a pen? I think I need to write that down."

She gave him a scrunched look and shook her head. "Let's go to the motel first, though. You could pick us up some dinner, and I'll get all my stuff packed. That way, if things don't go well, you don't end up packing my underwear for me."

"Sounds fair," Micah said. They stopped at a light, and he looked over at her, taking her hand in his. She looked from his hand to his eyes and tried really, really hard to ignore the intensity she felt at his touch. "But I'm not going back to Idaho without you, okay?"

She swallowed and could find no words, so she just nodded. He squeezed her hand and then pulled his away as the light turned green.

CHAPTER 92

~~~

$\mathcal{C}$hressaidia sat in the car, parked across the street. Waiting. Watching. It was almost five o'clock when the red-and-black Mazda pulled into the parking lot. She narrowed her eyes as the woman— the real Chressaidia—stepped out of the car, said something to the driver, and then shut the door. She watched for Micah Heet to get out as well, but instead, the reverse lights went on and he pulled out of the space and then the parking lot. She looked up in time to see the real Chressaidia go into room four.

"Follow him," she said to Eduardo as she threw her door open. They were in her car. The delivery truck would have been too noticeable. "I'll watch her. Don't do anything until we know where the parts are."

Eduardo nodded and scooted into the driver's seat before taking off after the red-and-black car. Chressaidia looked both ways for traffic and crossed the street, focusing her eyes on the motel room door as she approached.

After finding a spot amid some landscaping where she could

watch the door without being easily seen, she waited five minutes before calling Eduardo's phone.

"Where is he going?"

"Subway," Eduardo said. "He's inside getting sandwiches. The parts might be in the trunk."

"Stay with him," she said into the phone, stepping out of her shadowy hiding place. "I'll be with her."

CHAPTER 93

~~~

*Y*ou want onions *and* peppers?" Micah said into the phone.

"*Sí, señor, porciones de cebollas y pimientas,*" she said, stretching her back as she headed for her suitcase. "And jalapeños." She was tired of her skirt, and her shirt smelled nasty from the heat, humidity, and box hauling. She definitely needed to change her clothes. Her typical skirt and heels weren't what she wanted to wear to jail. Her stomach rolled again as she thought of what lay ahead. Maybe she'd have time for a quick shower before Micah got back.

There was a knock at the door, and she turned to face it.

"What's that?" Micah asked over the phone.

"Someone knocking," Chrissy said, heading for the door. She peered through the peephole but couldn't see anything. She leaned to the side and looked through the window. "There's no one there," she said, still scanning the sidewalk. The angle of the afternoon sun made it hard to see much.

"That's weird," Micah said. "Hang on." He must have moved his phone from his mouth, as his voice faded while he ordered their sandwiches, emphasizing lots of peppers and onions on the turkey on white.

Chrissy let the curtain fall back and headed for her suitcase again. She'd brought a pair of jeans and some sneakers. It would be drab and completely unflattering, but it was the best option, considering. A knock sounded again.

"Oh, for heaven's sake," she muttered. She walked quickly to the door and had her hand on the doorknob when she glanced at the "For Your Safety" plaque. Chrissy hooked the chain before pulling the door open about four inches.

"So sorry," the woman said, staring at Chrissy. "I am working the front desk tonight, and we are having a problem with our phones. Can I come in and call the manager? I am going through every room to find out which ones are affected."

She was a Latina and spoke excellent English. She had a trace of an accent, but not much. She was about Chrissy's height, but thinner, with angular features and her dark hair pulled into a braid. Chrissy reached up to undo the chain but hesitated, looking back at her visitor. There was something in the way the woman was looking at Chrissy that didn't seem right. She was too intent, too hard. Chrissy still had the phone open, out of view of the other woman, but pressed against her shoulder. She turned the phone around so that the conversation would be audible for Micah should he get back on his end of the line.

"My, uh, husband is coming back in a minute. Could we wait until then?"

The woman pursed her lips and continued staring. "I am very sorry. Please, if I could just check the phone. This is the last room on the list."

"Why don't I just check the phone for you?" Chrissy offered.

In the next instant the woman's hand flashed through the gap in the door, grabbed a handful of Chrissy's hair, and slammed her forehead into the edge of the door. Chrissy screamed but was suddenly silenced by the feel of metal against her cheek.

"You will open this door and let me in, Chressaidia Salazar, or the man following your *husband* will shoot him in the head."

CHAPTER 94

Chrissy!" Micah said loudly into the phone as his heart leapt to his throat. The people around him in line looked at him. "Chrissy!" he shouted again and began pushing his way out of line.

"Sir, your sandwiches!"

He pushed through the door and stood on the sidewalk. Her phone was still on, and he could hear muffled voices, but nothing definitive. He ran for the car, yelling her name into the phone, and fumbling in his pocket for the keys.

Seconds later he still had the phone to his ear as he pulled out of the parking lot. "Chrissy!" he yelled again, even though he knew she couldn't hear him. "Oh, please," he muttered under his breath as he looked both ways and cut through traffic in order to get into the far lane. A car honked as it swerved out of his way. The phone went dead. He glanced in his rearview mirror and saw a silver car pull into traffic behind him. He was just panicked enough to think the worst.

Micah was on the second 1 of 911 when his phone rang. It was Chrissy. He quickly answered it.

"Chrissy," he said breathlessly. "What's going on?" He made a right turn. He was only a few blocks from the motel now. The silver car was right behind him. His heart began beating so fast he couldn't feel the individual beats anymore.

"You will bring me my parts," a woman's voice said. "You will bring them to the motel, or I will kill her."

Kill her? Micah's heart pulsed wildly. "Who are you?"

"You should not have interfered."

This had to be the other Chressaidia. How had she found them? *What do I do?* "I don't have them," he stammered, then wondered why he'd lied.

"Bring the parts to me," the woman said calmly. "Or she dies."

Micah swallowed. "I want to talk to her."

"No." The woman's voice was tight and calm.

"How do I know she's still okay?" Micah said. He heard some muffled voices.

"I'm okay," Chrissy's voice said. She wasn't on the phone, but in the background somewhere, and her voice didn't sound scared; it sounded angry. For some reason her anger gave him confidence. "Don't come!" she yelled right before the woman got back on the line.

"Twenty minutes," the woman said. "And if the police come, I'll kill her."

The line went dead. Micah blinked while taking a breath and trying to get his thoughts lined up. He almost ran a red light and slammed on his brakes, already two feet into the intersection. The silver car was right behind him and had to slam on its brakes too.

In the next instant, Micah punched the gas, swerving around a SUV going through the intersection. The silver car wasn't quick enough. Micah flew past the motel and whipped around the corner before the silver car began to move.

He saw an underground parking lot and headed for it, scraping the bottom of the car on his way in. He pulled into a parking space and tried to catch his breath. The newspaper wedged between the passenger seat and the middle console caught his eye. He picked it up quickly, scanning the second page Chrissy had read to him that morning—the article about the investigation of the dead guy.

"Detective Long," he read out loud as he grabbed his cell phone. His own words rang back to him, "It's too big for us." He only hoped he was doing the right thing.

CHAPTER 95

$\mathscr{S}$it," the woman said, waving the toy-looking gun at Chrissy. But Chrissy had researched the gun purchased in her name and this one looked just like it, which led Chrissy to not take it for granted. The other woman had hung up with Micah a moment earlier and put Chrissy's cell phone in her pocket.

Chrissy took two steps backward and sat down when the back of her knees encountered the bed. She didn't take her eyes off the woman. The other Chressaidia. It was surreal to be in the same room with her—to realize the only name she knew for her was Chrissy's own. This was the woman who had turned Chrissy's world upside down. And this—Chressaidia—now had the power to end it if she chose to.

"Why did you do this to me?" Chrissy asked.

The woman had been scanning the room, but now she looked back at Chrissy. "To you?" she said as if disgusted. She took a few steps forward, but only to pull the motel phone cord from the wall. "You should not have come here."

"I *had* to come here," Chrissy said, glaring at the other woman.

"You turned what was a good life into something I don't even recognize. I have nothing left."

This brought what could almost be described as a smile to the other woman's face. "Except your life." She stared at Chrissy, then lifted her chin. "You should be proud of your contribution," she said after a few seconds had passed. "In your own way, you will have saved a nation."

Chrissy scrunched her eyebrows together. "Saved a nation?" This woman really was cracked.

"Guatemala," the woman said, the slightest touch of wistfulness in her tone. "My homeland. A country being swallowed by what you call the American Dream." She waved the gun around as if to indicate the room, or the state of California as a whole. "You are so worried about people coming into your country, but you do not care that you invade others. American, Chinese, and European industry comes and builds factories, takes over the government, institutes the Central American Free Trade Agreement, which only continues to force the true citizens into poverty and subordination. But I will change all that. I will make things right."

So, Jon Nasagi was right—she was Guatemalan. Not that it mattered right now. The woman continued. "And your name, your life, helped me do that. As I said, you should be proud."

"I see," Chrissy said slowly, scanning the room and racking her brain for a way out of this. "And are you proud? Are you proud of the fact that your child now belongs to the state of California and that his father is dead?"

The other Chressaidia's nostrils flared slightly, then her eyes narrowed, but she said nothing.

Chrissy's anger continued to build, pushing down the fear, leaving no room for any other emotion. Her common sense told her not to push this woman, and yet she'd destroyed so much, ruined—

and ended—lives. And she was okay with that? Because of some political agenda, this woman could write off all she had done? Baby Salazar came to mind. "What a blessing your son was born with a deformity that allowed him freedom from you."

The woman lunged forward, grabbing at Chrissy's shirt and pinning her to the headboard before Chrissy had time to react. She glared at Chrissy, their faces only inches apart. "That *mutante* was proof that my mission was to be different. And I have proved myself worthy of my appointment." Her voice grew louder, making it harder and harder for Chrissy to hide her terror. This woman was unhinged, and she had a gun. Why on earth was Chrissy provoking her?

Because she needed answers.

Even if she only had five minutes left on the earth, she needed those answers, she had to understand. The other Chressaidia continued, "You are not one to undo what I have created. You will not defeat me!"

She seemed to catch herself and her loss of control and let Chrissy go, stepping off the bed and turning toward the door for only a moment before turning to face Chrissy again, her demeanor calm once more. She held Chrissy's eyes and raised the gun. "I should kill you now," she said. "You are too much trouble."

What could Chrissy possibly say to that? She was spared begging for her life by a knock at the door. Chressaidia snapped her head to the side.

Is it Micah? Chrissy thought, tears coming to her eyes. She should want him to stay away—this wasn't about him—and yet she longed to have him here.

Chressaidia walked to the door and looked out the peephole. Whoever she saw made her inhale sharply and pull away. Chrissy took advantage of the distraction and scooted to the far side of the bed. Why would she react that way if it were Micah at the door?

A deep male voice said something in muffled Spanish from the other side of the door. Chressaidia suddenly looked terrified. After a few moments, she walked forward and pulled open the door as if she had no choice.

Chrissy took the opportunity to slide off the bed, stand, and scoot along the wall. Not that there was any way out other than the front door that was opening, but putting some distance between her and the other woman seemed to be a good idea. Having her feet underneath her seemed equally wise.

The door slammed shut almost as soon as it had opened enough to allow the man to enter. Chrissy tensed against the wall at the ease in which he entered. Was he an accomplice? He was older, short but thickly built with a gray-black beard that matched his hair. As soon as he was inside the room, he grabbed Chressaidia's left arm, pulling up the sleeve of her shirt. Chressaidia, who had been so severe, so fierce, was now scared, almost submissive.

Who was this man? Chrissy wondered. And how could his appearance, which was obviously a surprise to Chressaidia, work to her advantage?

The man stared at a tattoo on Chressaidia's arm. "What have you done?" he said in Spanish. "You indulge yourself to think you are worthy of a commission after what you have done!" He shook her arm as he issued the reprimand.

"Papa," Chressaidia said, causing Chrissy to raise her eyebrows. This man was her father? What, was this some kind of Guatemalan mob? Whatever else Chressaidia was going to say was cut off as the man raised his hand and slapped her hard enough that her hair arced, and her neck snapped to the side.

Chrissy gasped at the force behind the man's blow and wondered again how she could possibly get out of here.

He looked up, saw her standing there, and narrowed his eyes. "Who is this?" the man asked, causing Chrissy's mouth to go dry.

The other Chressaidia had only just raised her head. "No one," she said, shaking her head and not looking at Chrissy as she spoke. "Only insurance."

Her father looked back at her. "You should not need insurance," he said, glaring at her, his eyes drifting to the tattoo on her arm again. She lifted a hand to cover it.

What did it represent? Chrissy wondered. *Why was it so important?*

"You said everything was going well," he continued. "You dared tell me Frederico was killed by a dealer."

There was a pause for several seconds. Chrissy looked between the two of them in the silence.

When Chressaidia spoke, her tone was resigned, surrendered. "How long have you had Eduardo?" she asked, still in Spanish. Chrissy wondered if they thought she couldn't understand them.

"I sent Eduardo to Frederico long ago, to keep track of him, to oversee what he was doing in the U.S., to see how he cared for his father's business."

"Frederico was squandering it," Chressaidia said, her voice raising. "He was using the drugs, going to parties. His heart was not in our cause."

"That was not your job to decide!" her father yelled. "You were to bring me an heir! You should have come home when you failed, not killed your husband, not put the entire alliance at risk. What am I to tell his father? How am I to explain?"

"I was the only one who could fix things," she said back, though her tone showed her continued hesitation. "I was sent here to further our interests, to strengthen our armies. He stood to destroy all of it! I could not let that happen."

"And yet, you did not help our cause. The joining of our families is ruined now. There can be no trust, no alliance between us."

"I did help our cause!" she yelled as if forgetting herself entirely. "I found the parts. I fixed the trade. I did that—I did all of it!"

Chrissy edged even closer to the bathroom—or more appropriately—away from them.

"And then you lost the parts," her father said.

She fell silent and her eyes turned to Chrissy, who stopped as the woman's eyes narrowed. "I did not lose the parts," she said in English, presumably so that Chrissy would understand. "They were stolen from me, and they are coming back."

Her phone rang, and though she hesitated, she picked it up, keeping her eyes on Chrissy. She put the phone to her ear. "Where is he, Eduardo?"

After a moment her eyes drifted closed for only a second. "How could you have lost him?" she spat into the phone. "Or did betraying me get in the way of this mission entirely?"

Her father grabbed the phone and began speaking to Eduardo. Chressaidia was still staring at Chrissy, planning, plotting. It was all Chrissy could do not to shrink under her gaze, but she didn't dare move, didn't dare disrupt the tenuous climate of the room. Another moment passed, and then Chressaidia's face relaxed as she pulled Chrissy's cell phone from her pocket. She lifted her gun and pointed it at Chrissy again, then looked at the phone in quick glances while dialing something before putting it to her ear.

"Tell Eduardo to bring the other parts here," she said to her father over her shoulder.

Her father's fist spun out and hit her right ear, making Chrissy cringe. "Marked or not, you are not a general."

Chressaidia took a breath, and her eyes swung back to focus on Chrissy. She took a step forward, and Chrissy fell a step back, even though that only took her closer to the corner of the room. Her heart began racing as she tried to figure out what this woman was doing.

"You're running out of time," Chressaidia said into the phone. Then she shifted the gun ever so slightly to the right and pulled the trigger.

CHAPTER 96

Even though Chrissy watched the woman's finger squeeze the trigger as if time had stopped completely, the impact of the bullet still caught her off guard. She screamed when the bullet tore through the flesh of her upper arm. She stumbled and fell against the wall as her left arm erupted with fire. For the next few seconds she didn't know what had happened, what was going on. All she knew was pain unlike anything she'd ever felt as time and space began to spin around her.

"That shot won't kill her," Chressaidia said into the phone. "But the next one will, if she doesn't bleed to death first. I want my parts right now."

I can't lose it, she thought to herself. *Not now.* She took a deep breath and forced her eyes open. She clamped her right hand over her bleeding arm, nearly screaming out again at the pain the pressure caused.

My life is still my own, she told herself. *How badly do I want it?* She focused even more on pushing the clouds of pain and nausea from her mind, reinserting herself into this room, this moment. She could hear herself moaning, but couldn't seem to stop it.

Chressaidia paused, listening to the other person on the phone. "Oh, she's alive," she said. "For now."

Chressaidia closed the phone and turned to her father, who seemed to be regarding her with something akin to respect. Was her shooting Chrissy some kind of show? Some sort of test? "Is Eduardo coming?" Chressaidia asked him in Spanish.

"Yes," the man said. "He will be here soon, but you are no longer in charge of this mission."

Chressaidia hesitated, then lowered her head as if to accept the changing roles, though Chrissy saw the resentment in her eyes.

Chrissy pushed herself to her feet, her whole arm throbbing, her stomach rolling as her ankles wobbled. The man and woman began talking again, and Chrissy didn't try to listen in this time; it took too much energy. She had to stop the bleeding. She saw the oversized T-shirt she'd worn as pajamas the night before. It was laid neatly on the bed, likely put there by the maid. She picked it up and carefully wrapped it around her arm. The sight of her own blood covering her hand and clothing, seeping through the fabric of the T-shirt, made her head spin.

The phone rang again—not her phone, with the Shakira ring—but the other Chressaidia's. She looked up to see the man answer it; he spoke too quietly for her to hear for a moment, and then lowered the phone again. Chrissy was standing now, her back braced against the wall since the floor was still shifting.

"Eduardo is here," he said, turning to put his hand on the door-knob. He looked at Chrissy, then back at the other Chressaidia. "Can you take care of her?"

The "take care of" part didn't sound like the good kind of care.

"Of course," the other Chressaidia said back.

"I will go check the truck," the man said. He left, but as the door closed, a man passed by on the outside. Chrissy met his eye for just a moment, enough to see an almost imperceptible nod and to see the baseball cap he wore. The man wasn't Micah, but he wore Micah's Boise State cap and had communicated his awareness of her. She wasn't as alone as she felt. Chrissy's pulse increased as the man disappeared.

She looked at the other Chressaidia, who had gone to look out the window and left the door open a few inches. Despite her injury, Chrissy knew this would be her chance. As it was, her steps were shaky atop her Blahnik heels as she moved toward the door. She thought of Micah asking her how she could walk in them at all. Had that conversation only taken place this morning?

"Stop," the woman said when Chrissy was ten feet from freedom. With her hand, she pushed the door shut and Chrissy tried not to panic. "Sit," she said in a tense voice, but also a fearful one. She had a look of desperation about her, a tight, barely contained, angry fear.

Chrissy wondered who Micah had talked to. What was she expected to do? What could anyone else do to save her?

With no other options, Chrissy sat on the edge of the bed and increased the pressure on her arm which throbbed and burned. The pressure caused even more pain and nearly made Chrissy forget to breathe. She didn't know what to do and felt as if she were simply waiting for the next bullet, the final shot.

Don't go without a fight, she told herself.

"I guess your father doesn't know about the baby," she finally said, putting all she could into sounding casual, as if the bullet in her arm were of no consequence. Chressaidia turned to face her, as Chrissy had hoped she would. Chrissy didn't want her attention on the door and window that separated them from whatever and who-ever was outside.

"You speak Spanish?" Chressaidia asked, narrowing her eyes again as she realized Chrissy had heard everything. "No talking."

Chrissy shrugged, and tried to moisten her dry mouth. "Sure," she said. "But I wonder what he'd think if he knew the truth." Though never in a million years would Chrissy be the one to tell him. The idea that Baby Salazar was related to these people was a horrible thought. But bringing him up was the only weapon she had against this woman. It was the only thing that had garnered a reaction, and she wanted this woman's full attention. Chressaidia narrowed her eyes. Chrissy kept waiting for someone to rush through the door—a full SWAT team or something—but she had to remind herself she wasn't on a TV show.

Trust me.

She held on to those two words with every ounce of faith and determination she had and felt a small measure of peace wedge itself in between all the other emotions swirling in her chest. "I saw him, you know," Chrissy said. "He's beautiful."

Chressaidia hadn't expected that, and for only an instant Chrissy saw the other women's composure fall. Her face softened, her eyes changed; she *was* a mother after all. Though Chrissy couldn't imag-ine what kind of evil drove this woman to do the things she did, she'd always believed that birth was a moment when this life and the one before it touched for the briefest of moments. This woman had brought a blanket, expecting to take her child home. She must have felt something before her coldness and superstition took over. Her reaction now proved she had.

Now.

Before Chressaidia could recover from her momentary distrac-tion, Chrissy launched herself at the other woman's stomach. Her head caught the woman hard on the left side and sent both of them careening into the dresser against the wall. She moved fast enough, and with enough force, that the woman didn't have time to aim the gun she still held in her hand.

The pain that flared through Chrissy's body at the impact left her breathless and unable to move for a moment—not a good combination for a woman fighting for her life. But Chressaidia was pinned between Chrissy and the dresser so Chrissy dug the heels of her shoes into the carpet, bracing herself against the other woman. She knew she couldn't hold her for long and prayed for strength.

"You will not win this one," Chrissy said through clenched teeth as Chressaidia screamed against her confinement and tried to get the upper hand.

The door burst open and Chrissy panicked, thinking the father had returned and would finish her off. However, in the next instant she heard the voices of numerous men shouting and yelling orders to one another. She was pulled off the other Chressaidia and thrown onto one of the beds. She screamed, her arm feeling as if it had been ripped from her body.

Someone reached down and helped her to her feet, then rushed her from the room. With a man on either side of her, holding her up, she had no choice but to run with them. She was trying to take it all in, figure out what had happened, when she looked up to see a pair of bright blue eyes coming toward her. He wasn't wearing his Boise State hat, and she thought he'd never looked more handsome.

"Micah?" she asked, finally feeling herself crumble. Tears filled her eyes. He *was* here, he was part of . . . whatever this was.

He reached out for her and opened his mouth to speak as someone yelled from the motel room behind her and several shots rang out. She gasped and turned her head, but without a moment's hesitation, the two men guiding her threw her to the ground, where her head connected hard against the asphalt. As the parking lot and the people funneled into blackness, she held on to the thought that Micah hadn't left her, and that, in more ways than one, she had her life back.

CHAPTER 97

San Diego, California
Wednesday, June 4

Chrissy tried to open her eyes, but her eyelids were apparently weighed down with heavy stones. When she finally managed to keep them open long enough to see anything, she saw those blue eyes again. He had his hat back and she smiled to know that he was there, until everything flooded back to her. Micah must have seen her smile falter because she felt his hand in hers as she closed her eyes again. The words "What happened?" played behind her lips, but she didn't want to ask. She was sure she already knew.

Her mouth was so dry she wondered if she'd ever had a drink of water in her whole life. She tried to lick her lips, but Micah guided a straw to her mouth and helped her take a drink. "What time is it?" she asked.

"Well, you missed *General Hospital*—Sorry."

Chrissy tried to laugh, but it came out as a very unflattering snort. She attempted to move her left arm, but found it also felt weighed down with stones, yet the rest of her whole body felt strangely weightless at the same time. She was pretty sure she was at the hospital, seeing as how she remembered being shot and thrown to the ground. But that was as far as her clarity went.

"How did you know about *General Hospital?*" she asked.

"Amanda told me to turn it on earlier. She thought it might help you regain consciousness. She got real worried when even Jax and Lulu couldn't wake you up."

"Is Kate really going to leave Sonny to work on the magazine?"

Micah laughed. "I think you'll find out tomorrow."

"Oh, good," Chrissy said, attempting to smile again. "I'd be ticked if I missed anything important."

She'd forgotten that Micah was holding her right hand until he began rubbing his thumb across her knuckles. "So, do you want the good news or the bad news?" Micah asked.

"There's good news?" Chrissy asked. "I hope it's got something to do with limited-edition Beanie Babies after all. Or maybe those parts really were for sprinklers—there could be a reward, right?"

Micah laughed and moved his thumb over the back of her hand again. Maybe because of their circumstances, it seemed very intimate, warming her hand, her arm, and then the rest of her. Pain meds and Micah—could the good news get better than that?

"Okay, so you want the good news," he said. "The pistol was only a .22, and between the surgery and the two titanium pins, it's going to be okay . . . eventually."

Titanium? "I'd better still be able to mop my floors. That takes a lot of upper body strength, ya know."

"You won't be mopping for awhile," Micah said. "But one day, that mop will be all yours, so long as you complete your physical therapy. Had it been a bigger caliber weapon, you might not have been so lucky."

"So the good news is that I'm down to one arm for awhile. What's the bad news?"

"I wrecked your car."

Chrissy turned her head too fast and an explosion seemed to erupt in her skull. The Fourth of July in her brain. It took a few seconds to recover and by then her exclamation of shock had lost some punch. "What?"

"After I called the police, I was so anxious to get to you I forgot to put the car into reverse and I hit a cement beam. I'm sorry."

"I loved that car," Chrissy said, wondering if she could find another one like it online.

"Far more than it deserved."

"It was paid off."

"Its only redeeming quality. However, Amanda will be here later to pack up your underwear and you've got all kinds of police reports to prove who you are now."

Chrissy attempted a smile and they both went quiet. The IV hooked into Chrissy's arm clicked as it sent more medication into her body. It helped take her mind off the car. "Micah," she said quietly. He'd been looking at their hands entwined on the blanket but now he met her eyes. "She's dead, isn't she?"

Micah nodded. Chrissy turned her head to the front again, focused on a tile in the ceiling, and tried to decide how she should feel about that. The face she saw in her mind was that final one, the one where her demeanor slipped at the mention of her son being beautiful. "And the other two? The men?"

"I don't know," Micah said. "It all happened so fast, and I came with you in the ambulance so I didn't get to ask a lot of questions. Detective Long will be here later. He wanted to talk to you and get a statement." He leaned forward, and she turned so that they were facing one another. He reached up and brushed her hair from her face. "I'm so glad you're okay, Chrissy. I've never been so scared in my life."

Her insides began turning to Jell-O at the look on his face, the tenderness and compassion. She couldn't speak, so mesmerized by his words and expression.

He leaned forward and kissed her softly, gently, and yet it was a kiss she felt as completely as she'd ever felt anything. When he pulled back she held his eyes, trying to figure out the most appropriate way to tell him to do it again.

"I don't know what happens with us now," he whispered, the first trace of regret seeping into his words. "I meant it when I said my kids need me."

"I know," Chrissy said, but a little tornado of expectation was growing in her belly. There was a "but" coming, and she braced herself for it.

"But as I sat in that squad car, watching those officers move in on the motel, knowing you were in there, knowing you were hurt, I knew without a doubt that a life without you in it would be more than I could stand. I need the color, the life you breathe into me every time I'm with you."

It wasn't just the meds that made her head spin. She felt herself relax against the pillows as an amazing sense of *rightness* settled over her for the first time. She stared at him, the soft lines around his eyes, the concern that created slight creases in his forehead. He hadn't shaved in awhile and a red beard covered the lower half of his face, giving him an outdoorsman look.

"How?" she asked softly, well remembering his explanation of why he couldn't pursue a relationship. Well remembering her agreement with those reasons.

"Can you be patient with me?" Micah asked, placing one hand on the side of her face. "If we both understand the considerations, can we—"

"Knock, knock?"

Chrissy would have thrown a bedpan at the door if she'd had control of either of her arms. Instead, she turned her head to see Jon Nasagi standing in the doorway. Micah stood and welcomed him in, shaking his hand in greeting. Chrissy wondered if Micah was relieved at the interruption, or if, like her, he was wishing he could throw a bedpan too.

"Am I at your hospital?" Chrissy asked as Jon stepped to the end of the bed.

"It's the best one in the city," he said. "I hear you put up quite a fight."

"More like stood there shaking in my heels until someone rescued me."

He laughed, and Micah sat back down, placing his hand on her arm as if it belonged there. "You're going home in a couple days?" Jon asked.

Chrissy looked at Micah; she had no idea. He nodded. "We fly home at five o'clock on Thursday. The doctor will give you good drugs so you can make the flight."

"I demand my makeup kit before I leave this place. I really have no business talking to either of you in the state of undress my face is in right now."

Both men laughed. "Anything you want," Micah said.

Chrissy shared a look with him and raised an eyebrow that made him blush. She hadn't meant anything by it—not really—but his reaction made her wonder how he'd interpreted it.

There was quiet for a few moments, then Jon spoke. "I just wanted to offer—if you're interested—there's a certain someone in the NICU that would like to say good-bye before you go. Things are going to be better for him now."

Chrissy felt her spirits lift. "I can go see him again?" she asked. "That would be okay?"

"Better than okay." Jon looked at Micah, a question in his eyes.

Micah cleared his throat. "I mentioned that you might have some questions to ask, about . . . finding a home for Baby Salazar. I was telling Jon how nice Idaho Falls is this time of year, and that once your name is fully cleared, you might give in to some wacky thoughts you'd been having."

Chrissy's breath caught in her throat. She didn't want to get her hopes up—knowing it was a fantasy. Yet she was unable to forget all the times she'd wondered why *this* had happened to *her*. "It was just . . . a crazy idea."

"I wish more people had crazy ideas like that," Jon said. "No pressure, but know that I would go to bat for you in every way I could."

"But," she hesitated, then hurried forward. "It's . . . possible?"

Jon smiled a little wider and nodded.

"Anything's possible," Micah said, taking her hand again and smiling, the corners of his eyes crinkling as he did so. She imagined he was talking about more than Baby Salazar this time. "All it takes is a little work, a little faith, and perhaps a sturdy pair of heels."

AUTHOR NOTES

～～

*B*ased on a joint survey conducted by the Better Business Bureau and Javelin Strategy and Research, identity theft continues to be the fastest-growing crime in America for the eighth year in a row. Consumer awareness is finally making a dent; however, for 8.4 million victims in 2007 (down from 10.1 million in 2003), that is small comfort. I have always believed that education is the most powerful tool we have in fighting any form of evil—hence, author notes. ☺

Identity theft can be categorized in four different groups:

Financial Identity Theft—When someone uses another person's name and Social Security number to obtain goods and services. This is the most common—and most successful—type of identity theft. Examples include setting up credit card accounts, renting apartments or office buildings, taking out loans, using another person's health insurance, or gaining fraudulent access to existing accounts in the victim's name.

Criminal Identity Theft—When a person pretends to be someone else when arrested for a crime, creating a false criminal record for the victim. This is perhaps the oldest form of identity theft, and police agencies are well aware of the temptation for criminals to pin their crime on someone else, but there are still many instances where a person falsely verifies an identity to the extent where charges are filed, warrants are issues, and affidavits are filed against them.

Once this becomes a part of someone's criminal record, it can be very difficult to reverse and often takes several months to resolve, requiring substantial proof of the victim's identity, as well as proof of the identity of the perpetrator of the fraud, which can be difficult if the perpetrator was released and is not around to admit to his fraud.

Identity Cloning—When someone uses another person's information to assume his or her identity in daily life. They often obtain fake birth certificates and driver's licenses so as to fully assume the new identity. The people they interact with know them by the victim's name. Often this is used when someone is hiding their real identity for reasons of past criminal behavior or to protect themselves. This type of theft often leads to financial and/or criminal theft as well.

Business/Commercial Identity Theft—When a business uses another business's name to obtain credit. This is similar to financial identity theft, but is made on a business rather than a personal level and is just as debilitating to the business that ends up with a credit history that reflects another business's debt. It undermines the victim's credibility and reputation, often resulting in extreme losses or eventual loss of the business entirely.

Of those people affected by any one of these types of identity theft, only 15% will find out about the fraud through proactive steps taken by an involved business or institution such as a creditor, police officer, or bank. Eighty-five percent will discover the theft on their own. Seventy percent of thieves are friends or family members of the victims; people who would have easy access to otherwise private information.

In 2003, it was reported that 25% of all credit card theft was due to financial identity theft at a cost of 51.3 billion dollars. Ironically, however, despite such huge numbers, most thieves are not prosecuted because creditors find it is not cost effective. The lack of prosecution, and the increasing ways in which people can gain access to credit, makes identity theft a perfect crime—high reward and low risk. Often it only takes minimal consideration for a thief to cover his or her tracks and avoid any repercussions.

So what can we do?

The first thing we can do is protect ourselves:

- Keep personal information as private as possible. Lock up birth certificates, passports, unused credit cards, and children's Social Security cards. Only carry those items on your person that you must have, such as a driver's license and the credit cards you use on a regular basis.

- As often as possible, request electronic bills and statements rather than paper ones which can be intercepted through the mail or picked up from your desk by a visitor to your home.

- Set up passwords required to log on your computer so that other people cannot gain easy access to information stored there.

- Make sure PIN numbers don't include your Social Security number or important names and dates that someone familiar with you could know or easily guess. Choose PIN numbers at random and do not write them down in easily accessible locations.

- Fraudulent e-mails, commonly referred to as phishing e-mails, will often link you to replicated web sites, then capture your account and PIN number when you attempt to log in. Five percent of people respond to phishing e-mails, and hacking into another person's bank account is currently the fastest-growing version of financial identity theft. When receiving any kind of notice that looks legitimate, always go to the web site on your own, type in the address yourself, and then look for the same message. If it's official, there will be a copy available for you through the web site. If it is fraudulent, report it to the institution it's supposed to be from so that they are aware of the connection.

- Minimize your debt. Being aware of the status on three accounts is much easier than monitoring twenty accounts. Reduce the number of credit cards you own and carry with you. Pay off or consolidate accounts so that you can keep a closer eye on those that remain. We've been told repeatedly to get out of debt, and this is one more reason to do so, as it minimizes your exposure to identity theft.

The second level of protection is to responsibly monitor your accounts and credit score:

- Once a year, every person with a Social Security number is entitled to a free credit report. Take advantage of the options offered to you and look for new accounts opened in your name as well as changes in address you did not make.

- Be sure that the credit agencies have your current address, e-mail, and phone number so they can contact you if they are made aware of suspicious activity on your account.

- Set up e-mail alerts from your banks and lending institutions to alert you whenever a transfer or withdrawal takes place on your account. Should someone gain access to your account, you would be notified within minutes and the faster you act, the better chance there is of regaining your money and catching the perpetrator.

- Consider subscribing to a monitoring service that watches your credit report for you, issues ongoing alerts to protect your credit, and updates you on resources available.

- If, despite these measures, you find yourself a victim of identity theft, there are things you can do to minimize the damage and find resolution as quickly as possible.

- Act fast. Do not wait even twenty-four hours to begin working on the theft. Every seventeen minutes a new credit card is fraudulently approved and someone goes on a shopping spree. Waiting even one day can mean the difference of thousands of dollars.

- Immediately change PIN numbers to all your accounts—not just the one that was breached. You do not know who has your information, how they got it, and how much they know about you in general. Do not give the thief the option of trying a plan B on your existing credit.

- Notify creditors affected by the theft and put alerts on your other accounts in case the thief attempts to gain access to them.

- Place a "fraud alert" with any one of the three credit-reporting agencies. The notified agency will immediately inform the other two of your status. This alert will stay on your credit history for ninety days, and will spur credit-extending companies to demand further verification of anyone requesting credit in your name.

- Go to the FTC consumer web site at www.consumer.gov/idtheft and read up on the current information regarding identity theft. Policy and law varies from one state and one creditor to another, but there are general rules and regulations you need to be aware of. You will need to understand those things in your favor in order to successfully get the help you need from the credit institutions and in receiving a police report.

As with everything else, all things temporal are spiritual, and we can find comfort in the wise management of our financial resources through the Lord's promise that when we take our trials to him and lean upon his ample arm when our own strength seems depleted, he will comfort us. Good habits, both financially and spiritually, will not only help us avoid identity theft, but will give us strength should we need to respond to the criminal acts of others.

For more information, or to receive your free credit report, contact any one of the following agencies.

Equifax: 1–800–525–6285; www.equifax.com

Experian: 1–800–397–3742; www.experian.com

Transunion: 1–800–680–7289; www.transunion.com

About the Author

Josi Schofield Kilpack was born and raised in Salt Lake City, the third of nine children, and accounts much of her success to her mother always making oatmeal for breakfast.

In 1993, Josi married her high school sweetheart, Lee Kilpack, and together they raised their children in Salt Lake and then Willard, Utah, where the family currently lives. Josi loves to read and write, is the author of eight novels, the baker of many delicious confections, and the hobby farmer of a varying number of unfortunate chickens.

In her spare time, she likes to overwhelm herself with a multitude of projects and then complain that she never has any spare time; in this way she is rather masochistic.

She also enjoys traveling, cheering on her children, and sleeping in when the occasion presents itself. She loves to hear from her readers and can be reached at Kilpack@gmail.com.